THE ZEN

DETECTIVE

DEVORAH FOX

Mike Byrnes and Associates, Inc.
355 Keewaydin Lane
Port Aransas, Texas 78373

Also by Devorah Fox
The Bewildering Adventures of King Bewilliam series:
The Lost King, Book One
The King's Ransom, Book Two
The King's Redress, Book Three
The Redoubt, Book Four

Naked Came the Sharks with Jed Donellie
Masters of Time, A Science Fiction and Fantasy Time Travel Anthology
Magic Unveiled, An Anthology
Murder by the Book, A Mystery Mini
One Bad Apple, A Mystery Mini
Detour, A Big Rig Thriller

http://devorahfox.com
ISBN: 0-9778245-7-8
ISBN-13: 978-0-9778245-7-1

DEDICATION

to Mike Byrnes

AUTHOR'S NOTE

THANKS

This novel has been a work in progress for many years. I am grateful to:

Writers group members in Phoenix and Scottsdale, Arizona, who gave useful critique about the earliest drafts. In Corpus Christi, Texas, Jerry Bateman, Don Lowe, and Ellie Killian worked with me through yet another round of editing. Phyllis Harp gave every jot and tittle her close attention.
Brain Rust of the Northampton, Massachusetts Police Department and Ralph Asher, who answered questions about police practice, and Sam Marks who helped with my queries about firearms (all of which I took some liberties with, but this is a work of fiction not a procedural manual).
Stephanie Tade of the Stephanie Tade Agency for her initial interest in *The Zen Detective* and her renewed encouragement 16 years later. Beta readers Alice Marks and Michael Stephen Daigle for their valuable time, attention, and comments. (Alice and Mike are authors in their own right. Check out *Missing* by Alice Marks and the Frank Nagler detective series by Michael Stephen Daigle.)
My Street Team of Chip Cooper, Alan White, Ellie Killian, Joyce Walters, Theresa Guettler, Orville Ballard, Diana Knowlton Vondra, Hanna Brodie, David Abbe, and Andrea Dobson who are ever ready with helpful opinions and enthusiasm, and Barbara Sanchez and Alice Marks who relentlessly cheer me on.
The Art Center of Port Aransas, the Estelle Stair Gallery, the Family Center IGA, and to John Rojas for your support.

and Mike Byrnes, always.

The final mystery is oneself–Oscar Wilde

So I'm a liar so it seems
My desire could justify anything
So is there nothing that lies in between
This cold silence and a scream?–Glen Phillips

CHAPTER 1

Lightning splits the sky
In the flash of bright white light
I can see—nothing—Onomato

"Will? Hey, buddy, are you all right?"

Barely. In another minute I would have been deep in the throes of a flashback. Just in time I realized that the sizzling white light wasn't muzzle flash but lightning, and the window-rattling boom wasn't the fusillade of automatic weapons, only thunder. The false alarm has left me with clammy skin, knotted muscles, a headache, and thumping heart. My hand fumbles for a cigarette but comes up empty.

Dunk looks at me fisheyed. "I asked you if you wanted another."

"No thanks," I reply, my voice only slightly less shaky than my hands.

"Well if you need anything, just holler. I'll be in my office," Dunk says.

He disappears into a small room behind the bar. My blurred vision clears and I return to watching the rain carve wormy streaks down the front picture window. The morning rush is over and I am alone in Duncan Phyffe's Kaffeteria. Cars huddle against the curb, abandoned for the day by downtown office workers now busy at their desks, cups of Dunk's Paradise City Blend warming them against an unseasonably cold Yankee October.

I drag a spoon through my cup. I would savor it if it were coffee but it's green tea. Like most cops I practically mainlined coffee, but I gave it up when I found it impaired my attempts at meditation. It's hard enough to calm a mind that doesn't already buzz from caffeine.

The door chime gets my attention. An elfin old woman in a boxy coat hesitates at the threshold before crossing the polished wood floor. As she approaches, I see that she is neither as small nor as old as she first appeared. Short, wiry hair, the color of iron, frames a face that is lined but uncommonly serene. Her blue eyes are bright. She hoists herself up on the stool beside me and unbuttons her coat.

"Did you want to order something, Ma'am? I could get Dunk—"

"No, thank you, I'm fine. You're Detective Will Mansion, right?"

"Yes, ma'am." That she knows me even though I don't know her isn't that surprising. Only a few weeks ago my picture, the official one in dress uniform complete with ribbons, ran above-the-fold in the newspaper right next to reports about President Bill Clinton's bid for reelection. I experienced a spate of celebrity, thankfully brief.

"I could use your help, Detective," the woman says, "to find someone. A man I know. He's missing."

"Why are you asking me?"

"You are the one who was in the news, aren't you? Big drug bust? Recommended for a commendation? Wounded in the line of duty?"

At the too-fresh memory, my left thigh burns where a hot .25 caliber bullet punctured the flesh, clear-cut a bloody path through muscle, and ripped my femoral artery. My heart shifts into overdrive. Don't go there, I scream inwardly. I stave off the past by fixating on the present, cling fiercely to the lilt of the woman's voice, the burble of the coffee machine.

The shrink to whom the department sent me recommended just such a strategy for symptoms of post-traumatic stress disorder. I was skeptical until he related some impressive accounts of amazing body and mind control achieved by Zen Buddhists through meditation.

I shift on the wobbly stool. "Yes, ma'am, I'm Will Mansion but I'm not working. I'm on disability." Can she hear the quaver in my voice? Despite my attempts at meditation, the nightmares and flashbacks keep coming. Maybe I'm doing it wrong but I can't go back to the shrink for a refresher. While Department policy mandates counseling after a shooting, continue therapy beyond what's required and people snicker.

Still, I want the meditation to work. It would beat spending the rest of my life in a barbiturate fog.

"I'm sorry, Ma'am. Now if you'll go down to the station, you'll find—"

"A roomful of men who don't think my concerns merit much attention," she says, not as a complaint but as a simple statement of fact.

"This person you're looking for. How long has he been missing?"

"I haven't seen him in almost a week."

A man wouldn't have to be gone that long for us to consider him missing. Why was she turned away? "He's not a juvenile, is he?"

"Oh, no, he's an adult. Late forties, early fifties, it's hard to say. Older than you, though, definitely. His name is Hector. I don't know his last name."

"So this isn't your husband."

"No, I'm not married." She extends her hand. It's wrinkled and age-spotted but her skin is soft, her grip strong. "I'm Sister Clyde."

"Sister," I repeat. She isn't wearing a veil or a habit but rather a white blouse, black skirt, and black oxfords. Fur that looks like fox trims the collar of her short navy coat. Doesn't mean anything; lots of nuns these days wear civilian clothing.

"I run the Mercy Mission on the Miracle Mile," she says.

The red light district, barely a mile away, on a blighted stretch of North Hope Street. "That's hard duty, Ma'am."

She smiles. "I had become somewhat lax in my devotion. A lack of conviction, you might say. My superiors thought a little hard work would be a blessing."

"Sounds more like a curse."

"Exactly." Sister Clyde beams. "Hector's one of my regulars. Or was, until he disappeared."

"I take it nobody else has reported him missing." Could be he's a transient.

She shakes her head. "Only me. Isn't that enough? I'm worried about him and I'd like him found before it's too late."

"Too late for what?"

"To save him."

"You know it may already be too late."

"It's never too late. A man can be saved even as he takes his last breath."

I've read the same thing about enlightenment. There was more to the Zen book the shrink gave me than simply meditation instructions. Of course I read the whole thing. Who can leave a book half-read? Apparently, meditation leads to *kensho*, enlightenment. The masters maintained that it had to be personally experienced, that it couldn't be adequately described. That didn't stop them from trying. I don't know what attracted me the most. The reports of wild exhilaration, mind-blowing flashes of insight, and sublime liberation? Or was it the promise of unimaginable peace and contentment afterward? All I know is by the time I finished the book I had resolved to see for myself.

"I meant if he hasn't simply moved on, he may ... you realize he may be dead." The Miracle Mile is often the last stop before the morgue.

"Oh, I sincerely hope not." Again she gives me that bright smile.

"You really care about this guy, don't you, Sister?" Why? Apparently no one else does.

"I care about them all, Detective Mansion."

"That's your job, I suppose."

"My vocation."

"God's will be done? I understand."

She clasps my hand. "Do you? Are you sure? So few people understand their own intention, much less God's."

Her hands are gentle but insistent. I have to tug a little to get free.

"So you'll help me?" she asks. "You do find missing persons, don't you?"

Of course I have, including many who didn't want to be found and reacted violently when they were. Chasing down a wayward alkie or junkie sounds like a waste of time though, and I tell her so.

"But you would know the right questions to ask, it wouldn't take you long at all," she says.

She has a counter for every objection, it seems, and won't take 'no' for an answer. What is it about nuns? Is salesmanship part of the convent curriculum? "I'll bet you do the fund-raising for the Mission, too, don't you, Sister Clyde?"

She glows. "Why yes, I do. How perceptive of you, young man. I knew I picked the right person for the job."

"With all due respect, Sister, your clients are people with mental problems, problems with alcohol or drugs. It's not as if they have a regular routine, someplace they have to be——"

"Oh, but they do, their lives are quite regimented. They have to be at the shelter at eight to reserve a bed, at the clinic at ten for methadone, at my mission at noon for lunch——"

The discount store at 2:00 to do a little shoplifting, the alley at 4:00 for a fix, the sleazy bars at 10:00 to sell hot merchandise. She's right, of course. The job of supporting an addiction does give life purpose.

Sister Clyde says, "Some of my men do have mental problems. Hector is different, though. I don't believe he's schizophrenic. He's intelligent, alert. Also desperate and afraid. He may be running or hiding."

"From whom?"

"I don't know." She stands. "Come to the Mission and talk to some of the men. They'll convince you Hector didn't just get up and leave. Please. Won't you help me?" In an even softer voice she says, "Won't you help Hector?"

She can stop twisting my arm now. The doctor who patched me up told me to take it easy but, I'm already asking myself, "Who is this Hector and why is he running?"

I pick up my cup, set it back down untasted. When I checked out a book by one of those Zen masters the shrink mentioned, I learned that meditators are urged to avoid intoxicants. I figured that included caffeine, so out with coffee, in with tea. *Genmaicha* to be exact, a blend of green tea and popped rice. Zen monks rely on it to get through all-day practice sessions in unheated meditation halls. The trace carbohydrates in the brew are supposed to promote endurance and performance. All it's done for me this morning is go cold. The rice floats on the surface like scum on a still pond.

With a sigh of resignation I dismount my stool. "All right, Sister. I'll follow you."

"Oh, I don't think you want to do that. I took the bus."

In this morning's downpour? She doesn't have an umbrella and, I now realize, her dull blue coat is dry, the fur collar fluffy. "Well, I guess I can drive us," I say. At work I had a city car at my disposal. Not luxurious by any means, the old Crown Vic was still far better suited to these kinds of errands than my personal vehicle, an even older rattletrap International Scout which I've had practically since college. With its oxidized, rust-speckled finish it's more Old Paint than Scout but it suits my needs perfectly. Stuffed with all my gear it's taken me to the Berkshires' lakes and forests or the slopes of Vermont and New York without complaint. While I don't see Sister Clyde climbing up into it without a lot of awkwardness, it beats the bus.

*****

As I pilot Old Paint down Bridge Street, my muscles tense and my breath quickens, responding to old cues. My daily commute used to take me over the river at least twice. Crossing eastbound meant I was headed for work. The cross-eyed glare of the stone eagles atop the bridge's stanchions seemed to admonish me to get pumped.

Though Main Street has run through Paradise City for over a hundred years, it is now virtually indistinguishable from Main Streets everywhere. The brownstone and brick fronts of Woolworth's, Leuwen's Pharmacy and Soda Fountain, Masur's Meats, and Taranto's Shoe Repair have been replaced by the low-profile slump block construction of franchise operations designed to be recognized anywhere. As Sister Clyde and I get further east, vacant buildings, invitations to vandals and vagrants, hide crack labs and stash houses.

I turn left onto North Hope Street and flip the headlights on low. Even in daylight the stretch known as the Miracle Mile seems darker than any other part of the city. Hookers stand on the corners, shift their weight from foot to high-heeled foot, and keep a nervous eye out for their pimps. Derelicts slouch in doorways, their skin and clothing the same color as the sludge in the gutter. Their hooded eyes are as murky as the interior of the King Philip, once a cozy tavern, now a gin mill. A pawnbroker hangs back in the shadow of his doorway and smokes, a spider waiting for flies. The only people in motion are the hypes who dart into alleys. Even they walk slower when they come out.

Sister Clyde guides me to a gutted storefront wedged between a massage parlor and a liquor store, the Mercy Mission. I don't recall seeing it before, but on the Mile establishments spring up and wither like toadstools. Here, Sister Clyde says, she serves coffee all day, ladles out soup at noon, and dispenses hope around the clock. She indicates a group of men likely to have information about Hector. Gaunt and dirty, they sit on benches attached to a faded redwood table and hunch over their bowls, intent on getting enough nourishment to keep going until their next hit. None of them have bathed or shaved recently. Closing my nose to the stink of unwashed bodies and stale cigarette smoke, I loop my good leg over the bench, sit companionably close, and ask about Hector. What I get are their own sad stories, about how they used to have a life, a job, a family, a home—gone now. They express neither fear nor desperation, only anger and despondency.

"Ain't my fault," says a man whose slight frame is that of a twenty-year-old but whose eyes are old as misery. "My pop was a drunk. He throwed me out when I was just a kid and I didn't have nowhere to go." His story is only one variation on a theme.

Drink and the crimes it breeds—DWI, domestic violence, petty theft—used to be our biggest problem. Even at that, at least we knew who the drunks were, could keep an eye on them, and we knew whom to look for when there was trouble. Now we have a far more insidious devil to fight: smack. Junkies are harder to make. They hold down jobs, have families, manage just fine as long as they get their fix. For that they'll mortgage their integrity, their loved ones, their lives, for a debt that never decreases and is discharged only by death.

The next man I question has little to say about Hector. It's hard to tell if he genuinely has no information, is tired or uninterested, or simply resents that I don't have a cigarette. I wish I did, I could use one myself, but I swore off smoking when I found that nothing short-circuits *zazen* like a nicotine jones.

A man with a scraggly beard tips a spoonful of soup carefully down his gullet. His throat, he complains, is all closed up and he can't eat fast enough to slake his hunger. In answer to my question about Hector, he asks, "He in trouble?"

"Sister Clyde seems to think so."

He nods. "Yeah, he wasn't cut out for this, man with his white shirt and his shiny shoes."

"Ain't that the truth," says a fellow across the table from us. He scratches the top of his head, a barren island in a river of stringy brown hair. "If that man's in trouble, he needs help."

"Didn't look to need nothin' to me. Always seemed to get what he wanted," said the bearded man.

"Which was what?" I ask. *Girls? Booze? Drugs?*

The smirk I get from the bearded man implies I'm a fool for asking.

"What was he doing here then?" I ask. "Was he selling? Drugs, food stamps, something like that?"

The bearded man shakes his head. "Man was a buyer, not a seller." He laughs. "A regular consumer."

"What are you bitchin' about?" the balding man asks. "He always helped you out. Bought you a bottle. Gave you money."

"Yeah ... until lately." The bearded man shrugs.

"Until lately what?" I ask.

"Until he run out," says the balding man.

This is like pulling teeth, except he doesn't have any. With difficulty, he gums the meager solids in his soup.

"Ran out of drugs? Money?" I ask. This Hector could simply be crouched in an alley somewhere, shaking himself apart from withdrawal or as I first suggested to Sister Clyde, dead. She might look for him in the morgue.

"Ran out of luck, maybe," the bearded man says.

"You think he crossed him?" the balding man asks.

"Crossed Shrike?" the bearded man replies.

"Could be. Man had no sense whatsoever."

His voice sounds very far away, because Shrike's name has filled my ears with the crack of gunfire, the shouts of men—"Mansion's hit, Mansion's down!"—the wail of an ambulance, the white noise of unconsciousness, the deafening silence of death. My stomach churns, my vision clouds, the room spins away. Like a man falling off a cliff, I grip the edge of the table, focus on the solid feel of the wood against my fingers, call up every bit of nascent Zen concentration I can muster to haul myself back from the brink.

"You OK, man?" the balding man asks.

"I'm fine," I reply, though I'm cold and slimed with sweat.

"I dunno, man, you look like you could use somethin'. Shrike—"

A hot spark of anger vaporizes the mists of phantom terror. "What do you know about Shrike?" I ask.

"Hector, he a good man but he got no street smarts. Man wouldn't last a minute out there." The balding man points his spoon at the front door. "Hey, maybe that's what he was doing here, ya think?" he asks his bearded friend.

I grab his shirt front, pull his face toward mine. "Shrike! Tell me what you know about Shrike!"

The balding man reels back. "Me? Nothing. I don't got no truck with Shrike."

"You?" I ask the bearded man.

"Hell, me either. I got more sense than that."

"That Hector, he don't got no sense," says the stringy-haired man. "You want to know about Shrike, you ask Hector."

"Where do I find him?"

"He's gone," pipes up a grizzled man at the end of the table. His dark, unfocused gaze peers from a face mantled with a puffy gray beard and mustache. "Car's gone, too."

Hector had a car?

"Pretty, the car was. Gold, like a sunbeam." The man stares off into space. "He rode away on a sunbeam."

Stay with me, old man. I scoot down closer to him. "What kind of car?"

He says nothing but he pulls over a paper napkin and with a long yellow fingernail etches a symbol, a figure eight on its side.

An Eterniti. Some car!

CHAPTER 2

Pounding the old beat
Parlor windows yellow
Breath white as a ghost—Onomato

Stolen. It's got to be. Why else would a vagrant have a super-luxury car like an Eterniti unless he's dealing? The man at the mission said Hector was a buyer, not a seller, but he could be covering up. For Hector? For Shrike?

I time my arrival at City Hall's limestone edifice for right before lunch so as to run into as few people as possible. Still, I can't avoid the dispatcher in her fishbowl opposite the station's third floor public entrance. "Will, are you back?" she asks, half rising from her seat.

"No," I reply, and exaggerate my limp, which effectively quashes any further discussion.

Though it's been weeks since I was here last, the security door hinges still creak and a broken hallway bulb has yet to be replaced. Despite its weekly waxing, the linoleum floor is still hopelessly gray. The place smells familiarly of the yeast, tangy tomato, and garlic that seep through the old plaster walls from Tom's Pizza Parlor next door. Somehow I expected it all to be different.

There is a new item. In the lobby of our offices on City Hall's second floor, a brass-framed photo of me now hangs with those of other officers wounded in the line of duty. Heroes. Wounded I definitely was. Hero? That wasn't the idea. Swbyra was about to be blind-sided. I meant only to knock him out of the line of fire.

The display gives me the creeps but it could be worse. My picture could be on the other wall, among the black-draped photos of those who died in the line of duty. If not for the skill of some gifted EMTs and one saint of a surgeon, it would be.

Ace and Spade, two cops who have been working the Miracle Mile, straggle from the Patrol room, spot me, and meet me halfway down the hall. I barely recognize them out of the scuzzy rags they wear undercover. "What are you two doing back in the bag?" I ask.

"Captain pulled us off that detail weeks ago," Ace replies. He shifts his shoulders in closely tailored blues and scowls. "After your raid everyone went to ground. Wouldn't look right for us to still be out there."

That puts the kibosh on asking them if they've seen anyone on the Miracle Mile who matches the vague description I have of the AWOL Hector.

"And Shrike, man, he's been about as easy to find as fuckin' fish lips," says Spade. "We think we're onto him and every time he gives us the slip. Bet you'd like another crack at him after what he did to you."

Oh I do. Before, it was business. Now it's personal. The man killed me. Killed me! Even now, the mere thought chills me, leaves me feeling hollow, insubstantial as puff of smoke and as likely to blow away. The feeling of vulnerability is itself frightening. As soon as I'm well enough to return to work—

"Will, you're back!" The Chief's Admin. Assistant bolts from behind a cluttered desk and beams.

"Not exactly." I look over my shoulder into the detectives' office where my scarred desk hunkers in its corner, an old hound dog waiting patiently for its master's return. Unoccupied too are the desks of my fellow squad members.

"Where's Moe and Larry?" I ask her. They could tell me if there's a Hector look-alike in the cage, or if an Eterniti has been reported stolen lately.

She gives me a blank look, then chuckles. "Ah, the Three Stooges. What does that make you, 'Curly'?" Her glance goes to the top of my head, still covered with hair unlike my balding namesake's. "They're at the hospital. There was a shooting early this morning."

"I'll catch them there, thanks."

"It's great to see you again, Will. I've missed ..."

I hold my breath. Her attentions, though flattering, make me uncomfortable.

"That is, uh ... the place has been a madhouse since you ... since you went on leave."

No doubt Grady and Swbyra take up my slack. They should get another man on the squad. Maybe they can't unless my leave becomes permanent.

*****

The minute I enter the emergency room lobby and smell that cool dry acrid air, my pulse zooms. Outside, a siren wails, the automatic doors shudder open. My temperature plummets and the room swims. On legs of overcooked spaghetti I stagger to the nearest chair, put my head between knees that I can barely feel, and try to get blood to my brain before I black out. Breathe, I tell myself, breathe.

Beside me, a junkie vibrates with withdrawal symptoms, while nearby a wild-eyed street-tough presses a bloody bandage against his wound. The emergency room is a vignette of human suffering depicted in its most acute physical forms. Centuries ago, the sight of sick and wounded people set a sheltered Indian prince on the spiritual quest that led him to become the Buddha. Why was there suffering, he wondered? Desire, he realized, leads to suffering, but desire can be broken, through meditation.

Unlike the Buddha, I'm not here on a spiritual quest. It's Hector I'm looking for and he could be in the morgue or in a ward. Wobbling, I get to my feet and find a nurse.

"Will! It's great to see—hey, are you OK? Do you need to sit?"

"I'm fine," I tell her, and ask if they've admitted anyone like Hector lately.

"Not that I recall but I'll give it some thought, ask the other girls. Maybe on another shift? I'll call you if I come up with anything."

"I won't be there. I'm on disability."

"Does that mean you won't be coming around to brighten up our dismal hallways? I bet they miss you, too." She nods at my squad mates. Paper coffee cups in hand they stand within calling distance of the nurses' station. Grady spots me and waves me over. Swbyra glances over his shoulder and gives me a smile, lips parting over teeth like an old fence with broken and missing pickets.

"Hey guys, what's up?" I ask.

Grady, that human billboard, shrugs shoulders about as broad as he is tall. At six-one, I'm a little taller but nowhere near as beefy. By comparison, Swbyra looks downright beanpole-ish. "Nothin' much."

Swbyra says, "Mugger popped some woman out on Forbes in the wee hours. Just inside the city limits. Another couple of miles and the sheriff would have caught it."

"A pregnant woman," Grady adds. "Ambushed in her car in the parking lot of one of those no-tell motels. Scattergun—12-gauge repeater—sawed-off pump-action from the looks of things. Shooter just pounded double-aught buck through the fucking side window. What a mess."

"Gives new meaning to the term 'headliner'," Swbyra says.

Grady and I cackle without mirth at his joke. Gallows humor. At the first crime scenes I attended as a rookie, when I found the old timers cracking wise it angered and offended me. It wasn't long before I learned what it was about: getting distance. How would I react now that I seek the opposite, to be fully present?

"No witnesses, no leads," Swbyra continues. "Oh, we got some tire tracks, some brass. Not that it does us any fuckin' good."

"What was she doing out there that time of night?"

Grady shrugs. "What's any woman doing at a place like that?"

Once a main north-south route winding through our end of the county, Forbes Road is dotted with the relics of homey travelers' inns, hunting lodges, cafes. Long abandoned by traffic favoring fast straight highways and the even faster interstate, Forbes Road motels now accept guests by the hour.

A gowned and masked man with bloody gloves emerges from Triage. Across from the door, a young man in work boots and sturdy trousers rises from his perch on the edge of an orange molded chair, his face tight, his eyes wide with hope. The doctor shakes his head and the man caves into his seat, his face cracking like shattered safety glass.

The doctor approaches Grady. "We lost them both."

"It's a capital case now," Swbyra says.

Grady chugs his coffee and tosses the cup into a wastebasket. "You know what that means, guys. Happy hour."

Happy hour. Grady's black humor. As long as people keep killing each other, the world will continue to need cops.

"Come on, let's go get a drink." Grady heads for the automatic doors.

"You don't need to talk to the husband?" I ask.

"Boyfriend. Does he look in any condition to talk? Anyway, he wasn't anywhere near the place. We've already checked that out." Once outside Grady stops to turn his collar against a damp gust and lights a cigarette. "Mansion, you coming?"

"I'm not drinking these days, Grady."

"Ooh, yeah, bet you're happy enough with all the dope the docs gave you."

His observation gives me a guilty start. Does he suspect that I not only welcome but crave the narcotics I was given, and not just for their pain-relieving qualities? Drug-induced slumber in the hospital was the only nightmare-free sleep I've had since the shooting. "It's not that, Grady. I just quit, that's all."

"It's that Zen thing you're into, isn't it?" Swbyra asks.

Grady presses his big palms together, bows, and hums, "Ommmm."

"Grady!" Swbyra says.

"It's just fucking weird, man. It's like he got religion or something."

"If you died and came back to life, you'd probably get religion, too," Swbyra replies.

"I'd rather have a drink," Grady says. "You coming?" Without waiting for an answer, he charges off down the street.

We follow him around the corner to the Emergency Room. With its scarlet flocked wallpaper and crimson carpet, the place always looks lit by an ambulance's cherry. The bartender sets up three glasses of whiskey. "Mansion, haven't seen you in weeks. Been on vacation or something?"

"Or something." Before I'm even aware of it, I have taken a swallow.

Grady tosses back his drink, signals for another. While he waits, he lights another cigarette. The smoke teases me. "So what were you doing at the House of Pain, Mansion?" he asks. "Miss the action?"

"Actually, I was looking for you guys."

"Aw, you hear that?" Grady says. "He misses us. We miss you, too. And I ain't just saying that 'cause now we got to work twice as fucking hard." He leans into my face. "Which we do."

"I thought you might know something about a missing person I'm looking for. A woman asked me to—"

"You? Why you?" Grady asks.

"She tried at the station. A Sister Clyde. Looking for a guy named Hector. Know anything about that?" I take another sip. The liquid warmth flooding my system relaxes muscles and nerves tightened by the déjà vu of the emergency room. If I'm not careful, I could easily renew my former close friendship with alcohol. I push the glass out of easy reach.

"Oh, yeah, some little old lady. The complaint didn't have much merit," Grady says. "Anyway, now we got this double homicide and you know that's gonna take priority. There's just so much a two-man squad can do."

"Seems he might have a line on Shrike," I tell him.

"Shrike," Swbyra murmurs. His eyes go glassy, his gaze distant.

Four weeks ago, Grady, Swbyra, and I nearly had the scumsucker until our carefully engineered collar went all wrong. Shrike got away clean and I got hauled off in an ambulance. Now the city's most elusive drug dealer is free to resume his trade in "Nearvana," heroin so potent it's almost immediately addicting, so finely powdered it's smokable. No need for nasty needles.

Grady shakes his head. "You want this Hector looked for, you get your fuckin' ass back to work and help."

His bitterness baffles me. Why's he angry with me? I'd pin my badge back on right here and now if I could. "I ... need more time."

Grady taps the bar with a fingertip. The bartender replaces the empty glass with a full one. "That so?"

Swbyra says softly, "Relax, Mansion. We'll check out this Hector thing you think is so important."

"And Shrike," I reply.

"And Shrike," Swbyra says. He looks spooked.

"You might start with a stolen car," I tell them.

"Theft's taken a back seat now with this homicide." Grady empties his glass and lights another cigarette.

"I understand that. I'm not certain it is a theft. All I know is the man had a car. An Eterniti. Gold. Have any gold Eternitis been reported stolen lately?"

Grady glares at the bottles across the bar. I can't even catch his glance in the mirror. "Like I remember every car that's been swiped," he says.

But he does. That's the job. "You would remember this one if you saw it on the hot sheet," I tell him. Foreign cars are a rarity here. Yankees drive American.

"What's the matter with you, Grady?" Swbyra asks. "If you know something about a stolen car, tell the man." He looks at me with eyes that are almost doe-like.

I don't need him to defend me against Grady, who didn't use to attack me. As for Swbyra, I guess he feels he owes me since I was shot. He shouldn't. He would have taken a bullet for me, had the roles been reversed.

Swbyra rubs his temples. He's getting one of those migraines of his. At the start of the year he'd go home with it. By now, though, he's used up all his sick leave. If it were a slow day, he'd take his car somewhere outside radio range, lie down across the seat, and succumb, out of touch for hours. He'll have to tough this out.

Not Stooges in the least, Grady and Swbyra are good cops. They've worked hard, as did I. We started the job with the same ambitions: serve the community, keep the peace. No matter how many people we arrested, though, people still broke the law. So we worked harder and filled the jail until it could hold no more and the cons ended up back on the street, only this time smarter, with better connections and bigger guns. Trying to stop them became not only a futile exercise, but one that was increasingly likely to get us killed.

Catching the bad guys ceased to be a mission and became a minefield.

About that time, Swbyra began to get migraines and Grady started drinking. Neither of them can afford to quit or start over again in some other job. All they can do is hang on until retirement.

The big man takes a couple of thoughtful puffs. "No stolen Eternitis, Obi Wan," he finally announces. "But I'll keep my eyes open."

"Thanks. And thanks for the drink."

"Don't mention it, Yogi."

As I walk away, I hear Swbyra say, "Don't call him that" and Grady's muttered, "Fuck 'im."

So, no stolen Eternitis. Could such a car legitimately belong to someone who's been sucking down soup at the Mercy Mission? It's not hard to imagine what a man of means, however obtained, would be doing on the Miracle Mile. There's nothing about wealth, even legitimate, that immunizes a man from the lure of sex or drugs. But why would he be lunching at Sister Clyde's?

CHAPTER 3

Windy street corner
A patrolman chafes cold hands
A hooker shudders—S_zan

I'm surprised Grady didn't jump at the chance to pursue this possible lead to Shrike, but he's right; there's just so much that a two-man squad can handle. With a fresh homicide, I doubt he'll be able to tackle anything else anytime soon. Damn it, by the time he gets around to Hector, the trail will be cold.

Without a case number, much less a tag number, there's no use trying MVD for help finding the Eterniti so it's back to the Miracle Mile to nose around. The Mercy Mission can't be the only place Hector hung his hat, assuming he had a hat. Surely someone else around there has seen him.

I ask about the man at every establishment he might have frequented. Yes, they know him at the massage parlor and the liquor store, but by first name only. The plasma bank technician and the front desk man at the Algonquian simply shake their head.

In the musty pawnshop, I nose around the musical instruments and sports equipment before reaching the rear of the store. There the pawnbroker guards shelves of electronics, cameras, and jewelry, once treasured items whose worth paled in the light of some greater need. In answer to my question he grunts, "Don't know him."

In the King Philip as elsewhere on the Mile, Hector has done an admirable job of being simultaneously well known and anonymous.

Daylight thins to dusk. I stop being selective and knock on any door that shows signs of life, even the one on which hangs a ragged sheet of cardboard with the single word "Tattoos." For all the sign's crudeness, the hand-painted letters are artistic. A little bell overhead tinkles when I pull open the door and I step into a smog of dust, old cigarette smoke, stale sweat, sharp tarry ink fumes, and over it all, aromatic incense.

"Yeah?" asks a throaty voice.

Her back to the door, the tattoo artist stands in the center of the room under a suspended task lamp. Light shines in jet black wavy hair that brushes the ruffled collar of a dingy, gray satin blouse. Narrow shoulders hunch in a short, stiff ivory brocade vest that comes to the slim waist of black leather pants. A long drink of water.

"I'm looking for Hector," I say.

"He ain't here," the tattoo artist replies without turning around.

"He ain't here," not "Don't know him." Encouraged, I step farther into the room, peer over her shoulder. Her client lounges like an odalisque in a dilapidated barber's chair. She is topless and has an arm tucked under a head of fluffy blonde hair. With latex-gloved fingers, the tattooer positions the needle on the woman's breast, applies some color, lifts the needle, and wipes off the excess with a paper towel. The beginning of a pastel scallop hugs the edge of the aureole, embellishing a full creamy breast.

The tattooer applies the needle again. I wince with vicarious pain but the woman has a small smile on her face. She opens her eyes and her pupils are huge and dark. *Stoned.*

"Where can I find him?" I ask.

When the tattooer turns half toward me, I see with a start that she is not a woman but a man, albeit a small one with delicate features. The hair, the ruffled shirt, the slim shiny pants bring to mind Gainsborough's *The Blue Boy.* Shadowed eyelids fringed with thick curly lashes curtain dark glittering eyes that regard me out of a pinched heart-shaped face. Porcelain-pale skin stretches over high cheekbones and a sculpted jaw. Shiny rings pierce neat earlobes, an arched eyebrow, and one nostril. Full, lustrous dark lips form a perfect Cupid's bow.

Those lips are not smiling.

"Why should I tell you, cop?" she, no, he asks.

"Not a cop. Just a friend of a friend." *For now, at least.*

"Sure you are." He shows me his back, picks up his needle, and spreads his fingers out on the woman's breast again.

I find myself staring at it and force myself to look away at the walls instead. The unpainted gypsum, water-spotted and chipped in places, displays sample tattoos. Flowers, butterflies, death's heads, bike logos, nymphs, sword-pierced hearts, thorn-laced crosses, mandalas, dragons, snakes. They look mass-produced, like stencils, but there are also color photographs and pencil sketches. Custom work, I presume.

At last, the tattooer puts down his needle. "You're done, babe," he says to the woman on the chair.

She sits up, leans into him, and kisses him on the cheek. "Thanks, Lix." She hops down, struts over to me on high-heeled ankle boots, and swings her breasts. "What do you think?"

"Nice," I gasp.

"Come on, babe, the job's not finished 'till the paperwork's done," the tattooer says. He spreads clear gel on the fresh tattoo, tapes a folded sheet of paper towel over it, and pats it. "There ya go."

"He's the best," she tells me. She pulls on a fake fur jacket, zips it halfway up, and sashays to the door. "Till next time, Lix."

"See ya, babe."

I saunter over to a rolling supply cart and pick up a bottle of color. "So, 'Lex,' you want to tell me where Hector is?"

The needle man stops, leans toward me. "Put that down, man, that stuff's expensive."

"Is it?" If he knows something about Hector, he's going to tell me. I suspend the bottle over the floor and release it. Liquid spreads in a hot pink puddle. "Oops, I'm sorry."

"Ah, man, you don't gotta do that."

"Where is Hector?"

The tattooer glowers. I let a bottle of purple go next.

"Come on, man, cut it out," he says. "What are you planning to do, bust up the whole place?"

"If I have to." I pick up a bright lime green. "Look I've got no beef with you, Lex, I'm just trying to find somebody."

His glossy lips twist in a moue. "It's not Lex, it's Lix."

"Lix what?"

"Gemini."

"Lix Gemini. That your street name or your real name?"

"Sure you're not a cop? You ask questions like a cop."

"You dodge 'em like a man with something to hide. Now where can I find Hector?"

"I don't know. Around."

"Ah, hell." I drop the bottle of green. The pool at my feet becomes a psychedelic omelet.

"I'm telling you, man, I don't know! Honest."

Same old song. Seems everyone on the Miracle Mile is suffering from lip lock. "OK, have it your way, Lix Gemini. Be seeing you."

Gemini snatches up the roll of paper towels and kneels beside the spreading ink. "Damn, I hope not."

The night air is clammy after the suffocating warmth of the tattoo parlor. I button my coat and scan the street for unturned stones.

"Hey, Good Lookin'. Want a date?"

The voice belongs to a woman on the corner, the freshly illustrated blonde from the tattoo parlor. With her fleecy hair, fluffy white jacket, and pale bare legs, she looks like a dandelion swaying in the cold breeze. Since I'm the only other person within earshot, she must mean me. Not too long ago, I would have busted her for soliciting. Tonight, I simply say, "Sorry. I'm busy."

"Looking for Hector, huh?" she asks.

"Yeah. If you tell me where I can find him, that might free up my evening if you know what I mean."

She looks up at the starless sky. "Well, I can't do that, exactly. Been a long time since I've seen him. Too bad, too, he was one of my favorites. Till I met you, that is."

"I'd have an easier time finding him if I knew what name he was using these days."

"You mean, Waltann isn't his real name?"

Waltann? Hector Waltann? "Probably not any more than Smith or Jones," I reply, trying to keep my excitement out of my voice. "Thanks anyway."

"No problem. Now hurry up and find him so you can come back and take me someplace where we can crank up the heat."

I slip her a ten and tell her to go ahead without me.

Hector Waltann. Could he possibly be listed in the phone directory? Miracle Mile's lone phone booth doesn't have one—it doesn't have a phone either—but the desk man at the Algonquian lets me look at his. A Hector Waltann is listed on Columbus. Country Club Estates, a ritzy address. It's a straight shot down South Hope Street and across Mill Valley Lane. I could be there in under half an hour, easily.

I turn off Mill Valley into a subdivision illuminated by white street lamps. The houses' front windows glow yellow. Once, I was certain I'd have a house like this someday, along with a wife and kids, when I'd made the grade in the P.D., when I'd found a girl I could trust.

In Country Club Estates, mini villas with Spanish tile roofs and Mediterranean facades fringe the golf course. We've never had much trouble with this area. Domestic violence is waged discretely behind custom window coverings and there aren't even many burglaries. The pickings are good but the homes are too well protected. There are easier marks elsewhere in the city.

Manicured lawns devoid of toys say this is not a neighborhood of growing families. Children raised, corporate ladders climbed, these homeowners belong to the club, have home theater systems, vacation at summer cottages on the Cape, drink single malt scotch. Drive Eternitis. Could be the car is legitimately Waltann's.

Hector Waltann's house is as upscale as its neighbors, but weeds stubble the brown lawn. The birdbath is dry, the rose bushes are brambles. Shrubs have overgrown the windows.

At my knock, the yellow light that fills the front door peephole blinks out momentarily. The sneak-peek won't help whoever's behind the door; I'm standing off to the side. The door opens a crack and I glimpse a short middle-aged woman.

"Hector Waltann, please," I say.

"He's not here," she replies but doesn't close the door.

"When might he return?"

"I don't know," she says, and closes the door.

"So he is missing," I call out.

The door cracks open again. "Missing? What do you mean?"

"Ma'am, I'm happy to explain if I could have a few moments."

She opens the door as wide as the safety chain will allow and paints me from head to toe with her gaze. A kid in a toy store couldn't look more agog. As often as I get this reaction from women, it still makes me uneasy.

She asks, "You're not a bill collector, are you?"

"I assure you, I'm no threat to your husband or you."

After a moment, she slides the chain off. "Come in."

She's plainer than I imagined the wife of an Eterniti owner would be. Her navy slacks and sweater are the casual, at-home attire of a woman who wasn't expecting company. Her thin lips are pale, nails are unpolished, and graying hair is done in short slack curls. In contrast, huge earrings weigh down her earlobes and hunky ornate rings choke fingers that clasp a highball glass and a cigarette. The red, green, and crystal gemstones that glitter confidently in the foyer light are so large I wonder if they're genuine, though they probably are.

"Mrs. Waltann?"

"Yes."

She leads me into an unlighted living room. Overstuffed forms of furniture crouch in the gloom. Crystal vases and glazed porcelain figurines crowd the tables and shelves. Their shiny surfaces gleam in what little street light filters in through the front window's sheer curtains. I lean in close to examine the paintings on the walls: still lifes and landscapes, scenes from someone else's life. I'm no connoisseur but I doubt they are paint-by-number. There is a noticeable absence of family photos. The jewelry, the furnishings, the house and neighborhood all speak of money, even if the front yard's condition and Hector's presence at the Mercy Mission hint at a recent reversal of fortune.

"I don't know you. Are you a friend of my husband's?" Mrs. Waltann asks.

"A friend of a friend," I reply. "My name is Mansion."

"I see. Please, have a seat. Can I get you a drink?"

I choose the couch and struggle to get secure on slippery satin. "Thank you."

Without pausing to turn on a lamp she crosses to a wet bar, pours dark liquid from a crystal decanter that sparkles in the low light, and hands me a glass. It has the warm mellow aroma of fine whiskey. I don't plan to drink it but fingers that used to grip a cigarette appreciate having something to hold.

With the overly-precise movements of the inebriated, Mrs. Waltann settles into a dainty chair in a corner. "Feel free to smoke. There's an ashtray." She gestures vaguely at the cocktail table.

"Thank you but I quit." If I say it often enough, maybe even I'll believe it.

"Goody for you," she says. "Why do you think Hector is missing?"

"So you know where he is?"

Mrs. Waltann smokes silently for a minute or two. She sits with her shoulders squared, face-forward as if she were studying me though she can hardly see well in the grainy darkness. Finally she says, "Not exactly." She raises her glass to her lips and sips, follows it with a puff of cigarette. Just when I've decided she's slipped into a whiskey dream she says, "My husband and I are separated."

"I see. An acquaintance of his hasn't seen him lately and she's worried about him."

"She," Mrs. Waltann echoes.

Another moment of palpable silence passes. If a TV is on somewhere in the house, or a radio or stereo, I don't hear it. No appliances run. The phone doesn't ring. No children shout, no dogs bark. It is quiet as a museum. In the motionless air I smell no cooking aromas, no flowers, no perfume, only cigarettes and booze.

"You're not concerned about him, Mrs. Waltann?"

"Not anymore." She twists the glass in her hand. "I was at first, when he started acting strangely."

Oh? Maybe he's recently had a stroke or breakdown, is wandering around in some kind of dementia. Could be he's not as lucid as Sister Clyde made him out to be. "When was this?"

"About a year ago." Mrs. Waltann turns her head to glance out the front window. "One day, his clothes were suddenly too old and plain. Fine, get custom suits, custom shirts. And yes, they did look nice." She pauses. Thinking she's stalled, I'm about to prompt her when she restarts herself. "I didn't even tease him when he started using Rogaine, though even with hair he was still going to be Hector. You're young, handsome ..." She gives me a long look. "You wouldn't understand.

"Then the house was too shabby. It wasn't, but fine, get the house painted, get new carpeting, furniture, the home theater. I certainly didn't object. Then it was new golf clubs, a motorized cart ... I don't know why I'm telling you this." She tilts her head but she is too old and too drunk to pull off coquettish.

I know why. It's because I'm listening. "Would a new car have been part of the package?" I ask.

"The Eterniti?" she says. "Yes, he had to have that, too. Just walked into the dealership one day and bought it for cash—"

"Cash?"

"You'd think he was buying a new tie. It didn't scratch whatever was itching him. It wasn't good enough. Nothing was good enough."

She sips again. The clink of ice cubes against her glass is loud as a glacier cracking.

She sighs. "It got ... obsessive. I thought whatever was bothering him, he'd eventually get it out of his system. When he moved out, I left the door open. I held out hope." She drifts off again. When she resumes speaking, her voice is low, her tone spiteful. "But it only got worse. Stories got back to me: he was out partying all night. Drunk, crazy drunk." Her voice drops lower yet. "Involved with a woman." She smokes and sips some more.

"What about drugs?" I ask. She shrugs.

Not a stroke then, at least not to her knowledge. While she has described a man who's been living the high life, it's nothing that would explain his presence in a soup kitchen.

"You said it's a woman who wants him found?" she asks.

"Yes." I don't elaborate. I'm trying to obtain information, not give it.

She drains her drink, tips a cube into her mouth, and crunches down. It sounds like a floe yielding to an icebreaker. I ask her how to get in touch with her husband.

"Why would I try? He lost the business. Drained our finances, borrowed on the house and the insurance, then stopped paying on them. He's taken everything. I hope the sonofabitch is dead." She crushes another piece of ice. "You can tell his friend that."

Whoa, now that's harsh. This sounds more serious than a man trying to party away middle age. A bad drug habit, maybe. One that ran him into heavy debt. Owed to Shrike? Is that what the men at the mission hinted?

"Ma'am, if you don't mind, I'd like to borrow a picture of Mr. Waltann."

"I'll see what I have."

She leaves me alone in the unlit room. Time passes. More. Enough so I wonder what became of her. I set off down a hallway, slowly at first, more purposefully when I see light emanating from a doorway. In a classically-furnished study, Mrs. Waltann sits slumped over a writing desk, her head cradled in her right arm, snoring softly. *So much for asking any more questions tonight.*

Her left arm dangles at her side. Gently, I slip a card from her loose grasp.

CHAPTER 4

On a country road,
a single lamppost spotlights
wild asparagus—Soezi

I show myself out. Stunned by the brightness of the street lights and the vitriol in the woman's condemnation, I drift down the walk. Not until I'm in Old Paint do I shake off the spell and get my first good look at Hector Waltann. The map light shows I have a two-year-old color photo Christmas card. "To Our Valued Friends and Customers—May the beauties of the Christmas season be an inspiration to you all year, The Waltann family—Hector, Marybeth, and Terry."

In a green holiday dress with red plaid trim and lots of big jewelry, Marybeth Waltann is the picture's focal point. She sits flanked by two men in dark suits, each with a hand on her shoulder. The taller one gets my attention next. Mid-twenties, pasty-faced, long, thick dark blond hair slicked back in a style unsuited to its weight and length, a normally wild mane cleaned up as a concession for the photo. This must be Terry, their son. A young man wearing mature man's clothes with an arrogant smile that says he's doing the folks a favor, posing for this picture.

The head of the clan is fleshy-faced and fifty-ish. Dark hair worn in a nearly successful comb-over covers any bald spot Hector Waltann might have. Thick arms and a big stomach fill out a suit whose custom-tailoring makes him look robust rather than fat.

Chin up, he stares down the camera. The pose proclaims him a rich man. A powerful man. One with his hands on the controls. A man who should be driving an Eterniti, who, if he had even heard of the Mercy Mission, might donate to it, but not drink its soup.

Hector Waltann, prosperous businessman. *Now what is he doing in Sister Clyde's Mercy Mission?* It's too late to call at his business tonight. I head up Queen Street to Route 9. Floodlit billboards along the four-lane blacktop vie for my notice. One for Verve cigarettes shows a young attractive couple artfully arranged in a cheery den, heads thrown back, mouths open in delight. Not one bad odor, stained tooth, yellowed fingertip, or black lung spoils the image, even though Verves are unfiltered and about the highest tar brand around. By the looks on their faces, they have just had either a smoke or an orgasm. The hell with the orgasm, I could really use a cigarette. Lighting up is as much a part of driving as turning the ignition.

In another sign, Naiad Spring Water's buxom spokesnymph beckons me to partake of her mountain stream, conveniently packaged in twelve-ounce sport-top plastic bottles. One sip will no doubt transport me to her unsullied sylvan aerie, free from pollution and stress. A slug of bottled water is no substitute for an afternoon in the woods, for which I must be overdue as I find myself salivating.

Touchstones they are, for what we are told we must have in order to be happy. These days I am happiest when I practice zazen, sitting meditation. If I concentrate, for a brief moment the gory scene of the Terminal Road shootout stops replaying itself against the inside of my eyelids, and I can luxuriate in simply being alive.

Every other sign is for fast food. I'll be treated right, I can have it my way, I deserve a break. My Pavlovian stomach rumbles. The masters say a man functions best at two-thirds full but I believe I am one-hundred-percent empty. The pictures of juicy sandwiches are more than I can resist. Once over the bridge I detour north up River Way—Restaurant Row, threaded with fast food outlets like beads on a string. At the first one I come to, I pull up to the speaker, and order. "I'd like a Bingo Burger, no sauce."

A disembodied voice, scratchy and coarse, replies, "You say you want 'The Boss?'"

"No, a burger, hold the sauce."

"What you said. 'The Boss.'"

The Boss? Oh, I see, it's their meal-deal of the month: a triple burger, triple cheese, extra-large fries and drink. More food than I want, but I am too tired and hungry to argue. "Fine. Give me that."

"Pull up to the window, please."

Back on Bridge Street, I am so busy juggling my food I nearly overshoot my only chance to turn onto Crosspath and I cut off another driver so as not to miss it. He lays on the horn, I flip him off, and gnash my burger in fury the entire dark length of Crosspath to the T-intersection with Riverbank. A single street lamp casts a yellow circle on the corner, gilds the stubble of wild asparagus, the oaks and elms beside the river, and the ripples in the water below. It's a peaceful, soothing tableau, a scene I like coming home to, and that's why I live here, although the wood-frame colonial in which I rent rooms is drafty and expensive to heat.

My apartment is dark but I don't need a light to find my way to the attic bedroom. It's late, I'm weary, and logy from too much food. I shuck the tight and tired clothes I've worn all day and turn down the covers, ready to slip between the sheets.

But there is meditation practice.

In a hurry to get it done and get to sleep, I don't chant or light incense or perform any of the other rituals the Zen book described, and I definitely don't bow. Formal practice includes prostrations, forehead to floor, not once but three times, in homage to the Teacher, the Teaching, the others who follow the Teaching. The couple of times I made myself do this I felt anything but reverent. At best I felt embarrassed, ridiculous, at worst resentful, defiant. So no, I don't bow.

Instead I haul my *zafu* from its corner and plant my butt on it. The floor-sitting cushion is stiff and unyielding as a sandbag and it takes much wriggling to achieve a position that's even remotely comfortable. Against the black cotton case, the stuffing of buckwheat husks rustles softly as a woman's satin dress. Full lotus is the recommended position, but all I can manage is a quarter lotus, left foot over the right calf. I try sitting seiza, kneeling astride the cushion, feet behind with soles upturned, like a geisha girl. Torn nerves and muscles in my thigh protest even at that.

The breath. Pay attention to the breath.

My breath comes short and shallow. Like wild horses, stray thoughts canter over a prairie landmarked by the Mercy Mission, the Miracle Mile, the Waltann home. They gallop to the precipice that is tomorrow and peer over the edge. Sometimes when I sit I can hear the frogs outside in the grass or the wind in the trees. Tonight my ears ring with the scrunch of ice between Mrs. Waltann's teeth.

Waltann. Hector Waltann. Shrike. *No, not Shrike!* I drag my mind kicking and screaming back to the here and now. What is happening now?

What's happening now is that there's a piece of hamburger wedged in a back tooth and I'm gassy. Ate too much too fast and took in too much air while doing it. A burger is impossible to eat slowly and with attention. There's no way to put it down between bites without it falling apart, the shredded lettuce and the patties skidding out from between the buns. Once picked up all anyone can do with it is wolf it down. Not a food so much as a product calculatedly engineered to promote over-consumption.

My foot has fallen asleep and an irritating numbness extends to the ankle. From my reading I know that many Westerners find floor-sitting painful. We are advised to make the pain our practice, detach from it emotionally, accept it as a matter of the moment, a sensation that ebbs and flows, impermanent. Still, my strongest urge is to escape it.

My joriki, my power of concentration, must not be strong enough. Perhaps, without a teacher to guide me, I have gone too far too fast in my practice. I try counting breaths, which helps to dispel distracting thoughts. I focus on my breath not in my nose or chest but in my lower abdomen, the seat of psychic energy. My mind slows, stops, and for a moment there is peace, utter contentment. When I next check in with my foot it is still asleep. In fact, it's worse. The numbness has crept up to my calf. But for a second there, I had lost track of the pain.

*****

The Buddha said that on arising, we should be aware enough to know whether our first conscious breath is an inhalation or an exhalation. After a sleepless night, the question is moot. My first thought is for a cigarette. After I struggle with that craving, my mind turns to Hector Waltann's disappearance.

Light rain mists Old Paint's windshield on the drive downtown. The Kaffeteria rings with the shouts of patrons calling out their orders, the hiss of the espresso machines, and the clink of heavy white porcelain cups. The old red brick walls do little to muffle the noise. Freshly ground French roast and warm ginger spice the air.

Duncan Phyffe races back and forth behind the fruitwood counter, taking money and handing back to-go orders, his curly black ponytail bouncing against his white shirt collar. "Hey, Will! The usual?" he yells.

Dunk's shelves hold beans from Antigua to Zimbabwe and every caffeine-starved cell in my brain screams, "Java!" but I say, "Sure."

I sip my genmaicha, munch my muffin, and gaze at a corner table where sits a computer with access to the Internet. Dunk leaves it available to anyone who wants to cybersurf and it's as much an attraction as the coffee. From about three o'clock in the afternoon on, it's monopolized by rabid computer nerds; at this hour the people who dart into the shop are intent on hitting a real rather than a virtual highway, so it's available.

If I were at the office working an official case, I could use the department's computer to background Hector Waltann. Sure there are private data services on the Net that offer similar information— criminal record, financial background. They charge a fee, though. A cop's pay permits few extras, especially when that cop is drawing disability. Fortunately there are free sites that sometimes yield up good information, like the online archives of the Paradise City *Crier*.

A search on the keywords "Hector Waltann" provides hot links to several citations. One is from the business section. Six months ago, Hector Waltann, owner of Facets, a jewelry store in the Canterbury Bazaar, announced the promotion of comptroller Marvin Overshort to partner.

The article quotes Terry Waltann, Facets' gemologist, as wishing Marvin Overshort "a lot of luck" in his new position with the store. Somehow, the sentiment rings false.

*****

People buy at the mall but they shop at the Canterbury Bazaar, a plaza of upscale boutiques in "Noho," the recently gentrified corner of Nonotuck and Hobbes. I steer Old Paint under the Bazaar's entrance, a hatchmented arch of attractive but impractical alabaster allegedly quarried at great expense in Britain. A parking valet in Olde English footman's livery politely but authoritatively halts my progress.

"Can I self-park it?" I ask.

The valet casts a disdainful eye at Old Paint and points me to a remote lot behind the stores.

Heavy dark timbers X-brace the rough-surfaced stucco of the Canterbury's Tudor-style stores and eateries. Fancy but nonfunctional brass knockers decorate huge wooden batten doors. Second and third stories jut out over the first. In summer these tiers provide welcome shade, in winter they help keep the walkways clear of snow. Today they only magnify the claustrophobic feel of the low dark sky. In clear vinyl overshoes that transform them into glass-slippered Cinderellas, the ladies who lunch mince over slick cobblestones in groups of two and three and smile at me from under logo umbrellas.

A chime sounds when I enter Facets. Coffee aroma tempts me from a delicate table with a silver coffee and tea service just inside the door. Pearls, gold, colored gems, and diamonds glimmer in glass showcases ranged along the walls. Salespeople offer velvet trays of merchandise to customers who sit in plush armchairs and sip from china cups. A tall glass pillar at the room's center holds watches, pens, and glossy figurines and vases like the ones in the Waltann home.

From a door between two showcases a young blonde woman in a slim mint green linen dress and, no surprise, a lot of jewelry, emerges. Greeting me with smiling green eyes, she makes her graceful unhurried way across the dove gray carpeting. She offers me a long-fingered hand tipped with manicured nails the color of nacre.

"Welcome to Facets. I'm Heidi Quince."

So it says in script on a gold name badge that also identifies her as a certified gemologist.

"May I interest you in something? I see you've noticed our watches. We have some lovely Rolexes."

"No, not a watch—"

"Ah, a fountain pen, then. We have the Optima Oscar Wilde. Limited edition, of course."

Of course. Why else would anyone spend—could that be—damn near three months' pay! For a pen? "Why, did Oscar himself use it?"

Heidi Quince's green eyes twinkle as brightly as the emeralds in the showcases. "Only 15,000 were ever made." She unlocks the cabinet, removes the pen, and hands it to me. "You can see the edition number engraved right on it. It's a very fine instrument. The Optima name embossed on the clip is an assurance of quality craftsmanship that everyone recognizes."

"Everyone. Sure."

"The barrel is a monument to craftsmanship. It's all hand-painted, hand-lacquered, and hand-polished."

A tiny scene like something from a Japanese scroll encircles the pen. A tufted cliff looms over a robed monk and temple with a low-pitched roof. The painting's brush strokes are so fine they must have been laid on with a single bristle.

Heidi Quince points to the flagstone path in the painting. "See those paving stones? They're not painted on, they're actually inlaid flecks of abalone."

The minute stones are smaller than dandruff flakes. The human effort lavished on this pen, however beautiful, boggles the mind. The most attention I've ever given a pen was making sure none of the city's ever went home with me. "You sell a lot of these?"

"A fair number, to men especially. They understand the most important thing they have is their signature. After all, it's with your signature that you close deals, seal fate, change history. It should be done with an instrument that transforms simple writing into an act of self-expression. Would you like to try it?" she asks.

And soil it with mere ink? But she has already uncapped a bottle. She takes my hand in hers, turns it palm up, and with a stunning smile, lays the filled pen on it. She stands close to me and watches as I write, or rather as my hand moves with the pen that seems to glide effortlessly over the paper.

"It's a beauty," I tell Heidi Quince. "But I didn't come to shop. I'm here to see Mr. Waltann."

Her sweet smile fades and she puts a little space between us. "I'm sorry, he's not here."

"When will he be back?"

She doesn't respond and I ask, "Well, then, where can I find him?"

Her face clouds, she catches her lower lip between teeth as white as Facets' best pearls, and gives her head a little shake.

"In that case I'd like to see Terry Waltann."

"Terry? Terry's no longer with Facets."

"I thought he was the gemologist."

"He was. He ... moved on, out of state. I'm ..." She taps her name badge.

"His replacement. I see. How about Mr. Overshort?"

She glances to her right, her left, but no one, nothing, comes to her rescue. With resignation she says, "Just a minute," and heads for the door she originally came through. When she realizes I'm following, she turns and says, "If you'll wait here, I'll get him for you."

"I don't want to keep you from your work. Just show me where his office is."

Heidi sighs and opens the door marked "Staff" that leads into a short corridor. No soft gray carpeting here. The floor covering is thin industrial stuff the color of dirt. The door-less openings on my left show the offices to be small and cramped. To my right a heavy steel door seals the vault room. Next to it is the only office with a door. Small nail holes and a darkened rectangle hint where a sign once was.

Heidi Quince takes a deep breath and knocks. There is no answer. She hangs her head, raises her fist, and knocks again.

From behind the door, a man bellows, "That's it, you're dead. I said I didn't want to be disturbed." A second later the door opens so abruptly Heidi Quince almost falls in.

"What, dammit?" a fat man asks.

This is Facets' manager? Biker-bar bouncer is more like it.

"Mr. Overshort—"

Marvin Overshort notices me, stops in mid-tirade, and waits, his red face and puff-chested posture a challenge to me to explain myself. With his rotund body, round florid face, and deep-set eyes, he could be Porky Pig's evil twin.

"Mr. Overshort, he's asking about Hector," Heidi says quickly.

Overshort presses his lips together, dismisses her with a jerk of his head toward the door, and with another head jerk, directs me into his office. Stacks of catalogs litter the floor and fill the seat of a chrome-framed side chair. A fan-folded printout spills over the side of an avocado-green steel credenza piled high with brochures and other literature. Ranged along the credenza's top are gold statuettes of men with long guns. Trophies for hunting or marksmanship of some kind.

He lifts the telephone receiver, says, "I can't talk about that now," and hangs up. He props a broad butt encased in pilled black beltless slacks on the edge of a messy desk and folds his arms over a chest that strains a permanently not-quite-pressed shirt. "You a cop?"

"Were you expecting one, sir?"

He shrugs. "You got the look. We had a theft here a while back, thought you were one of those dicks here to tell me you'd gotten a lead on who done it, or maybe found some of the stuff."

A theft. Seems I remember something about that. It wasn't my case, though. Grady worked it, I think. So why did Grady act like he didn't know who Hector was? "Sorry, no, Mr. Overshort. Just someone who's looking for Hector Waltann."

"Is he missing?"

"You know where he is?"

Marvin Overshort's hunched shoulders lower slightly. "His condo? Somewhere partying? Hell do I know?"

"And you're in charge here, sir?"

"Damn I ought to be. I'm the owner."

"I thought you were a partner."

Overshort throws his head back and snorts. "'Was' is right. Now I'm the owner."

"Doesn't Hector still have some ownership?"

The phone rings. He turns his head and glares at it. It stops in mid-ring and chastened, goes silent.

"OK, so what? You see him here? What do you want with him, anyway? Who the hell are you?"

"I'm helping a friend of his who's concerned about him."

"Oh, private heat. Sorry, can't help you." He dismounts the desk and shows me his back.

"Well, thanks for your time, sir." As if in defeat, I start for the door, then ever so casually turn back. "About your theft ... any idea who did it?"

Still with his back to me, Overshort asks, "Why, you going to give me some kinda sales pitch for private eye service?"

"Not at all, sir. Just curious."

He shrugs. "Inventory shrinkage's my guess. I took care of that. Did me a little housecleaning, hired me all new people I can control is what I did."

Can terrorize into submission is more like it from the way Heidi Quince behaved.

He nods with satisfaction. "They're working out good, too, we're back in the black. So like I said, it doesn't matter about the theft."

Doesn't matter? Every other business owner I've dealt with on a theft has badgered me senseless over the case's progress. "You mentioned Hector's condo. What's the address?"

Overshort twists around and gives me a long look. He pounds the telephone's intercom button with his fist and shouts into the mic. "I'm sending some guy out there in a minute. Dig up Hector's new address and give it to him, will ya, babe?"

"Yes, sir, Mr. Overshort," a meek voice replies.

He turns back to me. "So, that everything you need? Ca'use I got work to do, you know. It ain't easy pushing these rocks." He grabs a fist full of paper, seizes a pen that appears to be a limited edition Optima Oscar Wilde, and pulls the hand-lacquered cap off with his teeth.

"I'll just find my way out."

Overshort doesn't respond. He has already dismissed me.

A young, pretty, nervous woman meets me in the corridor and hands me a folded note. I push through the door back out onto the sales floor. Heidi Quince walks me to the exit.

"Get what you came for?"

I hold up the note. "I guess so."

"You're sure? There isn't anything else here you like?"

She can't mean that the way it sounds, despite what her expectant smile and her hand on my arm suggest. I don't know. Could be she only wants to sell me a pen. I learned at a young age about the duplicity of women, at the shotgun wedding of a teenaged friend's older brother. "Let this be a lesson to you, son," my father said. "You can't trust women. When they want something from you, they'll do whatever it takes to get it."

"Thanks for your help," I tell Heidi.

The pressure of her hand on my arm increases. "If you find Hector, will you please let me know?" She sounds desperate.

"So you think he's missing, too, don't you?"

Before Heidi can answer, the "Staff Only" door opens and Overshort steps out.

"Can't talk now," Heidi says. She straightens her smile and hastens toward a young couple coming through the front door.

CHAPTER 5

People scurry home
through red, yellow, maroon leaves
to watch Tonight's News—S_zan

I'm eager to get to the little slip of paper burning a hole in my jacket pocket but there's something I want to check out first. Though I'm not far from the station, I don't want to create the wrong impression by showing up there every day. I'm only a few blocks from the Kaffeteria and if I go now, I can get onto the computer before the afternoon rush.

No need to hack into official police files, even if I could. The Paradise City *Crier* has plenty on the theft at Facets. The first article quotes Marvin Overshort who reports the unaccountable absence of "several loose and set stones." Included among them is a unique "marquise-cut emerald ring." It sounds expensive, although in the story Overshort is vague about its value. A follow-up report includes a statement from Overshort as well as a Facets employee who first discovered the theft, and from neighboring businesses, the janitorial service, and the Canterbury's roving security officer. None noticed any sign of a break-in. "Police maintained" to have questioned pawnbrokers to find out if the jewels had hit the streets. Sounds like a thorough-enough investigation, but the goods were indeed never recovered. There are no reports of anyone being arrested, much less charged.

Like the narratives I've written on my cases, the theft is reported in language that's meant to communicate facts, not opinions. Still, there's always more than what's in black and white—suspicions that couldn't be proved, impressions that couldn't be documented. By reading between the lines, the astute observer can see where the investigation was headed. The "pawnbrokers" that Grady questioned were probably street people or known fences pressed into service as informants. A subject re-interviewed or a location revisited shows who or what was under the microscope. The reporter interviewed only one person more than once: the complainant, Marvin Overshort.

Hector Waltann isn't even mentioned. No wonder the theft didn't come up in my initial query about Hector. Apparently Overshort was the one who was really in charge. That could explain why Hector's name didn't mean anything to Grady. He dealt with Overshort.

Just as when I spoke with him, in the reporter's story Overshort seems curiously dismissive, stating the loss was of no great importance and that he fully expects insurance to take care of it.

That done, I hustle on over to Hector's condo. Shays' Landing, in the crook of the river's elbow, is a newer development built to appeal to yuppies and comfortably-set empty-nesters who don't want yard work.

Even though it's on a cul-de-sac, bounded on one side by the river and gated, we get a fair number of intruder calls from this place. Walls are no real deterrents to thieves who find a way over, under, around, or through. Not even this one, designed to mimic stockade fencing. Instead, the so-called security gives a false sense of safety to the residents who then get lax about locking up.

The development's office is housed in a model. For accessibility to the public, the entrance is outside the gate. In the model's foyer, a well-groomed woman in a tailored pink wool suit rises from behind an antique writing desk, crosses the cushiony sand-colored carpet, and greets me with a pink-lipsticked smile.

"Hi, welcome to Shays' Landing. Were you interested in one of our units?" she asks.

"Why yes, I am." *That, in any event, is no lie.*

"How lucky for us," she says with a smile that is part flirtation, part salesmanship.

"One of your residents interested me in the place. Hector Waltann?"

"Ah, Hector ... yes. Is he on a business trip or on vacation or something?"

"I wouldn't know. We're not that well acquainted. Why?"

Her smile loses some of its brightness and she taps a long polished nail against another. "It's just that I haven't seen him lately. A week, maybe longer."

"You think something's happened to him?"

She flushes slightly and stands a little taller. "Oh, I wouldn't say that. I'm sure he's just out of town. He should have had his mail held. His lock box is crammed and the mailman's started leaving his mail with me."

"I could take it, give it to him when I see him."

"How sweet of you. But I probably should hold onto it." The leasing agent tugs the hem of her jacket and squares her shoulders. "Well, you said you were interested in our units."

"Hector made his sound very attractive. He invited me over but I've never had a chance to take him up on it. I wonder if I could see it now?" I give her my most appealing smile.

"Oh, I don't think I could do that. Why don't I show you a unit just like his?" She pulls on a trench coat and unlocks the access door to the complex's inner sanctum. Her pink high heels click loudly on rain-darkened brick walkways.

In a few years, the saplings they planted to replace the old trees they chopped down will mature and the ground cover will fill in the bulldozed meadow. Then the place will look as if it's been here for decades—if the buildings last that long. The brick veneered and dormered one-, two-, and three-bedroom townhouses mimic the architecture of old colonials but I doubt they have the same staying power.

"Naturally we have a pool, spa, a clubhouse, sport courts, all reserved for the residents," the leasing agent says. "But here's our signature feature: the view." She points to the river, visible through a rear gate. Ah yes, the river. I remember when the developers first narrowed the riverbed and shored up the bank with concrete retaining walls. Conservationists and environmentalists protested.

"The main security gate keeps solicitors out, not to mention the criminal element," she says. "You'll find it's very private here. Our residents mind their own business. Why you could go for weeks and never speak to a soul."

As if to prove it, people coming home from work look neither to the right nor left as they stream from their covered parking spaces to their respective warrens. Doors close and the blue light of television flicks on behind curtained windows.

"You don't think, maybe if neighbors knew and looked out for each other, we'd have less crime?" I ask.

The leasing agent looks at me with raised eyebrows. "Crime? We don't have any crime here. I told you, it's gated."

"Ah."

The vaulted ceilings of the one-bedroom unit she shows me draw the eyes up. Nevertheless I notice that the floors aren't quite level and walls aren't straight. Faux leaded-glass windows, cultured marble bathroom vanities with gilded faucets, and granite-like kitchen counter tops create a luxurious look that is only skin-deep.

I ask her if I could walk around the grounds on my own.

"But you haven't seen the upstairs." She grins. "Tell you what. See me before you leave. I'll show you the bedroom."

When she's out of sight, I make straight for Hector's unit.

A compact concrete walkway leads through a pocket yard of new winter rye and baby junipers. A short narrow flight of steps presents callers directly to the front door. Too vulnerable for my taste. I take up quarter stance as far to the side of the handkerchief-sized landing as the wrought iron railing will allow, reach across, and knock. No answer.

I jiggle the door handle. Locked.

I press my ear to the door. It's quiet inside which only piques my curiosity. Maybe I'd find something that would answer all the questions. So far this is my best lead.

A striking young woman in workout gear emerges from the unit next door. Halfway down her stairs she glances over at me and pauses, halted in mid-stride like a window shopper caught by a tempting display. I give my best impersonation of an impromptu visitor frustrated to find the resident not home, and she moves on.

Maybe there's a spare key. I check for any more uncharacteristically curious residents, then run my hand around the door frame. Flower pots flanking the door hold plants that have shriveled from neglect but do not hide a key.

Perhaps there's a way in around the back. The rear entry is at ground level at the end of a yard a little larger than the one in front. I sidle up to the door and wait for any sign my presence has been detected. A thorough survey of the surroundings reassures me I'm alone and can't be seen from the windows of the adjoining units.

I knock, listen, and try the door again but there's no answer and the door is still locked. A search of the few places to hide a spare key turns up nothing. With management relying so heavily on the vaunted security gate, they've probably skimped on the doors and locks. Sure enough, the door itself is thin steel, cheaper and flimsier than solid wood, and there is no deadbolt, just an entry lockset. It would be easy to break in, no special skills required. Only the most amateur thief would bother picking the lock; most would simply kick it in.

It's true that while nobody has seen Hector recently, the only one besides Sister Clyde who seems the least bit concerned about him is Facets' gemologist, Heidi Quince. But what if he's in trouble? He could be hurt or sick and who would know? Certainly not his bitter wife, absentee son, or blowhard business associate. Heidi Quince seemed too intimidated by Overshort to investigate, and Sister Clyde didn't know enough to get this far. That's why she asked me.

I want in so badly I can taste it. My conscience doesn't stand a chance against my craving to know what's inside. It's never a serious contest; even as I debate with myself, my right heel takes aim at the lock. My left leg protests the strain louder than my scruples but I have already felt the lock give. Two more quick kicks defeat it.

I open the door. A powerful stench assaults my nose.

CHAPTER 6

Cobwebbed ceilings,
dust bunnies in corners
in the rich man's house—Debisu

Organic putrefaction, thick and stifling, smells like trouble, possibly for me, but it's whoever is inside that concerns me. Anyway, I've smelled worse, so I steel myself and limp forward. No one attacks me nor does anyone call out.

Almost as a matter of reflex I go for my weapon and come up empty-handed. My sidearm, a chopped Beretta that conceals nicely, is home, stored high on a closet shelf with the intention that I would never need it again. So much for wishful thinking.

The rear door opens onto a breakfast nook furnished in ultramodern chrome and black leather that is truly too cool for the room. Dust dulls the table's smoky glass top.

The kitchen adjoins the breakfast nook. More shiny surfaces here. The black marble counter tops and gray granite floor have the solid, subtle sheen of real rock, unlike the man-made imitations I saw in the model. Not a single fingerprint or smudge mars them, nor the stainless steel sink, commercial-quality appliances, nor the leaded glass fronts and pewter trim of the cabinets. The pervasive odor doesn't seem to come from the garbage disposal. Maybe under the sink.

The cabinets don't have handles or knobs; they must work on magnetic touch latches. Just a nudge with a knee that with any luck won't leave too big a fabric impression pops the under-sink cabinet door open. There are none of the expected cleaners, rags or sponges but there is a wastebasket. Empty. I help myself to a white vinyl liner from an open box, wrap it a few times around my hand for a glove, and open the refrigerator. Inside I find a liter of tonic water, a quart of orange juice, a pizza box. The juice appears to have fermented; the sides of the plastic jug bulge ominously. I nudge open the lid of the pizza box. Either Speed-E Pizza is delivering a new green fuzzy topping these days or the thing has gone moldy.

As if prepared for an elegant dinner, the dining room table is already set with gold-trimmed plates, silverware, and wine goblets. Pastel cloth napkins stuffed into the glasses have lost their starch and droop like wilted tulips. The table itself, a pedestal-mounted high-gloss slab of seamless magenta laminate, wears a light veil of dust and is fingerprint-free. A wet bar glistens with cut crystal decanters, all empty. A hammered copper and brass trimmed espresso machine rivals anything I've seen at the Kaffeteria, but there's not a water spot on it.

The rest of the first floor—a living room that hasn't been lived in, a deserted den, a spotless half bath—is the same: showy, trendy furnishings and upgrades. Though Shays' Landing is undisputedly upscale, the money spent decorating this unit is way out of proportion. Except for someone with drug money. I've seen some humble facades hide palatial insides. Drug money could also explain the luxurious Eterniti bought for cash.

The furnishings scream "expensive" but whisper "unused." Dust frosts everything. Maybe Hector didn't buy everything for himself but took them in trade for drugs. He might have been running a stash house here.

I still haven't found what's causing the rotten smell but there is a second level. Cautiously I climb the stairs, a Goldilocks skulking around the home of three bears where everything is too big or too brilliant but nothing is quite right.

The stairs lead to a small library. Built-in bookcases are stuffed with leather-bound classics of the sort decorators buy in caseloads just to fill shelves. A chair-side table next to a sleek leather recliner holds a burled wood cigar humidor designed for serious smokers, with a hygro-thermometer set in the lid. I lift the lid with a vinyl-wrapped hand. The humidor is empty, but fresh tobacco aroma strong and sweet enough to assert itself over the stink in the condo floats up to my nose, making me almost dizzy with desire.

The other room is the master suite. A headboard of polished aluminum that arcs behind the king-sized bed reflects my image like a fun house mirror. More polished aluminum trims shiny white chests and nightstands as well as a seven-drawer dresser topped with a four-foot high mirror. Apparently this is the only room that got any use. Not only "any use"—all the use. I can't see the carpet for the clothes and papers that litter it. I believe I have found the source of the smell. Dirty dishes of spoiled half-eaten food lie all over the place along with empty liquor bottles and glasses glazed with sediment.

If Hector's into drugs, this is almost true to form. I've seen some successful dealers flush with cash and surrounded by luxury but living in squalor. That I haven't found any money or drugs makes me wonder if Hector fled in a major hurry, maybe mere minutes ahead of Shrike.

I pick my way around the clear paths between the door and the bed, the bed and the master bath. The medicine chest is crammed with over-the-counter remedies for headache, heartburn and hair loss, foul breath, itchy eyes, watery nose and burning feet, plus a diet aid for weight loss. "Appetite suppressant." That's a laugh. If appetites were so easily suppressed, a lot of people would be out of business. But there are no controlled substances here, legally prescribed or otherwise.

A loud short bang erupts somewhere at the rear of the condo. Instantly I'm on the floor, adrenalin rocketing, and lie there a long time, insensible. Only when the cold floor tile threatens to stamp my cheek permanently do I return to myself. No commandos have stormed the condo. All is quiet. Backfire from a car in the parking lot, that's all the noise was.

A blackout, a bad one. Not good, not good at all. Shaking my head, I return to the bedroom to resume my investigation. It's a good thing no one's life depends on my stability, or lack thereof.

On my knees I sift through the debris on the floor, lifting different layers away. The clothes are all men's. From the quantity here it appears that when something got too dirty or wrinkled to wear, Hector tossed it aside and simply bought a replacement. Plenty of credit card slips and men's store receipts back up that theory. The bottommost layer of May and June statements is covered by past due notices with July, August, and September issue dates. I collect samples from each stratum in the trash bag.

A folded sheet of coarse off-white paper gets my attention. I'm about to open it when I hear something downstairs. I shove the paper in my sack, stand in the bedroom's threshold, and concentrate all my alertness in my ears hoping the sound will come again to prove I'm not hallucinating. Yes! At the front door. A knock. The leasing agent? The inquisitive neighbor? I freeze with the cold awareness that I am not supposed to be here, must not be discovered. Maybe if I remain motionless, make no noise, whoever it is will go away.

Perhaps they have. In the silence, my heartbeats are so loud I can count them. I lift my foot to move toward the landing when another knock stops me where I stand, poised on one leg like an egret. My pulse metes out eight more beats. Twelve, sixteen. I lower my foot and hear a new noise. Metal on metal. A key in a lock? Hector? There's a creak of hinge and the door opens.

Someone steps inside. Blue ball cap, matching blue Windbreaker. Too slender to be Hector, he's carrying a flat shallow green and red carton. I flash on the Speed-E pizza box in the refrigerator. Pizza boy? He peers right, left, then gumshoes down the hall. Not wanting to be seen I step back but it is too late, he spots me. He stops, spins, and makes for the door. I race down the stairs and out the door after him because now I want to know, who called for the pizza? Did Hector? Was he here just before I arrived? Is he on his way?

"Hey, wait a minute!" I yell.

Pizza Boy lifts the box's lid, grabs the pizza, and flings it. I catch it full in the face. Hot sauce and cheese cling to my skin. I scrape it away before the gluey substance scalds my eyelids and cheeks. When I can see again there is no sign of Pizza Boy, only an empty carton abandoned on the walk.

Hector's fetching neighbor comes trotting around the bend, her workout gear daubed with perspiration. She slows as she nears me, a slightly raised eyebrow the only intimation of curiosity. I smile innocently as if not aware of the strange picture I present, panting man holding a trash bag and wearing a pizza, and she moves on.

I pick pepperoni slices off my shirt and wonder, since when do Speed-E delivery drivers have house keys?

CHAPTER 7

Deserted teashop
White rice puffs float in cold tea
I am not working—Debisu

Shays' Landing's exit gate doesn't have vehicle detection. With the leasing agent long gone and the office locked, I get out the way burglars get in, by vulturing the main entrance until a departing resident opens the gate and drives through. I tailgate and slip through before it closes.

With a pretext about being a dutiful Block Watcher, I tell the Speed-E Pizza store manager about how I surprised a delivery driver lurking around a neighbor's home and got a pie in the face for the effort. He assures me that Speed-E Pizza drivers don't have house keys.

With a wary eye on my face, which stings as though sunburned, he says, "Can't be one of our guys. Speed-E caps and jackets aren't blue. They're red, green, and white, like the boxes."

So I've noticed as carriers hustle in and out of the shop.

"And anyway, fella, all our delivery drivers are independent contractors. We're not liable for their actions," the manager yells as I exit.

Stealthy delivery boy with heat-seeking pizza. Deserted luxury condo. If I were working, I'd be telling the lieutenant right now that this missing person case has just increased in gravity.

When I reach the Mercy Mission, it is well past suppertime. Nothing remains of the evening meal except the salty, steamy smell of soup and unwashed humans. The room is empty.

"Sister Clyde?" I call. "It's Will Mansion."

A rear door opens and Sister Clyde enters the room. "Ah, Will," she says. She brushes her hands off against each other. "Just taking out the trash." She wears the same fox-fur-collared coat as before, for the trip out to the alley no doubt, as the room is warm enough. "I was just about to relax with a cup of tea. May I pour you one?"

"Sure."

She fixes two cups at one of two large stainless steel urns on the serving table and sets them on one of the redwood benches. "Please, sit. I don't know about you but it's been a long day. I need to get off my feet." She hands me my cup. The chestnut aroma and stray puffs of rice tell me the tea is genmaicha. Funny, I would have expected industrial strength Lipton.

Sister Clyde scrutinizes my face. "My word, what happened to you?"

"I surprised an intruder at Hector's condo."

"Let me get you something for that. I believe I have something in the first aid kit." She rummages around at the serving table and returns with a tube. "So, Hector had a condo?"

"Yeah, and that's not all he had." I tell her about the car, the wife, the Country Club villa, the jewelry store, the partner.

"And you believe this man, this Marvin Overshort?" she asks me.

"Not for a minute," is my unconsidered reply, yet the minute the words leave my mouth I know they're true. "Besides the store, it appears Hector had a nice little sideline going in drug trafficking."

"You don't say?" She sounds more interested than surprised.

"Looks like whatever poor-pitiful-me act Hector gave you was just that: an act."

"So you don't think he's in trouble?"

"I didn't say that. He may very well be." I'm less worried about Hector than I am about myself. What if I find him–what if I find Shrike—and black out?

"So? Isn't rooting out drug dealers your mission?" She looks around the room. "No pun intended."

"I told you, I'm on disability. At this point, I think the case should be handled through official channels."

She nods. "So, what you've learned so far will convince the police to open an investigation?"

Let's see. No complainant, save Sister Clyde. No body. Nothing's been stolen. No evidence of any crime at all, in fact, except my B & E at Hector's condo, and I'm not about to mention that. "Probably not."

She presses her lips together and nods again. "So you're still the best man for the job."

"Sister, I'm telling you. I've done all I can."

"I see." She taps pursed lips with an index finger. After a moment she says, "Detective, do you believe in predestination?"

"Couldn't say. Never gave it much thought."

"I do." She sips her tea.

"Well, of course. You would."

"What if I could prove to you that it's your destiny to look for Hector?"

"Prove?" I chuckle. "I guess I'd be pretty impressed."

"And you'd stay on the trail?"

There's something of the card shark in her twinkling eyes, her hint of a smile. Nevertheless, she's got my curiosity piqued. "Guess I'd have to, wouldn't I? It being my destiny."

"Great." She rises from her seat. "Give me a moment, would you?" she says, and stands with her eyes closed, her palms pressed together. Her breathing is slow and deep. She opens her eyes, reaches into her pocket, and holds out her hand. When she unclenches her fist I see she has a coin. "Heads, you will continue looking for Hector. Tails, you won't," she says, and tosses. The coin comes up heads.

"Aw, that's not Destiny, that's just chance," I tell her.

"Chance? Are you sure? Are you absolutely sure?"

Certain of my reply, I open my mouth to speak and discover I'm not.

"Carry on, then, Detective. Destiny holds you in its hand."

Sister Clyde was right about one thing. I don't trust Marvin Overshort. He's the one who sent me to Hector's condo, a fool's errand. Seems to me he owes me an explanation, and I mean to get it—first thing in the morning. All I want to do now, though, is get something for my face, which burns like fire, and my leg, which complains about kicking in doors and chasing Pizza Boy around Shays' Landing. Once home, I spread the benzocaine cream Sister Clyde gave me on my reddened skin and down two aspirins, then a third when the recommended dose fails to deliver the instant relief promised on the package.

While I wait for the painkiller to kick in, I empty the trash bag I took from Hector's condo onto the old Formica kitchen table and examine the contents. There are the utility bills, purchase receipts, and credit card statements with overdue balances, plus correspondence from Facets. The oldest of those are "Attention: Hector Waltann, copy to Marvin Overshort." They advise Hector on some development at the store and ask for his input. Then they become memos to Marvin, copy to Hector, painting a picture of Overshort and Waltann's chiasmatic trajectories. The most recent communications demand action from Hector. There's something about "withdrawal of partner" and other legalese. The formal language doesn't hide a menacing tone.

*****

Wednesday's dawn is less a matter of sunrise than darkness lightening to gray. In anticipation of the day's demands, I dress in a sport coat, shirt, and tie for more authority than a sweater and jeans can muster, and take a top coat against the threat of more cold wet weather.

My planned revisit of Facets is delayed by a follow-up appointment with the surgeon who worked on my leg. He checks the stitches and scowls. "I thought I told you to take it easy on this," he says, tapping my leg.

"You said I could—"

"I said you could walk. A mile or two. I didn't say you could run."

My protest vaporizes as I flash on my foot pursuit of the pie-flinging Pizza Boy.

"You're in pain, aren't you?" he asks. "And you look exhausted. Pain keeping you up at night? I can give you a prescription for that. You don't lose points if you take something to help you rest."

Except that it's not pain that robs me of sleep; it's the nightmares.

The doctor grunts. "Now I mean it. Take it easy. And how'd you get that burn on your face?"

"Don't ask."

"All right, I won't." He does ask how I'm treating it and sanctions the benzocaine cream Sister Clyde gave me. "And the PTSD? Still having blackouts, paramnesia?"

With reluctance, I admit that I am.

The doctor isn't pleased. "I was thinking of releasing you to return to work, but under the circumstances ... Additional counseling might help you with those flashbacks."

What will stop the flashbacks will be the sight of Shrike on his knees, begging me for mercy.

I head for the Canterbury Bazaar where yesterday's parking valet is again on duty. He starts toward Old Paint, then steps back and waves me on to the self-parking area.

This time I don't linger at Facets' coffee service or browse the pens and watches but head directly for the private offices. The corridor door opens and Heidi Quince and I collide.

"Oh, it's you! No, no, you can't go back there," she says and throws herself on me in a delightful body block.

"Why not?" I ask, not moving, content to remain in her embrace as long as she's willing to hold me. "I want to see Overshort. That address he gave me for Hector yesterday wasn't any help and I think he knew it."

"Shhh." She takes my elbow and leads me to a far corner of the sales floor. "What do you want with Hector, anyway?"

"I don't mean him any harm. Just tell me where I can find him."

"Maybe he doesn't want to be found. Maybe you should just leave him alone."

"You know something about this. Tell me."

She takes a step closer. "I know I'm glad to see you again. I know I wouldn't like you to get hurt."

"Well, I've already been hurt, in case you didn't notice," I say, although her delight at seeing me softens my rancor. I'm a cop, people are rarely glad to see me; offenders spit and claw at me, civilians revile me, politicians condemn me, victims denounce me. "I want to talk to Overshort about it. Now where is he?"

She sighs deeply. "He's at Knockers. Please, Mr.——"

"Mansion. Will Mansion."

"Will. Just forget about all this, can't you?"

"I'm afraid not." I head for the door and she follows along behind. "Don't worry, I'll tell you when I find Hector."

She latches onto my arm to stop me from leaving, scribbles on a business card, and slips it to me. "Call me." In a more relaxed tone she adds, "If you find him, that is."

I give her a reassuring smile and take off down the esplanade in the drizzle.

To harmonize with the Canterbury's pseudo-Tudor theme, Knockers is done up like an Olde English pub. The corporate line is that the bar's name derives from the extensive collection of antique door knockers decorating the lobby. When challenged, their spokesman always insists it's pure coincidence that their waitresses are all buxom. Also coincidental is that these attributes are prominently displayed by off-the-shoulder peasant blouses tucked into the mini-est of ruffled skirts. This is part, if not all, of Knocker's appeal. It's certainly not the food. Equally good if not better burgers and beer can be found elsewhere. The Buddha taught that sexuality is a powerful energy, one that can easily mislead. Sounds like my dad talking.

At the door, the hostess sticks out her chest and does a little curtsey. "How may I serve you, sir?" she asks with all the provocative ambiguity of a Victorian maid willing to sleep her way out of the scullery.

"I'm looking for someone," I tell her.

She wiggles bare shoulders. "You've found her." When I fail to flirt back, she giggles and says, "If you tell me whom, I can direct you, pub or dining room."

I describe Overshort.

"Mr. Overshort is in the pub."

I head that way with a backward glance for the hostess who waggles her fingers at me in a little wave.

The bar is dark wood, antique brass, and coats of arms with clumps of plastic straw swept into the corners. Across the room, Overshort and a man in a billowy shirt with sleeve garters face a wall-mounted dartboard. An arm's length away from them a high table ringed with stools holds schooners of beer and plates of food. In his rumpled shirt and baggy slacks, Overshort looks out of place here. He throws a dart and hits the twenty-point segment in the double ring, an excellent shot. Though he's got good aim, he's too beefy to be the blue-capped pizza slinger who attacked me yesterday at Shays' Landing.

"Nice shooting." I nearly have to shout over the noise. The Hopps Lite Golf Classic, the Verve Cigarettes' Pacer 500, and Redi-Chaw big time wrestling play across dozens of thoroughly modern television monitors suspended from the beamed ceiling.

Overshort turns around slowly. "Shit, that's nothing. I usually get a bull's-eye." He points a dart at the target. "Want to bet?"

"I'll take your word for it."

With a shrug, he sets his darts down, shakes out a cigarette from a pack of Verves, and lights up. The smoke tickles my nose. My whole body tenses. He tells his companion, "A beer for my friend, here."

Before I can decline, the man in the sleeve garters goes behind the bar, draws one, and sends it over with a cocktail waitress who carries her tray just under her ample breasts. She stops at Overshort's side.

"The beer's for him, but here's something for you, babe." He tucks some bills in her décolletage. She minces over to stand at my elbow, giving me a very good view, and departs for the bar with a flounce. Overshort tosses a dart after her. It sails over her shoulder and impales a support post. She lets out a shriek, which sounds genuine, then a giggle, which does not.

Overshort laughs. "I love a moving target." He takes a swig of his drink. "Find Hector?"

"'Fraid not. Got any other suggestions as to where I could look?"

"What do I look like, a detective?" He cackles.

I sample my drink, not room-temperature ale as would befit an English pub, but garden-variety American suds. The ice-cold effervescence goes down like tonic. "You don't sound very concerned."

Overshort chomps a huge bite of hamburger. "Hey, what's the big fucking deal? Hector's a big boy. I don't see how what he wants to do with his personal life is my business, or yours, or anyone else's. You being paid big bucks to look for him?"

"Actually, no."

"See, like I said. No big deal. "Anyway, I got to get back to work." He launches a dart and scores, but no bull's-eye. With a shrug, he steps away from the table.

"It's OK. I know what's going on."

He pauses. "Yeah?"

"Hector's in trouble and you're covering up for him to keep the store afloat. But wouldn't it be better if we got him some help?"

There's a slight but definite hesitation before he responds. "What would be better would be for you to just butt out," he says and makes to leave.

I call after him, "Your cigarettes—"

"You keep 'em," he says. Almost as an afterthought, he plucks a dart from a mug at the bar and flings it carelessly at the target. This time he hits the twenty but in the treble ring—bull's-eye. He gives me a cutting smile.

The waitress piles mugs and plates on her tray. She picks up the pack of Verves. "Want these?"

Yes! "No. Yes. No."

She grins, reaches inside my jacket, tucks them in the breast pocket, and pats my chest. "How 'bout the darts?"

Overshort pauses at the bar's entrance. I hand the waitress all the darts but one. With one eye on Overshort and one on the target, I fire. The dart misses the target entirely and nails the wall off to the side. Overshort smirks and gives a satisfied nod before exiting.

Butt out. There was a similar "butt out" quality to Overshort's comments about Facets' theft, both to me and to the *Crier's* reporter. I don't like it. The newspaper article made it sound as if the missing jewels were of some significant value though Overshort demurred. Admittedly, I don't know much about gems. However, I know someone who does. I put my hand in my pocket and finger the business card of "Heidi Quince, Certified Gemologist." I do believe I need to talk to her again. Later, and away from Facets, when she can talk freely. Meanwhile, perhaps I can learn something about the theft from the security company and the janitorial service mentioned in the article.

One small suite of a commercial strip on Dogwood is all Secur-It needs for a Paradise City office—this location is home to the local sales reps only. The personnel, dispatching, and monitoring are handled in Haviland, but maybe I can pick up some background here that will open doors down there. A young woman with orangey-red corkscrew curls and dangly-jangly earrings holds down the reception desk. I ask for the sales rep who handled Facet's account.

The redhead looks up from her work. Neon pink lips purse, an equally pink bubble forms, inflates, and pops. She sucks the gum back into her mouth, blinks, and stammers, "He's not here right now. Why don't you wait?" She bats eyes with impossibly long lashes. "Please."

I take one of two armchairs bracketing an end table against the foyer wall. She sets her elbow on the desk, props her chin in her palm, grins at me, and blows another bubble.

To avoid her unblinking scrutiny, I leaf through the magazines on the table: *People,* well-thumbed copies of *Sports Illustrated* I've already seen, and *Modern Locksmith.* I read a complete article on electrical access and exit control systems before the receptionist pipes up with, "I guess I should mention it could be some time."

Now she tells me. "I'd really like to talk with him about the system they used at Facets."

She replies, "I can have him get back to you just as soon as he checks in. You could look at a spec sheet if you want, only you can't take it with you." She bends to open a file drawer and the dangly earrings swing forward. I marvel they don't become tangled in her hair.

"Fine." I retake my seat. She resumes gazing at me and blowing bubbles until she's interrupted by the phone. With an annoyed frown, she takes the call, holding the receiver on an angle to clear her earrings.

While she talks, I study the system's specs. She finishes her call and I ask, "Do you know anything about these systems?"

"Try me."

"I see this has a door alarm. Why didn't it go off the night Facets was burgled?"

She unprops her chin and sits up straight. "Oh, you shouldn't let that worry you. There's nothing wrong with the system, believe me. I remember everything about that night. Ask me anything."

"Well, for starters, what went wrong?"

"Good question. Hell, it's still got us stumped," she says with a frown. "The alarm system didn't fail. It was never tripped. So like, that's not our fault, huh?"

"And the security camera showed nothing?"

"Not a thing. Once the store closed for the night, the showroom was quiet."

So only the showroom was monitored. "What about the inside security camera?"

She shrugs, which sets her earrings jangling. "They didn't have one. It's not like we didn't encourage them to get one. But Mr. Waltann said he trusted his help. So like, that's not our fault, huh?"

"Especially if the theft was an inside job. Besides Mr. Waltann, who had a key to the system?" *Another guess, but a safe one.*

"Code, you mean."

"Of course, the code."

"According to our records, Mr. Waltann and Mr. Overshort, the manager. Or, I guess he's in charge now. 'Course, they could have gotten careless or given the codes to whoever they wanted and not told us about it, but hey, that's not our fault, huh?"

"Who said it was?"

The receptionist leans back in her chair, crosses her arms over her chest, and tucks her chin. "Mr. Overshort, when he canceled our contract. That's what's got you worried, huh? That they fired us? Believe me, Mr. Waltann never would have done that to us. He would have worked with us, to find out what went wrong. He would have given us a chance to make it right. But Mr. Overshort, he just fired us, just like that." She pops a bubble. "Broke Corky's heart." Scott Corcoran, she explains, was the officer on duty that night, and he saw nothing unusual.

"Does he work out of this office? I thought the dispatching was done out of Haviland." *At least, that's where the PD's calls came from whenever Secur-It's alarms went off.*

"Oh, yeah, it is, but Corky was a local guy. Lived in a trailer park over in Linfield."

"Lived? Did he move?" *Maybe there's something he would tell me that he couldn't tell the police or reporters.*

"Unh uh," she says. "He died."

CHAPTER 8

Shriveled pumpkin shells,
dry corn husks in autumn fields
All Hallows' Even—S_zan

My "spider sense" tingles. "Dead? How?" *Must have been natural causes or I'd know about it, unless it was within the past few weeks.*

"Killed himself." The receptionist shakes her head sadly.

A ruling of suicide, no further investigation warranted. No wonder I don't know about it. "Oh, I'm sorry to hear that. Guess he did take it hard."

"Guess so," she replies. "All those years with the sheriff's department, you'd think he'd be tougher than that."

Indeed. Not that I haven't heard of a lawman taking his own life, but over an incident that could hardly be considered his fault? Perhaps next-of-kin could shed some light on it. Unfortunately no Scott Corcoran is listed in Linfield, which doesn't surprise me. Many officers I know aren't listed; I'm not.

The drive up River Way should be pleasant, the fallow fields to the left dotted with bright orange pumpkins in honor-system farm stands. Under a low sky though, the earth is dun and there are no pumpkins, perhaps due to a dearth of honor. To the right, the river's deceptively lazy appearance masks a current that is deep and strong enough to have once supported shipping and milling, fast enough for white water rafting and sculling.

At the third trailer park in Linfield, I find a mailbox cluster. Number Seventeen is labeled Corcoran. On the off-chance the mailbox and lot numbers match, I knock on the door of the corresponding trailer. The woman who answers proves to be the dead security officer's wife. The widow Corcoran has pure white hair and the weariness of someone depleted by grief. I give her my name and state I'd like to ask her a few questions about Scott without saying why. It doesn't seem to matter; she invites me in with the eagerness of the recently bereaved trying to keep the memory of the newly departed fresh by talking about him.

"I'm fixing some tea," she says. "Would you care for some? It's caffeine-free."

While she prepares it at a galley kitchen range, I take a seat at a compact dining table against the window. To my left is a living room, casually-furnished but neat and clean. Bowling trophies line the wall shelves. Hung beside them are family photos and formal portraits of Mrs. and, I presume, Mr. Corcoran. One shows him in uniform, standing at attention, his right hand at his forehead in a salute, the left arm at his side bowed slightly around the sidearm at his hip. Framed certificates commend him on various achievements with the Sheriff's Department. A hardwood gun case with a formidable brass lock stands in a corner. Corcoran had a nice collection of long guns.

Mrs. Corcoran brings a small pot and two cups. "There's sugar on the table."

So there is. "Raw" sugar in little brown packets fills a yellow bowl next to a container of salt substitute and bottles of vitamins and herbal supplements.

"Or would you rather have honey? That's healthier," Mrs. Corcoran says.

"This is fine."

"It's chamomile. It's supposed to be relaxing. I seem to be having a little trouble in that department since Scott—died. Why exactly are you interested in him?"

"It's Hector Waltann I'm interested in, Ma'am. From Facets? I'm talking to everyone who knew or worked with him. Apparently he's missing. He hasn't been at work, at home, or at his condo."

"Missing? I guess Scott had mentioned seeing less and less of him at the store, which was unfortunate. He liked Hector. Couldn't say the same for that Mr. Overshort." Mrs. Corcoran shakes her head. "Lemon? Milk? Milk has a sedative effect. It's the calcium, you know."

"No. Thank you. About Mr. Waltann?"

Mrs. Corcoran doctors her tea. "Well, I really couldn't say. I don't know what Scott could tell you if he were still—still—" Tears start to flow. She sniffs and blots them with a paper napkin. "I'm sorry. I'm not adjusting well."

"I think you're doing just fine, Ma'am."

She smiles faintly. "It's just that Scott was so close to retiring, and then this. It was so sudden, so unexpected."

"Hadn't Scott been depressed?"

"Depressed?" she says, anger flash-drying her tears. "You've been talking to someone from the department! Scott wasn't depressed; he was looking forward to retiring. We had plans, we were going to travel. Yes, I know. His death was ruled a suicide, but I don't believe it, not for a minute. And with a stolen shotgun? Scott would never steal. Now I can't explain what he was doing in some no-tell motel—" She gives me a stern look. "Oh, I know what you're thinking but I don't believe that either. I'll bet he was working a sting. The department denies it, of course. I think they're afraid of the liability."

She takes a breath and says, "Sorry, I didn't mean to rant. I'm afraid I haven't been much help. With finding Hector, that is."

"Not at all, you've been a big help, Mrs. Corcoran. Thank you for the tea, and your time. One last thing. What did your husband say to you about the theft at Facets?"

Mrs. Corcoran shakes her head. "That's what so strange. It was such an uneventful night, he didn't even know there had been one until after they discovered inventory missing."

I'm tempted to believe her but wives often see what they want to see. Besides, it sounds like she has a beef with the sheriff's department. Scott Corcoran could have been depressed about the

Facets theft. Maybe there had been something to see and he missed it. The stolen gun doesn't make much sense, it's true. He had a case full of guns, any one of which would have done the job. Maybe he didn't want to sully his collection. *Who's to say what makes sense to a man bent on doing away with himself?*

It may have nothing to do with Hector's disappearance but this theft at Facets stinks. Whatever happened that night, one other person might have seen something significant and not realized it: the cleaning lady. She could even have been in on it. Much as I hate to admit it, Overshort could be right. It could have been an inside job. The fact that Scott Corcoran saw nothing on his rounds and that the Secur-It alarm wasn't tripped implicate someone with legitimate access to the store. That would include the cleaning lady.

North on Pleasant Street, a gently curved thoroughfare, single-family detached homes are increasingly being converted into small business offices: an insurance agent, a tax accountant, a dentist. A wood-framed bungalow houses Clean Sweep, the cleaning service mentioned in the *Crier* article. An inexpensive upholstered settee-and-side-chair suite has turned a home's front room into an office waiting area. Cluttered with full ashtrays and untidy piles of dog-eared magazines, it could use a good cleaning itself.

A heavy-set woman in her early thirties scurries in from the back of the house to greet me. Her clothes, a navy double knit pants suit and high-necked bowed blouse, fit as if they're wearing her rather than the other way around.

She introduces herself as the manager. "Did we have an appointment?" she asks. Her frantic air borders on panic.

"No. I'm sorry. I was in the area and saw your sign—"

She lets out a sigh of relief. "Thank goodness. I didn't think so. See, normally I'd come to your place. If I'm on site, I can better assess your needs." She wrings wrinkled hands that look older than the rest of her. "I'd hate for you to judge our service by the condition of this room. Growing pains, you see, new clients and I— not that I'm overextended or understaffed or anything like that, although I am short one person but—well, I like to put our clients' needs before our own and—"

She has a lisp, her L's come out like Double-Us. "Clients" sounds like "cwients."

"No problem."

"Come on back, we'll talk in my office."

I follow her down a short hall that branches off into a kitchen on the right. What was probably a bedroom on the left now serves as an office. Instead of a bed, a desk, swivel chair, folding chair, and file cabinet furnish a room just as cluttered as the front. Office equipment crowds the desk. Unsteady stacks of file folders stand on the floor. She plucks a pink smock from the folding chair, motions for me to sit, and takes her seat behind the desk.

"How did you learn about our service?" she asks.

"Through one of your clients. Facets?" I reply.

She frowns. "Is Hector back?"

"Had he left?"

More to herself than to me she says, "'Cause if he's back, maybe he could have a talk with that partner of his." Her eyes narrow and she stares into space.

"Overshort?"

Her gaze comes back into focus. "Sorry. Just thinking aloud there."

"Thinking Hector could get him to renew your contract?"

She presses her lips together.

"Don't be embarrassed on my account, ma'am. I understand. New management almost always starts by cleaning house. No pun intended."

"No pun ... Oh!" She chuckles. A phone rings. She pushes aside some papers to get to it. "Cwean Sweep, this is—Yes, I'm working on that. See, I had an unexpected, uh, resignation. I'm trying to fill that position just as soon as I can. Say, can I call you back? I'm with another customer. Yes, thanks." She hangs up. "So, is Hector back?"

"As I said, I wasn't aware he had left. When would that have been?"

She gazes into the distance again. "Well, I can't pinpoint the date exactly. Our last day at Facets was about a month ago. Right after the ..." She stops abruptly.

"Theft," I finish for her. "And it was Overshort you heard from."

"That's right. I tried to speak with Hector but I was told he wasn't around. And Mr. Overshort did have authority so there wasn't anything I could do."

Hector not around. Where have I heard that before? "Overshort made you feel like it was your fault, didn't he? The theft, I mean."

She wriggles on her chair. "I assure you we had nothing to do with it. Pwease bewieve me. My girls are all bonded and insured. I screen my personnel carefuwwy. Monetta had worked at Facets for years, they were very satisfied with her work."

The phone rings again and I wait impatiently for her to issue a quick promise to call back. I want to hear more about this Monetta. But the manager says, "Cwean Sweep. Yes, I'm aware of that. I'll get someone else to you this afternoon, I promise."

When I have her full attention again, I ask, "Is, uh, Monetta, uh, available? To work other locations?" If the manager says "yes" and wants to write up a contract, I'm in big trouble.

She replies, "I'm afraid not. See, uh, Monetta's no longer with us."

I feign great disappointment. "That's too bad. Has she gone with another service?"

The phone rings yet again. The manager holds up a forefinger, mouths "Wait," and takes the call. I shift on my chair and nod as politely as I can.

Finally she finishes the conversation, turns to me, and smiles. "Where were we?"

"Monetta. You were about to tell me whom she's working for now."

"Working for? ... Oh, I'm sorry. You misunderstood. I mean, she's no longer with us. She's, um mm, well, dead."

"Dead," I echo in the same calm, professional tone I've used all afternoon, although now the hairs on the back of my neck are standing straight up and my pulse is racing.

"Some mugger attacked her out on Forbes Road in the middle of the night earlier this week," the manager says. "With a shotgun. A carjacking, I guess. You know, I don't even think whoever did it got away with much, just Monetta's purse. What a shame. She was just getting her life back together." She tsks and shakes her head.

Forbes Road? *Earlier this week? The pregnant woman who died in the hospital? Could it be?* "How's that?" I don't have to pretend to be interested, I have to reign in what must look like an obsession with the woman.

The manager folds her arms on her desk and leans forward. "I guess she thought Mr. Overshort canceled our contract because of her and took it personally. It was like she disappeared overnight. She didn't come back to work. I called her house, her references, but no one knew where she was. Then last week, she just showed up again. Said she had been so upset about what happened at Facets, she went a little crazy, left town for a while. But now she was back and could she come back to work? See, she was pregnant and she and her boyfriend decided to stay together, have the baby."

The young man in the hospital. A baby. "We lost them both," the doctor had said.

"Well, she had been dependable up to this point and seeing as how I need all the good help I can find—"

As if to prove her point, the phone rings again. The manager rolls her eyes and puts the caller on hold. To me she says, "Poor Monetta. She had just come back to work for me and then that horrible shooting. Let me finish this call and then I'll be right with you." She gives me a broad wink. "Your place I will do personally myself."

"That's OK." I get to my feet. "I can see you're busy and I did drop in without an appointment. I'll call and schedule a site visit." I take a business card from a caddy that peeps out from under a pile of papers. "I'll let myself out."

*****

I don't know what I expected to hear. In an investigation I've learned it's best not to have expectations. Then I'm free to see reality for what it is instead of what I would like it to be, and I avoid going down the wrong path of inquiry. It's difficult when neon arrows flash "This Way." That seductive light only deepens the blackness of the shadows where secrets hide.

More than ever, I want to talk to Heidi Quince. I try the number she wrote on the back of her business card. She's hesitant but she agrees to meet me. "Someplace public, where it might look like we simply ran into each other," she says.

"Where would you suggest?"

There's a moment of silence. Then she says, "Under the covers."

CHAPTER 9

A dog's distant howl
An empty yard, a full moon
A night heron—S_zan

"I beg your pardon?"

She giggles. "It's a bookstore, silly. Used books, half-price or less." She gives me an address on Ironwood.

A bookstore. No cigarettes, no alcohol, and well away from the Canterbury Bazaar. Sounds like a safe place for a meet.

A concrete block divided into identical individual suites, the Ironwood Industrial Park houses a discount carpet outlet, a computer sales and service shop, an auto parts store. Each has a warehouse with a bay door and separate office entrance. Except for the bookstore, the businesses don't keep late hours so they're all dark. The flood light over the bookstore's windowless front door is a beacon in the misty night.

I scope out the place from a spot just inside the door, find Heidi in the warehouse space beside a wooden rack of old *National Geographics*. She wears a body-clinging black lace top and tight purple jeans. Her only jewelry is a cameo on a black velvet ribbon around her neck. Her blonde hair, tucked behind her ears, falls to her shoulders. She sees me, smiles, and signals with a tiny nod that it's all right to approach.

"Well, if it isn't Will Mansion," she says in that hushed tone everyone adopts in libraries and, by extension, bookstores. "So, did you find Hector?" she asks in an even fainter whisper.

"No. And I'm beginning to think that when I do, it's not going to be good."

Her smile fades. "Oh?" She glances to the left and right. "Um, want to help me find a book?"

I follow her into the stacks of six-foot tall utility shelves. Dusty hardbacks, moldy leather-bound classics, and obsolete textbooks reek of mildew and cigarettes. We pass aisles of scuffed paperbacks until Heidi makes a sudden left. As if I have stepped into the parlor of a bordello, I find myself surrounded by dozens of half-clad couples locked in a variety of passionate poses on books displayed face-out. *Romances.*

Heidi pulls a book off a shelf. On its cover, a man with dark wavy hair and an open poet's shirt embraces a fair-skinned blonde woman. His hands almost cup breasts mounded like whipped cream above the ruffled neckline of her gown.

"What did you find out about Hector?" she asks, flipping through the pages.

"Not much. Tell me about the theft at Facets."

"Before my time. I don't know much about it, just what Mr. Overshort told me." She replaces the book, selects another. This one has a Tarzan theme. Heidi makes a face. "His hair's longer than hers. And blonder. I like my heroes to have dark hair."

I have dark hair, I think with inordinate pride.

She picks up another book whose cover suggests one way in which the West might have been won. An Indian brave kneels at the feet of a frontier woman, his head buried in her skirts.

"Will?"

"Huh? Oh, right. The stuff that was taken—just how valuable was it?"

"I'm not sure," Heidi says. "Apparently Hector used to do all the ordering, and checked the merchandise when it came in. Now Mr. Overshort does that."

"You don't assess the stones?"

"Not every one. Just when a customer requests it."

"Is it possible the stolen items were of a different value than what was reported?"

"Different how?"

"Overshort made it sound like they weren't worth very much. What if they were worth more than he said?"

"Why would he do that?" she asks. "They were insured. He'd want to put in a claim for every penny of loss. What are you getting at?"

"I'm not sure." The book-cover models' parted lips and rapturous faces have derailed my train of thought. "I understand it was an inside job."

She turns away from me to shop the books on the opposite shelf. Her body muffles her voice. "Could have been. I guess that's why Mr. Overshort got all new staff, people he could trust."

"Like you?"

Heidi pivots to flash a modest smile. "I'm grateful for the opportunity."

"Well, was anyone working late that night? Was Hector?"

"I don't know. All I know is, I wasn't." She considers another book, rejects it, and reclaims the dark-haired poet and blonde damsel.

"You actually read those?" I ask.

"Why not?" she replies. "They're sexy, and in the end, the heroine always gets what she wants. I like happy endings." She turns on her heel and marches to the cashier.

I walk her out to her car. She pauses alongside a dark BMW and lights a cigarette.

"You're not telling me very much, Heidi Quince."

"There isn't much I can tell you." She peers up through her lashes. While her tone is apologetic, her expression is worried.

From across Ironwood, an unexpected glint steals my attention from Heidi's pretty, troubled face. A car emerges slowly from the easement beside a warehouse. What's a car doing there at this time of night? The car's golden gleam is incongruous in the dark, industrial setting.

The car inches into the street with a caution that the absence of traffic doesn't warrant. It creeps into the lane parallel to the bookstore. *It's a gold Eterniti!* I should get closer, get a look at the driver but the vehicle's inappropriately slow speed and proximity to the curb trigger my internal alarms.

"Down!" I tackle Heidi Quince, sandwich her between the bookstore's concrete wall and my body. Shot pellets fill the air over where our heads were a second ago.

Heidi screams. "What's happening?"

"Stay down!" I keep us low until even the scrunch of the tires can no longer be heard. The car is out of sight and I didn't come anywhere near making the driver or the plate. Slowly we get to our feet.

Her arms around my neck, Heidi looks up into my face, her eyes wide. "What was that? A street gang drive-by?"

Dizzy, I can barely reply.

"Ohmigod, we could have been killed!"

"Back in the store. Call police," I gasp.

"No! We can't. If the cops come out there'll be a big scene. It'll be on TV, in the paper. Overshort will find out about our meeting."

"Call—"

"Besides, I didn't see the car," she says. "All I saw was the wall coming to meet my face."

I'm going down.

"I'm fine. I mean, I will be fine, once I get home. I'm not hurt, thanks to you. Just like on the book covers." She cries, "My hero!" Her arms still around my neck, she kisses my cheek. "Please, I'd really like to go home now. Sit down before I fall down."

I mumble something.

"No, no need to escort me," she says. "You've been hero enough for one night." She kisses me again, this time on the lips, but I don't feel it.

She releases me and before her car's taillights have even vanished around the corner, I sink to the curb. Ironwood Street dematerializes and I am on Terminal Road. Lit by muzzle flashes, chaotic scenes flicker before my eyes like slides in a fitful carousel. Me sprinting down the side of the stash house. Swbyra rounding the corner from the rear.

Men and bullets burst from the back door, Swbyra in their sights. No time to shout a warning he can't hear. I pitch myself at Swbyra in a flying tackle, then scramble to my feet, run for cover.

From behind, a rocket tunnels into my leg, burning, ripping. The leg gives out, I fall. Hot blood. Cold shock. I black out knowing it's over, I'm dead. My last sensation is gritty pavement against my cheek and the smell of asphalt, dust, gunpowder, and blood. My blood.

The balky slide carousel grinds to a stop. The show is over. I find myself once again on Ironwood, collapsed on the curb. The bookstore is dark, the store is closed. *How long was I out of it? How many people drove past me on their way out of the lot? Was I raving, too scary to approach?* In the dark, the surroundings come back into focus slowly.

The Eterniti. Was it Hector Waltann's car? Who was the driver? Hector? The person he's running from? Shrike? Overshort?

Force of habit directs my gaze to the street. There are probably tire tracks but I can't see them and have nothing to capture them with anyway. Something metallic winks in the misty moonlight. A spent twelve-gauge shotgun shell casing. Unsteadily I stand, pick it up. It feels warm but I must be projecting. It can't be from this shooting. Those rounds should have been ejected into the car. I put it in my trouser pocket anyway.

Hector Waltann's disappearance has taken on deadly proportions. Grady and Swbyra will have to take it from here. Effective immediately.

*****

The Mercy Mission's door opens to a deserted room. No one sits at the redwood bench, no one stands at the coffee urn. This close to midnight even the homeless have found a home. Yet the lights, the coffee are on. Sister Clyde has to be here.

Perhaps she's in the alley, taking out trash. My steps echo as I cross the empty room. I open the rear door to the alley. The creak of rusty hinges flushes an animal from behind the trash cans. A fox, I think at first when it darts across the alley into the shadows. *No, it couldn't be. Not that we don't have foxes in the area and not that we don't see them in the city, but this far downtown? Must have been a small stray dog. With a tawny coat. And a bushy tail.*

There's no Sister Clyde, however, so I go back inside to find two men huddled at the redwood bench, sipping coffee. They must have come in while I was in the alley.

"Sister Clyde here?" I ask.

"Yup," one of the men replies without looking up.

I scan the room but all I see are the two men. I step closer, lean over, and repeat, "Sister Clyde here?"

"Someone looking for me?"

I spin around. There she stands in the familiar blue coat. Where did she come from? She had to have been out back. How did I miss her?

"Oh, it's you, Detective Mansion. So good to see you. How are you coming on finding Hector?" she asks.

"I quit."

She laughs. "No, no, no. We've had this discussion."

"Not this one, we haven't. I think Hector wants to stay lost. Plus, there's apparently someone who's willing to do whatever it takes to keep him lost, maybe Hector himself." I tell her about Heidi Quince, the meeting at the bookstore, the shotgun sniper attack. "It's gotten too dangerous. Someone could die. Like me."

She appears relieved. "Well, we all have to die sometime."

"Been there. Done that. Don't want to do that again, not for a very long time."

Her laughter is light and merry. "As if you have anything to say about that."

"I don't have to walk in front of a loaded gun, that's for sure."

She shakes her head and tsks. "So you're not going to help me."

I'm not up to it, is my mute protest. "If I keep poking around, I could end up dead."

"And what about Ms. Quince?"

I open my mouth to rebut but I'm speechless. *Yes, what about Heidi?* Her life was threatened. It's obvious she knows something, and it's equally clear someone wants to keep her quiet. Wants that badly enough to kill her. Whoever it is may not stop trying simply because I've quit looking for Hector.

"So basically you're saying that I'm damned if I do, damned if I don't."

Sister Clyde smiles. "Or blessed. You decide. The sword that kills the man is the sword that saves the man."

I don't know what the hell that means but I do know one thing: I'm trapped. However, the weakness, the sin, of heading next to Knockers is not that I want a drink to calm my nerves, to numb my brain, and banish the night's horror. It's not even that I give in to that desire. It's that I allow myself to believe I'm looking for Marvin Overshort, for Hector.

Canterbury's shops are closed for the night. Knockers and the Bazaar's restaurants are open, though, so a valet is on duty. In spite of the abundant empty spaces in front, he insists if I'm self-parking that I take Old Paint around to the rear.

Knockers at night is even louder than during the day. Tangerine-colored bulbs make it appear lit by fire. It's crammed with noisy customers. The smoke stings my eyes and I feel a cue-induced craving coming on. I find the bar by radar and hoist my butt onto a padded stool.

The bartender lays a cocktail napkin in front of me. "Ah, Mr. Overshort's new friend. What can I get you?"

"Seagrams. Make it a double."

I raise it in a vague toast, drink it too fast to taste it, order another. While I'm waiting, automatically I pat my pockets in search of cigarettes. Just as I remember that I've quit, I find the Verves that Overshort left me. Nicotine-addicted nerves rejoice. I turn the pack over and over in my hand. The bartender watches me with a bemused expression. It's unlikely he's seen anyone regard a cigarette pack with such a mixture of longing and trepidation. With a shaking hand, I put it back in my coat pocket.

"Is he here?" I ask.

"Marvin? 'Fraid not."

No, of course not. He's home reloading his shotgun. "How about Hector?" I put the second drink away nearly as fast as the first. The liquid warmth unkinks muscles. Vapors veil the grisly pictures in my mind. A third should disperse them altogether.

"Mr. Waltann? Not tonight," the bartender replies.

Not tonight. But maybe on other nights? Recently? I drink the third whiskey, ask for another. I want to hear more of what this man knows about Hector. Drinking will justify my staying here.

The bartender slides a glass toward me. "Really putting it away tonight, aren't ya, fella?"

I waggle the glass at him. "If you'd quit watering it down, maybe I wouldn't have to."

"Water?" He scowls. "Hey, this is a class place."

"Yeah, well don't you have something with a little kick to it?"

"Got some kind of big hurt, huh buddy?"

"You don't know the half."

"Kick, huh?" The bartender busies himself with some glass-washing behind the bar and avoids my glance.

I catch the tease in his tone. "Yeah, you know, like what Hector was into." *Whatever it was, there's a better than outside chance this man knew something about it.*

He raises his eyebrows. "Who said anything about Hector?" *It sounds more like, "Go on."*

Act twitchy, I think, like a junkie looking to score. It's not hard, I want one of the Verve cigarettes about as badly. "Come on, we both know what the man was into. Nearvana?" It's a long cast but I figure there's a fifty-fifty chance the bartender will bite.

"Don't know what you're talking about. Sorry, I can't help you," he says, but he seems to nod at a man in a black raincoat sitting alone at a booth, his face shadowed by a limp rain hat.

I shrug, pay for my drinks, and leave. The night is blue-black after Knockers' radioactive orange. I amble to Old Paint and lean against it, make like a man taking some night air in the misguided attempt to sober up enough to drive. I don't have to wait long. Footfalls announce the raincoated man's approach long before he appears at my left elbow.

"Nice place, that Knockers," he says.

"S'all right as far as it goes. They didn't really have what I'm looking for, though."

"Girls ain't friendly enough, huh?"

"Girls are fine. It's not girls I'm after. You know, an hour with a girl is, well, it's just an hour with a girl. I'm looking for something with staying power."

"Ain't we all," says the man by my side. He lights a cigarette, takes a puff. "Trouble is, there's them what thinks them kind of thrills shouldn't ought to be allowed."

I know the words to this tune. "You mean like cops?"

"You ought to know, you being one." Against the black of his hat and coat, his unremarkable face is moon-pale.

"Was," I tell him. "They canned my ass. See, I got me this little problem, know what I mean? The job, it gets to ya after a while. I just wanted a little something to take the edge off. So I could keep going. You know?"

"I hear you."

"Sonsabitches, I give 'em the best years o' my life, you think they could cut me a little slack."

"Fuck 'em."

"Fuck 'em is right. So how about it? This Nearvana Hector Waltann was into?"

The man smokes some more. "Trouble is, cops make the stuff hard to find these days. I mean, I got some, but it's my last." He looks away, takes another couple of puffs. "Ah, what the hell." He fishes a cigarette pack from inside his raincoat, taps one out, and hands it to me. It looks normal but if I'm right, it will be supercharged with the heroin.

"What do I owe you?" I ask.

"Nothing. Oh, it's worth two bills."

"For one hit?"

"It's worth it."

I don't ask him why he's giving it away. He's not the dealer, he's just a steerer. He'll expect me to smoke it, though, right here and now, to prove this isn't a sting.

We don't usually enter these transactions at the retail level. We send a CI in and don't come into play until it's time to talk wholesale. At that point it's understood—we're dealers. And while users often deal, dealers rarely use, not if they're true professionals. So we never actually have to do the stuff.

But there will be no getting away with that here. All I can do is light up.

CHAPTER 10

Dark vacant lot
Autumn leaves prance and spin
under a street light—Debisu

A chill gust sweeps across the Canterbury's self-parking lot and stirs the dead leaves. With a stick of turbocharged weed clamped between my fingers I search my pockets for a light. The steerer waits patiently. He's seen me put away four doubles at Knockers; he must not have high expectations of me.

I don't find a lighter but I do find Overshort's cast-off cigarettes. "Would you believe I don't have a light?" I tell him.

While he searches his own pockets, I fumble a Verve from the pack and swap it for the Nearvana-spiked smoke.

The steerer gets my cigarette lit, then watches while I inhale deeply. "This is funny. I ain't never watched a cop get high before."

Yes, the long-denied nicotine is almost that good. Much as I would be happy to stand here and suck the cigarette down to my fingertips, there's something I've got to find out. "I got to get some more of this Nearvana stuff," I tell him. He won't have any, but his connection will. His connection might be my connection to Hector.

"Yeah, well, like I said, I ain't got no more," the steerer replies. "I might know where you can get some. It'll cost you."

A twenty buys me an address on South Hope Street not far from a railroad spur. I know the area: machine shops and small fabricators punctuated by grinder takeouts and stuffy taverns. Heavy industry and heavier drinking. Fights that start soon after the five o'clock whistle and continue past last call keep the evening tour lively. At this hour the bars will be long closed, the area relatively quiet.

'Lotta Cars for Less takes up half a block. The sales lot isn't fenced, but it is roped off with a bulky chain to keep browsers from taking unauthorized test drives. Old iron horses sit forlornly in the lot, their bumpers dull pewter.

I'm familiar with this place, and its owner: Carlotta Trephino. We have long suspected she's up to something. She makes entirely too much money selling lemons. We've never caught her at anything big and haven't been able to make the small stuff stick. She buys high-priced representation and she gets her money's worth.

There's no showroom, just an office in a trailer planted in the far corner. The iron grates over the windows detract from the trailer's gingerbreading. When I'm within two feet of the trailer, an overhead spotlight comes on. *Motion detector.* The light temporarily blinds me.

The steel door looks more solid than the body. The mail slot is roughly at eye level. From the bottom of the steps, I reach up and knock on the door. It resounds with a clang. There is no response. After a moment, I try again. Still no response, and I'm starting to think I got burned for my twenty. I try one more time. "Hey, Hector sent me," I holler.

"Hector, huh?" asks someone from inside and the door opens a crack. I wait. A dark-skinned man puts first his head, then his body through the opening. He greets me with a Ruger 9mm reception stick in his fist.

"Hey, what gives?" I ask with the nonchalance of someone too drunk to be afraid. Four doubles admirably buffer me from a PTSD fugue.

The sentry is six-eight and two thirty at least, much of it packed into in his shoulders, arms, and chest. With a physique like that he could play basketball, and he does, or did, before he got sidelined by a drug problem he's supposed to be in rehab for. It's Airol Jones, star center for the Rebels, namesake of pricey athletic shoes. *Airol*

Jones! Rebels tickets have always been out of my reach so the closest I've ever gotten to him has been the small screen. Yet here he is in a used car lot trailer in Paradise City. *My lucky day!*

Three battered and scarred work desks with chairs cram the thinly carpeted space just inside the door. Airol Jones doesn't give me time to snoop around but nudges me down the short corridor to my left. At its end, a door bears an oak sign with the name "Carlotta" and an ivy-and-flower border burned into it. Airol Jones opens the door and ushers me inside with the Ruger.

It's like passing through Alice's looking glass. A fog envelops me, one that smells pleasantly of tobacco and cognac. Cigars. I blink against the smoke. Furry yellow light glows from a single source in the center of the room at about table height.

I draw closer to the light, a desk lamp. Wearing a trim dark suit, Carlotta Trephino sits in a leather side chair in front of a long desk. Her face in the lamp's shadow is recognizable from night-owl TV when she stars in her own commercials. Fifty-ish, she is so attractive it doesn't matter that her face has that taut look of aggressive cosmetic surgery. The white blaze that accents her carefully styled gunpowder black hair has earned her the nickname "Skunk" from those she has wronged.

She holds a shot glass in one hand and a fat cigar in the other. *Cigars.* My brain is trying to tell me something about cigars that I can't put my finger on.

"And who might you be, good lookin'?" Carlotta asks.

I briefly consider giving a moniker. But Carlotta Trephino can't hide, and neither can Airol Jones so I answer, "Will Mansion. I'm a friend of Hector Waltann's."

"No you're not, honey," she says.

Uh oh, busted! My back breaks out in goose bumps. It's a relief to hear her say, "Hector didn't have friends. Toys, maybe, not friends." She pats a second side chair next to her. "But you can be my friend, honey. Sit down. Or am I too old for you?"

"A beautiful woman is ageless," I answer with glibness I'd never attempt sober.

"And a powerful one, immortal," she replies, just as glib, or drunk.

The chair's leather creaks as I take my seat.

"Have a drink?" She hoists the shot glass. "We have nothing but the best."

Indeed they do. The desk lamp shines on a humidor, a marble box, a crystal ashtray, and several bottles. One holds wormwood, purely illegal. Another contains something clear. Tequila, maybe— the label pictures a spiky cactus plant.

Carlotta says, "Airol, be an angel and pour the man something good."

Jones gives her the menacing scowl that always intimidated on the court. "Woman, I ain't here to be your Step'n Fetchit," he says. Nevertheless, he goes behind the desk for another shot glass that he fills with the colorless liquid. I knock it back in one bullet-to-the-brain gulp. It's tequila all right but from the taste of it, not the kind that has to be chased with lime and salt. It slides down like satin, puts the Seagrams to shame.

"Easy, honey, that's blue agave," Carlotta says. "It should be savored, not chugged."

No kidding. Distilled from a rare Central American plant, the liquor is more expensive than the best single malt and I could probably buy two weeks' worth of food with what one shot goes for. I've often wondered if it could possibly be as good as advertised. It is.

Carlotta pours us more. "So how is Hector?"

"Don't know. Haven't seen him. Kinda thought I'd find him here." Hector was into cigars. He had a humidor in the condo.

"He hasn't made this scene in about six weeks," Jones says.

My glass is full again. *Am I due for another already? Must be.*

Airol Jones picks up the humidor and holds it out to me. "Go ahead. That's what you here for, ain't it?"

Damned if I know. I lift the lid.

The cigars nestle snugly against rose-colored satin. The warm aroma has me salivating. I haven't had a cigar since the chief's assistant had her baby and brought some to the office, a cardboard boxful of cellophane-wrapped stubby stogies. Each of us had one and some got sick on them. Something tells me these are not likely to produce the same watery eyes, hacking coughs, and burning-rags smell.

"Cohibas," Airol says. "Fidel's favorite."

Real Havana cigars. Not made of domestic tobacco grown from Cuban seed, but the genuine article, smuggled in. At the moment, though, I'm not thinking about unlawful importation. I'm thinking, how can I get one of those cigars? Because what I want now, what I crave with every fiber of my trembling being, is a smoke. The cigarette I had behind Knockers only whetted my appetite.

With deliberate movements reminiscent of Japanese tea ceremonies, Carlotta takes a cigar from the box and slices off its tip with a cutter whose blades gleam gold. She gently tamps the cigar in a crystal dish powdered with a thin layer of white ash and hands it to me. The cigar's outer wrapper is soft ocher, velvety, as tender to the touch as an old woman's hand. Carlotta takes a match from the marble box. No butane lighters here; the fluid's fumes would sully the earthy scent of the carefully tended tobacco. She strikes the match and the head ignites with a lightning crackle. I take two tentative puffs, then fill my lungs.

Airol Jones blows a smoke ring and says, "Rolled against the inner thighs of young virgins."

I laugh away the cliché but not before picturing a clutch of young women sitting on a wooden bench, sarongs parted over firm flesh, and taste the salt of their sweat.

"Ah, but this is better. How's the phrase go?" I ask. "'A girl is just a girl, but a good cigar is a smoke'?"

Carlotta chuckles. "That's 'woman,' not 'girl.'" She lays a hand high up on my leg. "What's the matter, Will? Don't you like women?"

Jones snorts. "Get real, Carlotta. With his looks, he probably gets all the cooz he wants. No, I'm betting it takes something a little stronger to get our boy Will going." He settles back in Carlotta's desk chair with a drink and a cigar. Carlotta strokes my thigh.

CHAPTER 11

The sculls' oarsmen
straining against the mist,
cutting the fog—Onomato

There must be something more than mere mystique to Havana cigars and blue agave tequila. A lack of contaminants perhaps, resulting in a cleaner higher high. Whatever. Except for the slow burn Carlotta's stroking started in my pants, I am so totally relaxed I could float on the cigar smoke clouds.

Jones says, "Dammit, Carlotta, this just not doing it for me."

Chill, man, this is good. Premium liquor, the best cigars in the world—

Jones waves his cigar and scowls. "You step on this?" he asks Carlotta.

"Of course I did," she replies. "Don't look at me like that. It was for your own good. This Nearvana is that pure. You wouldn't be able to take it if I didn't cut it."

"Own good, my ass. Look, Carlotta, don't do me no favors. I know what I can take and what I can't."

And they go on like that, about who's got whose best interest at heart, but I am stalled in the first part of the argument, the part that seems to be about how at this very moment I am smoking a cigar dusted with turbocharged heroin. Heroin! Of course I've seen it before but always where I expected it, at drug busts and shooting galleries, not on the end of my cigar. But, it's OK. I'm cool. I am so cool.

"So, honey, where is Hector keeping himself these days?" Carlotta asks me.

"Don't know," I reply.

"What you mean, you don't know?" All bent out of shape, Jones springs from his chair, stands over me, and glowers.

"Hey!"

Carlotta says, "Airol—"

"I wouldn't let this fool in here 'cept he got a notion where that muthafucka is." He gets in my face and says, "Waltann in serious trouble. You want to be there with him?"

"What kind of trouble?" I appeal to Carlotta. "Look, I don't know anything about this."

"Now, Airol, no reason to get testy." Carlotta scoots her chair closer, pats my leg with more than simple reassurance. "Honey, Hector just owes me a little money, that's all. We want you to tell him to pay up and all will be forgiven."

Jones adds, "If he don't—"

"Airol!" Carlotta smiles, baring her teeth.

My, what big teeth you have! "I'm going now," I announce. Someplace I can just be mellow, where women don't have barracuda smiles and big men won't slam dunk me. I rise from my chair and put my cigar stub in the crystal dish of heroin.

"Honey! Already? And we were just getting to know each other." Carlotta sniffs loudly. "But if you must, you must. Let's settle up then—"

"Settle up?"

"You invited yourself to this party, remember?" Airol says.

Carlotta purses her lips. "I'd like to say we extended all this hospitality for the sheer pleasure of your company, honey, but I'm afraid that's not the case. A grand ought to about cover it."

"A grand?"

Carlotta smiles.

I edge toward the doorway. "Um, I don't have a grand."

Jones produces the piece he met me at the door with. "Where you think you going, sucker?"

I'd let myself out with my own sidearm only I don't have it on me.

Fortunately, Carlotta tells Airol to put his gun away. To me she says, "That's OK, honey, you can deliver it tomorrow. No later than five p.m."

"Oh, sure. OK."

"And I know you will, honey. Airol, will you do the honors?"

Jones plucks my cigar stub from the ashtray and my glass from the table. He drops them into a zipper-lock plastic bag.

"Just in case, we have this little memento of your evening with us. I'm sure someone would be interested in that, *Detective* Mansion."

Someone must have dumped a bucket of ice water on my head, I go that suddenly cold.

Airol Jones stows the bag in Carlotta's desk.

Given enough time, condensation inside the bag will spoil the prints on the glass, but right now I'm not thinking evidence preservation. I'm not thinking at all. "I said I'll be there," I tell them.

"And we'll keep your membership in our little club a secret," Carlotta replies.

Already chilled, I stumble out into the frosty predawn air. The sky isn't black or blue, it's yellow, mad-dog yellow. Somehow I arrive at Riverbank Road although I can't recall getting in the truck much less merging onto Route 9 or stopping at the stop sign to make my left off Bridge Street. To my right, the river is a mercury streak. Wisps of mist rise from the water's surface and drift toward shore like hungry ghosts restless with greed and desire, floating up from the depths of Hell.

It's just a few steps through fallen leaves and bracken to the water's edge. I find a rock large enough to sit on. It is no more comfortable than my buckwheat-stuffed *zafu*. Cold seeps through even my coat. Though the air is frosty, my shifting and shivering are less from the cold than from craving. Tension is an ache in my shoulders, a pounding in my head. Lungs searching desperately for more of that sweet smoke take short, shallow gasps only to receive icy air scented with humus. Muscles twitch.

Heroin. I've just had heroin. And I liked it. Never have I felt more serene. Already I want more.

Two reproachful eyes glitter at me from the underbrush. A pointed snout sniffs, tapered ears flick. A fox? The thought, "Man, I must be really stoned, I'm hallucinating," presents itself.

"What the hell do you want?" I yell.

The apparition gives me a sad-eyed stare, then vanishes.

*****

The cry of a mourning dove intrudes on something more like a doze than sleep. Awake, I realize it's the distant, muffled "Stroke, stroke," from the coxswain of a crew team on the river below my bedroom window.

In the bathroom, the mirror reflects a slack stubbly pale jaw, flushed cheeks, squinty eyes with narrowed pupils. While I clean up, I reflect that I have about nine hours to raise a thousand simoleons, from where I don't know.

Now I know why Hector can't be found. His family, his condo, his job, all appeared abandoned not because he was abducted, nor did he simply drift away. He ran, from Carlotta, maybe even from Shrike. If I thought I could get away with it, I would, too.

At the Kaffeteria, the morning rush is over. Route-men grab a coffee break before they get back on the road, stock market players drink double lattes while they check the quotes on the computer, ladies of leisure fuel up on croissants and cappuccinos for a day of shopping. Steam threads its way to the ceiling from multiple brewers.

"You look like hell, my man," Dunk tells me. "Tie one on last night?"

"'Fraid so." Now I remember what was nice about laying off the booze: no hangovers. This morning, my head is a bowling ball.

"Hair of the dog that bit you, or would you just like the usual?" He narrows his eyes at me.

It's not a question of "want," I *need* some caffeine. "What's the brew of the day? Never mind, I don't care. Give me a large one, whatever it is."

"Muffin with that? I made Praline Pecan Crunch today."

I should be hungry, but I don't have any appetite. "Just the coffee." The brew is mellow as wine but pastes my eyelids to my forehead. "God, Dunk, this is strong enough to put in my gas tank."

He squares his shoulders. "I call it Seismic Blend. It's light roast. Dark roasts have the caffeine burned off of them. I steep it in caffeinated water for an extra kick. My own invention. Good, huh?"

"Do you have a license to sell this stuff?" I ask. The caffeine has jump-started my pulse and I feel a little more human. A cigarette would really put me right. Overshort's pack of Verves thrums in my coat pocket but I leave it there. Cigarettes have gotten me into enough trouble already and anyway, Dunk keeps his place smoke-free.

The coffee gone, I can put off the inevitable no longer. I square my shoulders, make sure my tie is straight and my hair is combed, and drive to the bank.

There's been a bank in this granite building on Nonotuck Street as long as there's been a city but recently the ownership has changed more often than the traffic light. The name becomes more acronymic each time.

I know the bad news even before I slip my banking card into the ATM: my account holds only a few hundred and my credit card is maxed out. If I had ever bothered setting up a loan line, I could borrow against my debit card. I wish now I hadn't thrown out all those "courtesy checks" the credit card company keeps sending me, urging me to "Do It! Get It! Have It All!" Well, there's no time like the present to start trading on my future. While the prospect of having a debt hanging over my head doesn't thrill me, I tell myself it's only temporary. As soon as I straighten out this mess with Carlotta Trephino, I'll pay it off.

While I wait in line for a teller, I study the other customers, try to determine from their dress or demeanor whether they're depositing or withdrawing. That done, I study the art on the walls. Norman Rockwellish drawings picture a young girl with Shirley Temple curls feeding a piggy bank, freckled brothers with a lemonade stand, a ball-capped boy with a bicycle and a bag of newspapers. Gnashing my teeth with impatience, I read and reread all the signs enough times to memorize today's CD rate, the terms of home loans, even the track record of the bank's investment advisors. I'm in the middle of trying to origami a withdrawal slip into a paper airplane when at last it is my turn. I explain my predicament.

"Ah, you need a loan officer," the teller says.

"Fine. Where can I find one?"

She points behind me. Across the lobby, bulky desks and leather-looking chairs stand empty. *Are they hiding under the desks? Behind the drapes? How do I tell her I don't see them without sounding like an imbecile?*

To my relief, the teller says, "However, they're out."

"All of them? Together?"

"In-service training," she says with an apologetic smile. "They'll be back after lunch."

That will make it one o'clock. Still, plenty of time to get to Carlotta's.

"You can come back, of course, or if you'd prefer to wait—" She extends her hand to a cluster of easy chairs in the lobby. "You can at least get your application filled out."

"I'll wait. No, on second thought, I'll be back. Can I take this?"

"Sure." She hands me a form on a clipboard, and a pen.

At a convenience store halfway down the block I buy a foam cup of coffee. Typically I'd buy cigarettes, too, but I still have Overshort's. Since I don't plan to smoke them, I'm not sure why I continue to carry them around. Perhaps it's because every time I resist having one, I feel I've achieved some sort of victory.

I settle on a bus stop bench to wait. The steel shelter that provides protection from the cold breeze is lined with an eight-foot tall poster of a barely-dressed supermodel selling—what? The only other element in the poster besides her attention-riveting body is one word. *Is it a brand of athletic shoe? Cigarettes? Perfume? What?* Silky blonde hair draped over a rounded shoulder cocked provocatively forward reminds me of Heidi Quince.

Heidi. My problems have so preoccupied me I haven't given a thought to hers. Is she all right? At this hour she's still at work. Leery of calling her there and getting her in trouble with Overshort, I promise myself I'll contact her later.

Across the street, an electronic display marks the time and temperature minute by minute. Between ogles at the poster, time checks, and sips of nasty too-hot coffee, I get the application filled out. Soon after one o'clock I find myself in front of a loan officer. A pimply kid about ten years my junior, he has fine blond hair and pale blue eyes.

He folds his hands on his walnut desk. "I'm sorry, Mr. Mansion. We'd like to help, but I'm afraid you haven't given us much to work with. Your credit card is charged to the limit, you don't own a home, you have no assets to speak of for collateral."

"I've got my truck. That's all paid off, free and clear."

The loan officer scans the application form, then gives me a look that is sympathetic and at the same time, resolute. "You'd do better to sell it than borrow against it. I'm afraid it's not much help."

I point out that I've never borrowed a red cent before but pay for everything in cash, and on time.

He replies, "It would be better if you had debts. You'd have a stronger credit rating then."

I try to make a case for strength of character, remind him I'm a peace officer, with commendations.

"Yes, I wanted to ask you about that. You've indicated you're on temporary disability. When do you plan to return to work?"

"I'm not sure."

"Because if you plan to make it permanent, you should revise these income figures. Don't you have some insurance policies you can borrow from or cash out? Some friends you could borrow from, or who could cosign a loan?"

"If I did, would I be here?"

The kid tips his pimpled chin up. "Hey, don't take it out on me, fella. I'm here to help you."

"Sorry." Though I get a grip on my mounting anxiety, further appeals do no good. The kid either has a stone heart or is stone deaf. Even I can hear the desperation in my voice.

Out on the street, I stop to contemplate my next move. Only when I search for a light and come up empty-handed do I realize I have automatically fished out a cigarette. I put it back. The time-and-temperature sign tells me I have three hours and fewer options.

I can walk the few blocks east to City Hall faster than I can drive and find a place to park. The city cashier is one floor up from the police department. Double doors open onto a crowded bull pen of people shuffling paper and talking on phones that aren't quiet for long between calls. A chest-high counter divided into cells by Plexiglass partitions separates the public from the bull pen. The nearest available cell is staffed by an older woman whose eyeglasses hang from her neck on a chain of pearly beads.

"Hello, Ma'am. I'm a police officer—"

"You're a policeman? You're too handsome to be a policeman, dear."

For a moment I'm speechless. I finally manage, "Well, um, be that as it may, I'd like to see about borrowing on my pension."

"I'm afraid that's not possible. That money's for your retirement, and you are a long way from that."

"But it's an emergency. If I don't get that money, I won't be around to enjoy my retirement!"

"Piffle!" she says.

"Ma'am, I need that money, now what do I have to do to get it? Quit? Fine. I quit."

"Oh, don't be silly. You have many good years of service still ahead of you, you could have a brilliant career, maybe make detective—"

"Ma'am!"

She blinks.

"I am a detective. But I quit. Now I want to cash out my pension."

She blinks again. "Oh, I'm afraid you can't do that."

"What? Of course I can."

"If you do, you can't come back until you redeposit it, every penny, and that could prove a real hardship. You'll find you spent it all, many people do, and can't put together such a large sum of cash so we really try to discourage—"

"But I will pay it back. I just need it temporarily."

"Yes, I'm sure you think you will, everyone does. However, in our experience—"

"The hell with your experience. Look, I'm not coming back! All right?"

"You sound very sure—"

"I want my pension and I want it now!"

She presses pale lips together in a thin line. "Well, if that's how you feel about it."

"I do."

"You're sure?"

"Yes, I'm sure. And I'm in kind of a hurry, so can we get on with it?"

She shrugs. "All right. I hope you know what you're doing." She reaches under the counter, brings up a multi-copy form, and hands it to me with a pen. "Go to Personnel and fill out a resignation form. Indicate the effective date of your resignation. Then you'll need to fill this out. Press down hard, now, it has to come out clear on all the copies."

As instructed, I go down the hall to Personnel and fill out the form, which they give me without argument or lecture. Just to be on the safe side, I put yesterday as the date of my resignation. I return to the cashier's office, take the pension withdrawal form to a stack chair, and hurriedly fill in the blanks. Overhead, the large wall clock ticks. 3:45, 3:46 ...

"Done already?" the woman asks when I bring the form back. "My, you are in a hurry." She puts on her glasses and examines the form. "This seems to be in order." She peers at me over the top of her glasses and scowls. "You might have been a bit neater." She gives the form another going-over. With a sigh, she says, "You'll have your check as soon as your resignation is accepted."

"What do you mean, 'accepted'?"

"Well, it has to be approved by the Chief and the Mayor has to sign off on it, too. They may not accept your requested resignation date." She scans the form and glowers. "Yesterday, really? I'm sure they'll need you for several weeks just to transition—"

"Several weeks? No way. I've got to have the money now."

"Now? Oh, that's just not possible."

I ball my hands into fists and pound the counter. "Dammit, I need that money."

She backs away, the form clutched to her chest. Her coworkers at their desks look up in dismay. "We'll mail it. Four to six weeks. That's the best we can do. Now I'm sorry but you'll have to leave." She adds the form to a towering pile and scurries away to the sanctuary of the rear offices.

I'm still standing there, stunned, when she peeps out into the bull pen, accompanied by a gentleman wearing a threadbare vested suit and the look of a bureaucrat.

"I'm going, I'm going," I assure them, and head for the stairs. It's quicker than the sluggish elevator, not that there's any reason to hurry. I may as well slow down and enjoy the time I have left. Halfway down I stop for a cigarette. I earned it, I deserve it. I need it.

But there's someone else in the stairwell, slumped against the wall on the second floor landing. I put the cigarette away.

"Hey, Swbyra."

"Hey, Mansion!" He rises slowly to meet me. "What you doing here?"

"Came to cash out my pension."

"Cash out? But you can only cash out if you ... ohmigod, you quit? I'll be damned."

"Yeah." The enormity of what I've just done sinks in.

Swbyra says, "Hell, who could blame you after what you've been through. Probably a good thing, give you a chance to heal. Come to mention it, you don't look so good."

"Neither do you." Cheekbones jut from an already-thin face and his eyes are sunk deep in dark sockets. "Migraine?"

"Yeah, migraine. Trying to get it under control here. What's your excuse?"

"Had a little too much to drink last night, that's all."

"Thought you stopped drinking. Smoking, too."

"Well, you know how that goes. Say, uh, you know that missing guy I asked you about? You find out anything about him?"

"Nah. We've been busy."

"Well, turns out it's Hector Waltann."

Swbyra looks thoughtful. "Waltann?"

"You know. Used to own Facets, the jewelry store. Got burgled a few weeks ago."

"Oh, right. How'd you find out?" Swbyra asks.

"Just, uh, asked around."

"Ah." Swbyra leans against the wall. He looks to be in serious pain.

I glance at my watch. My pulse quickens when I see how late it's gotten. "Say, you wouldn't be able to lend me a few bucks, would you?"

"A couple of bucks? For you, buddy? Sure." He takes his money clip from his pocket.

"Like, four hundred?"

"Four *hundred?*" He searches my face. "What the fuck did you get into? You knock up some girl, you horny bastard? Drop one too many at poker? You have been busy."

"No, nothing like that. It's, it's about Shrike. I told you. I might have a line on him." *Not the whole truth and nothing but the truth, but I'm not under oath here, I'm under pressure.*

"Shrike? You just said you quit working."

"I did—"

"You know something about Shrike, you tell me!"

"I will, I will. But I'm still asking questions. And the answers cost, you know that. Now can you lend me the money or not?"

"Four hundred? I—"

I grab the bills and bolt down the stairs.

"Mansion!"

"Thanks, Swbyra, I owe you."

"Mansion! Get back here and tell me about Shrike!"

*****

Four hundred bucks and then some. Why Swbyra's pocket was so full between pay days doesn't concern me at the moment. What does is that I'm two hundred dollars short. I can come up with the rest tomorrow, sure I can. Maybe I could borrow from Grady, or Heidi. If I deliver what I have, Carlotta will see I'm good for it and will carry me a few more hours. Surely she won't kill me over the shortfall. More likely charge me some exorbitant interest. And have her muscle break one of my limbs just to demonstrate her seriousness.

I sprint back to Old Paint and race across town. So intent on getting to Carlotta's by 5:00 am I that I don't even notice my speed until a patrol car comes up behind me, lights flashing. *Dammit!* I can't afford the fine, much less the delay. My watch reads 4:45.

The redheaded rookie who steps up to my window does her uniform justice. "License and reg—hey, aren't you Detective Mansion? Yes, you are! You know, I got called to that scene on Terminal. What a mess. I didn't realize you were out of the hospital. Gosh it's good to know you're up and about and driving around. But speeding ..." She crosses her arms over her chest, tucks her chin in, and gives me a stern look. "Did you realize you were doing 50 in a 35, sir?"

"I'm sorry, I—"

"You know, you don't look so good. With all due respect, sir, should you be out driving around so soon after ... you know?"

"I am in a hurry."

"To get home? Yeah, you probably should get off the road. Go home and get some rest, you look like you could use it, sir."

"Thanks, Officer."

"But take it slow, you want to get there in one piece."

"I'll do that."

"Hope to see you back on duty soon, sir." She waves as I merge back into traffic, my palms slick on the wheel.

4:50. My pulse races faster than the car, I'm panting, and my vision is a blur. Oh, no, not a stress reaction, not now! Quick, what did the doc say? "It's fight-or-flight syndrome, rapid respiration caused by the release of adrenaline." What did the Zen masters say? "Change your breathing and you can change your mind." At the light, I deliberately slow my breathing. By the time I reach Carlotta's I'm somewhat calmer.

At 4:55, the car lot is full of merchandise but no shoppers. I trot directly toward the trailer. A burly salesman in a light top coat blocks my path. A pink shirt collar shows at the unbuttoned neck.

"Hey, how ya doing? Great day to be buying a car, isn't it? And you're in luck. Seeing as how it's late in the day, I'm in the mood to make you a great deal."

If it gets any later ... "I'm not interested."

"In this baby? I don't blame you. Piece of junk. But over here, I got something you'll really like." He gets me in a salesman's half-nelson, his left arm across my back, my arm vised in his right hand.

"No, see, I'm really here to see Carlotta."

"Yeah, well, we'll see Carlotta in a minute but first let me tell you what a great deal—"

"Look, I already have an appointment." The huge watch on his wrist reads 4:48.

"Oh, so you're the one?" He gives my face a long hard look. "Ok, fella, you watch your step. I got my eye on you." The hand that grips my arm falls away and I'm free to finish my dead man's walk to the trailer. "Run" is what I should do, and in the other direction. If I do, though, I'll have to keep on running. Like Hector.

The trailer is open but the door to Carlotta's office is closed. When I knock, her husky voice from behind it calls, "That better be you, Will Mansion. Come on in, honey."

The room still smells of cigars but the smoke has cleared. Carlotta Trephino sits in a mauve high-back leather chair with her high-heeled feet on a desk so big the trailer must have been built around it. She takes a long drag from a cigar. Not one of last night's Cohibas, it's a panatella but it smells almost as good and I want one. She glances at a wall clock. "What's your rush, honey? You've got at least two more minutes."

"I was out of cigars. Thought I'd find one here."

"Oh, how rude of me. May I offer you one?" She takes one from a small marble box.

"With or without Nearvana?" I ask her.

"What do you think, honey? I know what you like."

I tell myself I've got to take it to keep up the pretense. I tell myself it will calm my nerves, stave off a flashback. The truth is I want one, that's all. As I smoke, I stroll around the office. Plaques and framed testimonials to Carlotta's success in business and support of various charities hang on walls papered in pastel stripes the color of Necco wafers. Out a rear window I spot several flashy cars: not part of the inventory, more likely hers and those of her staff.

"So, have you found Hector?" Carlotta asks.

"Not yet."

"Detective Mansion, I'm disappointed in you. I thought surely, someone of your caliber ..."

"If I'm going to find Hector for you, I need to know when and where you last saw him." I don't have to fake calm and confidence. My voice flows like molasses. Muscles feel like taffy. I'm drowsy.

"He used to come here, but not in the last couple of weeks," Carlotta says. "Been spending quite a lot of time on the Miracle Mile, I understand. Got tied up with someone named Nicky, last I heard. Does that help?" She lays her cigar in an ashtray, slowly rises, and steps up close to me. She puts her hands in my coat pockets and gropes around. Not finding what she wants, she makes for my pants' pockets.

I grab her hands. "This what you're looking for?" I ask, and produce the money.

"Well, that too." She smiles, but as she counts the bills, her smile fades. "Will, honey, you're short."

"No I'm not. I'm above-average height for the American male."

I hear someone giggle but Carlotta's mouth is twisted in non-amusement. The joker must be me. "Look, this was the best I could do on short notice. You guys cleaned me out last night."

"Honey, we can't really be held to blame for your excesses, now can we? Well, what are we going to do?"

"I'm good for it. I've got more coming. A few weeks ..."

"Now where have I heard that before? You are a friend of Hector's, aren't you?" She picks up her cigar, takes a puff.

"Believe me, I'll get the rest, I promise."

"Well, that would be good enough for me, honey, but I'm afraid it won't wash with my, uh, manager."

Manager. Got to be Shrike. No one else wholesales Nearvana, at least no one who wants to go on living.

She smokes silently for another minute or two. "You couldn't borrow some?"

"My friends are as tapped out as I am."

"Honey, I'm not tapped out." She presses against me and strokes my chest. "And I told you, we can be friends. I'll lend you the rest. And I think you'll find my terms very generous."

CHAPTER 12

Catbird feathers,
tufts of fur on the grass.
The yard is silent—Onomato

She jerks my shirt out of my pants, tugs at my belt. The grazing of fingernails sets off ripples of gooseflesh, shattering my mellow. I wrest myself free and put my clothes back in place.

Carlotta pouts. "Now where do you think you're going, honey? You still owe me and tomorrow just won't do. So there's a little errand you will run for me."

"I'll get you your money, Carlotta."

"It's too late for that, I'm afraid. Now I could take my little baggie of souvenirs from your visit last night and pass it along. I'm sure there's someone who would be interested to know you were there. Drinking tequila. Smoking Havanas. Doing smack. Or would you prefer we just keep that our little secret?"

"You were there too."

"Let me assure you, that's not a problem."

"Your fingerprints as well as mine are on the glass and the cigar."

"My fingerprints? Airol Jones's, you mean. As I recall, he handed you the glass, and the humidor."

Damn, she's right.

"I'm making it easy on you, honey. Just exchange one little package," she brandishes a wad of bills, "for another little package. See the man." She mentions a name that is more a moniker: Shrike. "Do this little favor for me and we're even." She wraps both arms around my waist, stuffs the wad of bills into one rear pocket, pinches my cheek through the other. "Run along now. The sooner you get back, the sooner we can dust our cigars. Now if I can't convince you to do this, I have some very persuasive salesmen on the lot I'm sure could sell you on the idea. They are good closers, that you can believe."

Like the bruiser I met on the way in? I can imagine the high-pressure tactics he might use.

Just yesterday, the mere mention of Shrike's name sent me into a tailspin. With Nearvana soothing my nerves, I calmly say, "So where do I find this Shrike?"

"Last I heard, honey, he was running a stash house on the Miracle Mile."

"That covers a lot of territory. Can you be more specific?"

"A month ago I could have. Lately, though, Shrike's been keeping a low profile. 'Don't call him, he'll call you?' Except I'm in something of a bind, so you'll have to find him. Big time detective that you are, it should be easy."

Big time detective. More than ever I need that to be true if I'm to find Shrike. Gone to ground, as easy to find as fish lips, Ace and Spade said. If they with all their resources can't find him, how can I, one man alone? My usual informants won't help. Having resigned I no longer have any influence to offer them and they're not known for their altruism. I drive around for a while meaning to ponder the alternatives, but all I do is waste precious gas. Finally, I simply head for the Miracle Mile.

After dark, even the fullest moon and brightest stars can't compete with the neon, so the sky appears black. There are a few people on the sidewalks, mostly with something to sell, and more cruise the street—the buyers. They drive just above idle in their Continentals and Blazers.

Just another lemming, I'm cruising, too: for Hector, for this Nicky whom Carlotta said he was connected with. And for Shrike. Not that I want to find him. I don't. I must find him.

There's enough space in front of the Mercy Mission for Old Paint but I don't have what it takes to parallel park it so I simply steer in as best I can. I turn up my topcoat collar against the drizzle and plod along the sidewalk. The buildings seem to lean toward the street, hemming me in. Seemingly from nowhere, hookers and pushers start toward me, their leering faces garish in the neon. The homeless, drunks, and derelicts beg me for a cigarette. For once, I don't want one myself. Nearvana satisfies all cravings, except the craving for more Nearvana.

Catty-corner across the street, a noisy game of three-card monte is in progress in front of the coffee shop. The dealer and his shill look like they were born and raised on the Miracle Mile, but I've made them. Ace and Spade, back on their undercover assignment. *They mustn't see me!* I make for the Algonquian. A man slumped across the doorway grabs my ankle.

"Help me, man," he says. "You got a dollar? Anything you can spare? I need to fix, man, I'm hurtin' bad."

"Let me go." I tear loose and cleave to the wall, slide along to the pawnshop hoping to duck in there but it's closed. Only the night trade window is open. Panicking, I continue to inchworm my way south along the wall and try the plasma bank but it's closed, too. Two men locked in mortal combat block my entrance to the neighboring King Phil.

I push, then pull on the next door I come to. It opens and a little bell tinkles overhead. Air stuffy with smoke, petrochemicals, and incense fills my nose.

"Oh, no," cries a throaty voice that's vaguely familiar.

Lix Gemini. I've worked my way down to the tattoo parlor.

"Get out," he says.

"Hey, Lix."

"I said 'get out!'" He backs away from me. Beaded fringes sway from a balding hip-length suede vest. A tank shirt under the sleeveless garment leaves his lean arms bare. Pale skin stretched over small bunched muscles is blue-white. Ankh and peace symbol pendants hang from his neck on bead necklaces. He looks like a ragged remnant of the seventies. At his small feet booted in scuffed snake skin, the ink I spilled on the floor is a dry but still Technicolor Rorschach.

"No, look, you got it all wrong," I tell him. "I'm not here to hassle ya." He's got to let me hang here just a little while longer. Ace and Spade won't man that corner all night. In fact, they could soon be going off shift. What time is it, anyway? Nearly eleven on my watch. "In fact, I, uh, I feel bad about the other night. That's uh, why I came back. To make it up to you. Pay you for the ink. What do I owe you?"

He was right, the stuff is expensive. The small bills in my wallet won't cover it. A big bill from the stake Carlotta gave me will, though.

"That's some wad you got there," Lix Gemini says.

"Huh?"

"Money. You're loaded."

"Oh, it's not mine. I'm just, uh, running a little errand. For a friend." The words nearly choke me.

"Uh huh. I understand."

"No, it's not what you think."

"Hey, you don't have to explain nothing to me."

Indeed I don't. But a peep out the door shows Ace and Spade are still holding down their corner. I need to keep the conversation going so I can hang here a while longer. "Say, you don't have any tattoos yourself. What's this, a case of the cobbler's kids going barefoot?" Other than the multiple piercings he has no distinguishing marks.

Lix blinks obsidian eyes. "Cobbler? What's pie got to do with it?"

"You're so busy working you can't give yourself a tattoo?"

"Oh, I'm busy enough, but that ain't it. I can't do myself, I got to get someone else. I just can't get anyone else to do me." He looks up at me through his lashes. "You want to take a poke at me?"

He may not mean that the way it sounds. Nevertheless I don't like the direction this is taking. Time to be moving on. "So, where can I find Nicky?"

He ambles to a shelf tucked into a corner, returns with an apple and a carving knife. One-handed, he cuts a wedge from the apple and eats it before replying. "I thought you was looking for Hector."

"And I thought you didn't know where he was."

His eyes on the apple, Lix says, "I don't."

"So I didn't ask you about Hector, I asked you about Nicky."

He considers that a moment. "And you'll leave my name out of it? I got to live here, you know."

"Just tell me. Where can I find Nicky?"

He gives me a sly smile. "Only one by that name on the Mile worth talking about is Nikki Saint Clair. She dances at the Metro."

The Metro is at the top of the Mile. "Thanks a heap, Lix Gemini. Be seeing you."

"I hope not."

I exit the tattoo parlor and start back north to the Metro. Not so fast. Ace and Spade are still at work. *Putting in a little O.T.?* They want Shrike badly, but I'd better find him first. Carlotta said he runs a stash house here. Lots of good candidates for that on this street but I can hardly go door-to-door asking. *Think, think.*

The fight in front of the King Phil has broken up. Nikki St. Clair will have to wait. I slip inside.

The tavern is bathed in a blood-red light usually reserved for darkrooms. Drinkers line the bar from end to end; more fill the banquettes and tables. Toward the rear, small-time dealers without their own cell phones vie for the pay phone.

Phone. I was supposed to call Heidi Quince. At the first break in the action, I drop my coin.

"Heidi? It's Will Mansion."

"Will, I'm so glad you called. I've been worried about you all day."

"I'm fine. Are you OK? It's not every night a woman finds herself ducking gunfire."

"Don't remind me. I'm still shaking. I have nightmares."

Join the club.

A broad-shouldered man in a black leather coat and cap comes to stand very close to me and fixes me with feral bloodshot eyes. He drapes an arm over the top of the phone.

"So there haven't been any further ... incidents?"

Heidi says, "No. I'm fine, really. Tell me where to meet you and I'll show you I'm perfectly all right."

"I'll have to take your word for it. I don't want you down here." I smile politely at my leather-coated companion.

"Where is 'here'?" Heidi asks.

"The Miracle Mile."

There's a pause before she says, "I don't like you being there."

"Well, this is where the trail led."

With a curled lip, the leather-coated man says, "Now," and I mouth, "Just a minute."

"The trail to Hector?" Heidi asks.

"Yes, and I have a lead. Someone named Nikki St. Clair."

There's another pause before she says, "You're not giving up, are you?"

Leather Coat clasps my wrist with a gloved hand that clamps tight as a talon.

"Maybe the next time I talk to you I'll be able to tell you I found him."

"Will, it sounds dangerous. Get away from there. Meet me—"

"Gotta go." Leather Coat's grip is cutting off my circulation. He forces me to hang up. "All yours," I tell him. He growls, I retreat.

A thin man in an equally thin Windbreaker jostles me. Under his arm he carries a VCR, its cables flapping like rudely severed umbilical cords. "Stolen" pops to the forefront of my brain.

"Hey, man," he says to me. "Got a helluva bargain for you here. Four head, full-track audio, dual deck." Rheumy eyes in a drawn face beseech me. "Just two bills."

"Sorry, man," I tell him. "I don't even have a TV."

He wastes no more time with me but approaches one patron after another, holding out the VCR and having a brief conversation. All end in a head shake. No one, apparently, will buy despite the fact that the King Phil's clientele is known to appreciate a bargain, never mind the merchandise's provenance. VCR man tries Leather Coat, my friend at the pay phone. He also shakes his head. But he points to the door. VCR Man smiles, nods vigorously, and leaves.

When Leather Coat reclaims his seat at the bar, I take off my watch, put it in my pocket, and sidle up to him.

"Hey, Bud, I got a little problem I think you can help me with," I tell him. "See, I'm getting desperate. Can you help me?"

He narrows his eyes and looks me up and down. "What do I look like, the Red Cross?"

"No, no, man. You heard me on the phone. I can't find my man, my regular man. You look like someone willing to do business."

"Oh, so now I look like a businessman."

"Come on, buddy, don't play games. I'm looking to go to Heaven."

"Keep buggin' me, man, I'll send you to hell."

"You know what I mean. I want to experience Nearvana. They tell me you're the man. What do you say?"

"I say you want to go to Heaven, you got to pay the price."

"Well, see, that's just it. I'm a little tapped. Got cash flow problems, you know? My regular man, he understands. He'll take something on trade." I fish my watch from my pocket. "I got this. It's worth something. It's Swiss."

"Oh, so now I look like a pawn shop. Try down the street, asshole."

"Aw, come on, man. Give me a break. I'm hurting."

"You're breaking my heart. Cash only, dirtbag. Now get out of my face." He picks up his drink.

"Come on, man, you gotta help me." Mimicking the man who grabbed me in front of the Algonquian, I whine, "I need to fix, man, I'm hurting bad."

My distress is genuine and far more convincing than any con I've ever pulled because Leather Coat gives me a long look and says, "Go see a movie."

"Ah, man—"

"I said, go see a movie. Now beat it or you'll really be hurting."

With my hands up in surrender, I back away and leave the King Phil. A quick glance up the street is reassuring: the monte game is gone, the sidewalk in front of the coffee shop clear.

Opposite the coffee shop stands the Paradise Theater, its 1920s plaster facade crumbling, its ticket window shuttered. Like single-screen theaters across the country, it has been long abandoned. The last time I was here might have been the '70s for midnight showing of "The Rocky Horror Picture Show."

"Go see a movie," said Leather Coat. VCR Man did and it must have been a real sleeper. He sits on the ground slumped against the wall below a faded poster for "The Secret of DG," chin on chest, no VCR in sight.

"Where's Shrike?" I ask him.

VCR Man looks up with eyes that don't quite focus and jerks a thumb down the alley. I peer down the dark passageway but don't see anything. Hugging the wall, I take a few cautious steps over stinking piles that rustle alarmingly. A shadow moves. Out of what must be a learned response to dark alleys I go for my piece although I'm not aware of being afraid. Good thing I'm not; I don't have the weapon on me. Anyway, nothing jumps out at me except vermin.

There is no one in the alley and no VCRs, nothing in the vacant lot beyond except knee-high weeds. The north side of the coffee shop at my back and the south side of the theater opposite are both windowless brick walls, each broken only by a side door. The coffee shop's side door has an eye-level wire glass window and a doorknob. While the theater's side door may have once had a window, it's since been opaqued, and there is no doorknob.

While I stand before it wondering how to get in, I hear an electromechanical click. Overhead I spot the red eye of a night vision surveillance camera tucked in the eaves. As if by magic, the door opens. When I step inside, it closes behind me just as magically.

Inside, it is no brighter or warmer than the alley. Red spots glow in the corners as if the place were infested with hot-eyed rats. I bump into something thigh-high: a theater seat. Cold metal presses against my temple.

"Mansion, if you got a prayer, say it. You about to die." The disembodied voice is more like a croak. Shrike! The Nearvana high from Carlotta's evaporates. It drops me faster than a runaway elevator, leaving me with the same hollow stomach.

"Shrike, you got me wrong. Carlotta sent me."

"Sure."

"I swear it, I'm just here to make a buy." I couldn't be any more sincere if my life depended on it. And it does. "You got to believe me. I have a package I'm supposed to exchange for another package." A kid making his first score wouldn't whimper this badly, but I don't care. This isn't a sting and I don't have to impress him, don't ever have to see him again. I just have to get out of here alive.

"You got half a second to convince me this ain't a bust."

"Bust? I'm not even armed."

The pressure of the gun barrel against my temple eases off. A shadow moves into my line of sight: a tall man with a sharp nose, hard glittering eyes, and a swarthy face under a black leather slouch hat. A dark raincoat hangs on his thin frame. Shrike. He holds a semiautomatic pistol big as a quart milk carton. Its T-shaped silhouette suggests a Cobray M-11. Fitted with an extra-long magazine, the weapon is mean and ugly as a rabid Rottweiler and about as easy to control.

Beside him a skinny junkie points an automatic with a Swiss-cheesed barrel shroud at my chest. A TEC-9 maybe, just as nasty.

Shrike says, "Lose the coat. Up against the wall." He smacks my head with his weapon.

Having never been on the receiving end of a pat-down, I've failed to appreciate the enfeebling humiliation the subject must feel. Shrike, however, capitalizes on it. He takes his time, feels me up like he enjoys it. Hums. Takes my wallet, keys, small change, and Carlotta's bankroll. He's got the cash, he could kill me now.

"You in the business now?" Shrike asks.

"No, I ... just owe Carlotta some money."

"You using?"

"Yes, yes!" *Whatever!* I turn my head to catch his next move and see him pick up my topcoat, go through the pockets, find Overshort's cigarette pack. Shrike chuckles. His lieutenant wags his gun at me and I turn my face back to the wall. Sparks of phantom light signal an oncoming flashback.

"What you got here?" Shrike holds a cigarette under my nose. It's the Nearvana sample Carlotta's steerer gave me in the Knockers parking lot, the one I swapped for a cigarette from Overshort's pack. "You ain't done this yet?"

"I was saving it for when times get rough." Like now, when my vision mists, blurs, and I find myself spinning toward Terminal Road in the strobing light.

Shrike laughs. "Yeah, you new at this. You find out, it all rough times. OK, maybe you on the level, but I ain't falling for no narco trap."

"No trap, I swear." *Terminal Road, it's a trap, it's a trap!*

"Prove it." From his raincoat, Shrike produces a plastic straw, sealed at both ends. "Do it."

"What is it?" I ask, but I know damn well. It's "HIS," heroin-in-a-straw.

"Just do it." He opens the straw, shoves it up my right nostril, and clamps the left closed with his thumb. "Snort, sucker."

Death by OD, that's the plan. Smart. I'll be just another dead junkie. I squeeze my eyes shut but the light and noise of little explosions only come faster. My ears throb with the beating of a vulture's wings, his shrill caw. *I don't want to die!* Tears trickle down my cheeks.

"C'mon, Mansion, breathe!"

His second pokes my kidney. Though I intend to take the tiniest whiff, I breathe deeply because oh, yes, Nearvana—I want it! Something powdery goes up my nose. I sink to my knees and wait to die.

But I don't die. Instead, the nausea, dizziness, and disorientation that signal a flashback subside. Tension ebbs away, respiration slows. Light-spirited rather than lightheaded, I open my eyes. The cackling vulture has taken flight; there is only Shrike in his raincoat, laughing.

He counts Carlotta's cash. "You short," he says.

The money I gave to Lix Gemini! "A few dollars. But ... but ... I got something worth more than that."

"Yeah, what's that?"

"Information. Uh, you know that monte game on the corner? It's a plant."

"Shit, you might be all right, Mansion." Shrike tells his associate to give me the dope. "Better'n that other errand boy Carlotta had, that Hector."

"Oh yeah? What'd he do?" I ask.

"Sonofabitch stiffed me, big time," Shrike says. "Pay me with some worthless junk, man must have some kind of death wish. Tell you what. You find him for me, I just might let you live."

Shrike sweeps toward the exit. On the wall to the left of the door, a small green light glows above a chest-high panel studded with ten buttons. Shrike fingers the buttons, the light changes to red, and the door opens. His second flings me and my coat out the door. With a noisy flap of fabric, Shrike and his second are gone and I am alone in the alley. I nod off until a fit of shivers shakes me awake and prompts me to pick up my coat. I return to the street, calm, relaxed, just another stoner with a load of heroin in my pocket. Miracle Mile is quiet, dark, save for the sputtering neon of the Metro at the corner.

I'm supposed to go there, although I can't exactly remember why until I reach the door. It's hung with a full-length, full color poster of the headliner, a tall redhead, damn near naked with a hungry look that is both daring and dangerous. Nikki St. Clair. Oh yes, that's why I'm here. Hector's "Nicky."

The door takes a hard shove to open, the place is so densely packed. I elbow my way closer to the front through a fog of cigarette smoke. Most of the men, transfixed by the dancer currently on stage, let me nudge by. Those who feel I should stay back give me dirty looks and curses but no one picks a fight. They sit or stand in a trance, numb and dumb.

I worm my way to a spot with a good view of the runway. The man at my side takes one step to the left to put some space between us and for a moment there is eye contact. His eyes are red, his round pale face sheened with sweat in the close, smoky atmosphere.

A roving cigarette girl approaches wearing only a G-string. Instead of a bra she wears a halter-slung tray of smokes. "Cigars, cigarettes?" she asks.

"Got any premium brands?" the man next to me asks.

"Toward the back."

The man hands over a large bill. Even in a place like this it's an exorbitant amount for a pack. He reaches in to the back of the tray and takes a long time about making his selection. The cigarette girl waits patiently, her mouth stretched in a rictus of feigned pleasure.

Oh I see what's going on here. The cigarette girl is naked behind her tray. A bill buys a feel. Our eyes meet and in hers I see hopelessness, resignation, and loathing.

"You?" she asks when he's done.

I shake my head.

With raised eyebrows she asks, "You sure there ain't something here you want?"

"I'm sure."

She shrugs and shoulders her way into the throng.

The dancer leaves the stage and the crowd hoots and stamps for the next act. The house lights dim, heavy metal rock music comes up. A spotlight hits the curtain and follows the woman who strides across the stage dressed in a tight white nurse's uniform. No nurse who ever attended me wore a uniform this form-fitting, much less shiny red four-inch heels.

Nikki St. Clair is tall, especially from this angle. Toned, with slim arms. Strong legs long enough to wrap around a man twice stretch from the bottom of her micro mini skirt all the way to the floor. She peels her nurse's costume to reveal something else the poster didn't show: she is abundantly tattooed. Flowers vine up her calves. A firebird is spread eagled across her shoulder blades. A pair of winged serpents with forked tongues forms a caduceus from G-string to navel. I saw the same picture on Lix Gemini's wall, a custom design, and picture her stretched out naked on the old barber chair while he applies it, then picture her simply stretched out naked.

She removes the rest of her costume. The men fall silent again, mouths firmly shut, arms crossed over chests or bellies. No one speaks, no one smiles, as if the smallest movement would betray arousal.

Which they must be because Nikki Saint Clair is good. Oh, she has all the usual moves. She flows from a backbend into a split, turns her back on the audience, bends from the waist, and shakes her white buttocks. Turns again and, perched precariously on those spike heels, sinks into a squat so deep her thighs are at right angles to her hips. Swirls her hands around her body, shivers in ecstasy. Rubs her crotch against the pole at stage left, then at stage right in a pantomime of humping. Her eyes are not fixed on the back wall or staring off into space, turned inward in self-absorption, or glazed in a drugged stupor. They bore into mine, tell me this performance is for me, only for me. My pulse pounds with the heavy metal beat. An erection presses against my trousers. Even my skin throbs. A night with her would reduce us both to cinders, I am convinced.

Her act draws to a close and with a roar, the crowd tosses bills of large denomination onto the stage. Nikki throws kisses and disappears through the curtains, only to reappear on the floor wrapped in the customary short kimono. She is not to touch the patrons, nor they her, but that doesn't stop anyone any more than it restricted the cigarette girl's trade.

Nikki comes to stand before us. Bills fan out of her belt and neckline like parrot feathers. She glances at the sweaty man next to me, then at me, and I feel her thigh press against mine.

"Did you like Nikki's act?" she asks me.

"Yeah," the man at my side answers breathlessly, and slips a fifty into her robe.

"How 'bout you, Good Lookin'?" Nikki asks me.

"I'll come backstage and tell you how much," I reply.

She licks her lips and squeezes against me, close enough to smell her: sweat and pheromones.

"Nikki would like that, sugar, but if she let you, she'd have to let all these other guys."

"But I'm special. I'm a friend of Hector Waltann's."

"Don't know any Hector Waltann." She steps away and I grab her arm. "Hey!"

"Lix Gemini said you did."

CHAPTER 13

Sunday morning
Brown glass shards in the gutter
How the street sparkles!—Onomato

Nikki St. Clair stops in mid-stride. "Lix said that?"

"Well, not in so many words."

"Maybe you ought to tell Nikki exactly what he did say. Give her five minutes to change, then come to the dressing room." She plunges into the crowd which parts briefly to let her pass, then meshes again.

"Let me go with you," the man next to me pleads.

"This is business, pal."

"Sure it is."

Nikki must have told the bouncer to let me by because I make my way back to the dressing room unimpeded. When I enter the room—a space about the size of a walk-in closet—Nikki sits enthroned on a vanity chair with flaking brass colored paint and a cracked pink vinyl seat. She faces a mirror over a waist-high shelf. The makeshift vanity holds pink and lavender brushes and combs, frosted jars of makeup, cans of hair spray, and jewel-toned bottles of booze. A black leather motorcycle cap and a G-string, both with Harley Davidson insignias, drape an old black phone set.

Breathless, Nikki pants, "Please, make yourself comfortable." She suggests a shabby armchair wedged against a rolling metal clothing rack crammed with capes, lengths of filmy material, sparkly fabric, and feathered hats. Costumes, as if the regulars might get bored watching the girls take off the same things all the time. A feathered boa slithers from the rack onto my shoulder.

"Nikki was just about to have a drink," she says. "How about one for you, sugar? It's creme de menthe. Very refreshing. That riser is the smokiest place in the house. Dancing leaves Nikki with quite a cough."

Which would go far to explain the many bottles of what appears to be prescription cough syrup among the other vials and jars. She swivels toward the mirror and fusses with the jumble on the vanity. The effort loosens the sash to her robe which slips from her shoulders. "Nikki really must find another line of work. This job is likely to be the death." She swings back around, steps over to present me with a drink, and stands so close I can see the sweat beaded between her breasts. "Well, sugar, what was it you wanted from Nikki?"

My immediate thought is physical and primal. I take a healthy slug of creme de menthe. It's all sugar and sting. "I'm looking for Hector. Where can I find him?"

She settles back into her chair. "Nikki told you she doesn't know any such person. Shame on Lix for spreading such nasty lies."

"Actually, Lix didn't say you knew where Hector is. He only told me where I could find you."

"As if Nikki is hard to find." She spreads her shapely arms and parts her legs to show just how accessible she is. "So who did give you this sadly mistaken impression?"

"Carlotta Trephino."

"Ah, Carlotta."

"So you know her?" It's getting increasingly hard to sit knee to knee with a nearly-naked Nikki Saint Clair and keep my mind on the subject. Another minute and I'll be all over her like hot syrup on johnnycakes.

"Just from the TV, sugar. Carlotta and Nikki live in different worlds. She's a successful business woman. Nikki's just a lowly dancer in a cheesy strip bar." She skims sweat from her body with the side of her hand. A huge rectangular green sparkler glints on her right ring finger. If she wore it on stage, I somehow failed to notice it. Then again I wasn't paying much attention to her hands. "Ooo, Nikki is hot. Feel." She presses my palm against her breastbone.

"Not lowly," is all I can manage to say. My tongue feels thick, my speech sounds slow.

"Oh, aren't you sweet, sugar? Let Nikki get you another drink."

Another? I don't even remember drinking this one and now I'm sorry I did, it's made me sick. Irresistibly drowsy, I just want to conk out. "No thanks. I, uh, I think I'd better be going."

"There's a fire exit just at the end of the hall if you don't want to go through the crowd."

"I'll do that."

"You come back, stay a while," she calls after me.

I stagger down the corridor, lean on the crash bar, and tumble out the dented aluminum door into the chilly drizzle. I'm just emerging from the alley onto Putnam when a gold sedan creeps down the street from my right and drifts into the opposite lane. Something not quite right about it brings me to instant alertness. The passenger side window. It's down. On a cold night like this? I dive back into the alley under a burst of shot. I hit the ground, slide for home, and collide headfirst into something sharp-edged and immovable.

*****

A hand jostles my shoulder. An aromatic scent fills my nostrils. Is someone trying to revive me? I open my eyes to the face of Lix Gemini. Rain drips onto my face from the bill of his black cap.

"Hey, man, you OK?"

No, I'm rain-soaked and half-frozen. My topcoat is gone. Gone with it are my goddamn cigarettes, one of which I could use right now. My head is killing me. There's a sticky gash in my scalp where I collided with the sharp edge of the Dumpster that looms beside me. "Call an ambulance. I hit my head. I may have a concussion."

"An ambulance, that's rich," Lix says. "The only ambulance that'll come here is the meat wagon. You're breathin', you're talkin', you must be OK. Maybe if we get you inside, you'll feel better. You're probably just cold."

He gives me a hand-up and I stumble along to his studio. The room is especially stuffy after the cold wet air in the alley and it doesn't do my headache any good. Lix tosses his damp jacket and cap onto a chair. Underneath he wears a muscle tee, not that he has many muscles, his black leather pants and vest, and lots of silver chains. "How'd you find me?"

"Oh, I was on my way to see Nikki."

"Why are you helping me after I messed up your studio?"

"Hell, I don't know, man. You paid me back for that—I guess you're all right."

I sink onto an old wooden bench and rest my back against the wall. The lump my wallet usually makes in my rear pants pocket is conspicuous by its absence. I reach behind to check. Sure enough, it's gone. Worse, so is the heroin I got from Shrike for Carlotta.

"Wallet's gone, huh?" Lix says. "Someone rolled you. Man, the look on your face, you'd think it was the end of the world."

"It is."

"Lost that pile you had on you, too, didn't you?"

"Looks that way."

He turns his palms up and hunches his shoulders in an extravagant shrug. "Tough break, man." He strolls across the room to a corner nook where he has a double-burner hot plate set up on a shelf. "Say, you want some coffee? Make you feel better."

"No thanks," I say quickly.

He wheels around, hands on narrow hips. "You think I'm gonna poison you? Hey, get it yourself then. But make me a cup while you're at it."

On the shelf I find a double burner hot plate, a half-empty box of doughnuts, the apple carving knife, some paper napkins, an open pack of Verves, and an assortment of orphan crockery. Not quite out of sight are a syringe, a scorched metal spoon, and a length of yellowed rubber tubing. Works. Lix Gemini has himself more than a little heroin habit.

I find the two cleanest mugs among a collection stained with coffee on the inside and ink on the outside and fix two cups of instant. I sit back down on the bench, gripping my cup with both hands like a lifeline. Dead again, I could have been dead again. The bench, the floor, do not feel all that solid yet.

Lix holds out a cigarette. The smoke curling from its tip is a wraith with a gaping maw, Edvard Munch's *Scream*. "Want it? It's Nearvana. It's the only one I got but you look like you could use it, man."

I could. We smoke and sip together in silence, until the warmth of the room and the coffee and the balm of the drug causes the shifting walls to settle into soft focus. After some time, Lix speaks.

"So, you find that dude you was looking for?"

"Hector Waltann?"

"Yeah, Hector. You want him pretty bad. What's he to you?"

A lead to Shrike, not that I need that anymore. "Nothing."

"Got to be somethin' for you to get yourself all busted up and strung out over it."

"I'm not strung out." Not anymore.

He gives me that extravagant shrug again. "Yeah, like your hands always shake like that."

"Other people are involved. Some have been hurt. Killed. There may be more killings yet."

Heidi Quince. Her kiss did more for me than Carlotta's hands on my body, Nikki Saint Clair's moist flesh against my palm. Now Ace and Spade are in trouble, too. When I tipped Shrike to their plant, at the very least I blew their cover. Worse, I may have endangered their lives.

Lix says, "So how's that any of your business? I don't know, man, to me it looks like the only one in danger is you. Why don't you just forget it?"

Why indeed? To protect Heidi? Why not let the cops do it? That's their job. I'll tell them where to find Shrike and to look out for Hector who's on his hit list.

I finish the cigarette and coffee and set my cup on the bench. "Thanks, Lix Gemini. Be seeing you."

He smiles. "I hope so."

CHAPTER 14

Searching for the moon
I saw instead
a shooting star—Onomato

The sword that kills the man, saves the man.

Sister Clyde's cryptic comment still makes no sense. It's not swords I'm worried about, it's shotguns. The blast behind the Metro makes it clear the one at the bookstore was meant for me, as well as Heidi. It's damn hard to aim a shotgun, even a sawed-off, and drive at the same time, which might explain why the shooter missed but I'm not sticking around while he improves his aim. How did he know just when and where to find me? Had he been following me all night? If so, he had several other, better opportunities to take a shot at me. He couldn't have known when I left Nikki's, and that I'd be in that alley. Not unless she told him.

The Metro is dark. Nikki is gone. A setting moon tells me I am already well into today. I lurch home in Old Paint, thinking I will get some rest, knowing I will get none.

In the bedroom, pre-dawn light sifts through half-open vertical blinds and turns the white walls, the beige carpet, to mottled gray. Over a drafty window, the blind's slats sway gently like piano keys pressed by invisible fingers. The neglected zafu languishes in its corner, its stolid lump both sternly disapproving and humbly beseeching. I sit on it but could no more meditate tonight than fly to the moon.

"Sit, rest, work," the Buddha prescribed, "Alone with yourself, never weary. On the edge of the forest live joyfully, without desire."

On the edge of the forest. Yes. With a nice girl, maybe a pretty gemologist. Become a farmer or an accountant, something tame. Live to be a hundred and one and pass away peacefully, asleep in bed, not breathless and cowering in the street at the business end of a gun, heart squeezed by fear and guts turned to water.

I awake from a dreamless Nearvana-deep sleep to discover I fell asleep on the floor, my head on the zafu, which is no more comfortable a pillow than it is a sitting cushion. My neck is stiff. I scrounge around in pants pockets and junk drawers, on dresser tops and under seat cushions for stray singles and spare change. Unshowered, unshaved, I dash up to the convenience mart for coffee, which I no longer have in the house, cigarettes, and matches. I don't plan to smoke, but when I lost my topcoat, I lost the pack of Verves Overshort left me and I need a new talisman. Home again, I take the coffee out to the stair landing and sit, sipping. Forty yards away, dead leaves cruising on the river's surface belie the swift currents that roil underneath.

It's time I got busy. I'm not looking forward to what I have decided to do. But I fix my gaze on the promise of freedom at the end of it.

It takes a nerve-wracking hour on the phone to report my stolen credit cards to the appropriate companies, a laborious task made no easier by a stiff neck. By the time I get to the last one, I'm slamming the receiver down, teeth throbbing from grinding them.

The next call promises to be almost as painful. I dial Heidi's private number. A recording in a man's voice tells me I have reached the intended number and instructs me to leave a message.

"Heidi, it's Will Mansion—"

"Will!" It's Heidi, sounding somewhat out of breath.

"Oh, you're there."

"I was, you know, screening calls."

"Well, I got that man's voice. Your husband?"

She giggles. "No, Will, I'm not married. I got a friend to record that for me. Cuts down on the number of obscene messages that get left. Why advertise a woman living alone?"

"Good thinking. I called to tell you, I'm not looking for Hector anymore."

"You're quitting?"

Why did she have to say "quitting?" I can almost hear her thinking, "Will Mansion, gutless wonder."

Instead, she says, "Glad to hear it. I think that's very wise."

"You do?"

"Yes, I do. Why take unnecessary risks?"

"Yeah. Uh, exactly. Anyway, I have a few loose ends to tie up, but then, uh, I wonder if we could get together later."

"I'd like that. Call me."

I hang up the phone with a somewhat lighter heart and head for the freeway and Haviland to jump through the hoops at DMV. Traffic makes the nineteen miles of rain-slick I-91 travel like ninety, especially without a smoke. More than once I go through the motions of lighting up, stopping just short of actually doing so. Trees which should be in full autumn glory have already lost their leaves; penitent prodigals, they reach for the sky with naked limbs. Drivetime radio is buckshot with commercials. The cell phone companies offer to sell me time, as if time could be sold in slices, like pizza, of which I could order more if I didn't have enough. *If only I could sell my past, buy my future.*

At DMV, a big wall clock authoritatively segments time into minutes past, minutes yet to come. The minute hand never lingers long enough for me to acknowledge the present moment. When a flashback descends, the past is more real than the present and the future doesn't exist.

Duplicate driver's license finally in hand, I leave DMV and return home, my shoulders heavy with the task that faces me next. Carlotta Trephino expects me to bring her a fifteen-hundred-dollar packet of heroin, a packet I no longer have. Though I've thought about it throughout the interminable wait at DMV, I can see no other course of action.

It takes hours to disconnect the stereo, gather up mountain bike, skis, camera, binoculars, camping equipment, fishing tackle, hunting rifle. The work is hard and painful; torn muscles and nerves not completely healed protest the bending and stretching. On an upper shelf in the closet, the Beretta lies wrapped in its holster. I take that down, too, and load it with the other gear into Old Paint. I work up quite a sweat doing it, but it doesn't matter. Where I'm going, they're not likely to care about my disheveled appearance. The air is cold on my now damp shirt, though, so I return to the closet one more time to unearth an old leather bomber jacket.

*****

The squinty-eyed proprietor of the Miracle Mile pawnshop removes his thick-lensed glasses and peers through my binoculars, fiddles with the focus. "Nice stuff. What did you do, knock over a sporting goods store?"

"It's my stuff."

"That's what they all say." He writes a figure on a scrap of paper, examines the camera.

"It is. What are you telling me, that you'd accept stolen merchandise?"

He replies, "Didn't you just tell me this is your stuff?"

"Yes—"

"See?"

Beaten, I ask, "So, what's it all worth?"

A lot less than what I originally paid and a lot less than what the gear is worth to me, but it nets me the fifteen hundred I need. Though my pockets are full of cash, I leave the shop feeling denuded. One robe, one bowl, is all a Zen monk needs, but that's little consolation.

No sooner am I out the door than a hooker sidles up to me with a suggestion as to how I might spend some of the newly acquired capital. I send her away only to be approached by a pusher. He's harder to turn down but I do.

On a Friday afternoon, business is brisk at 'Lotta Cars for Less and the sales staff is out in force. I barely set foot on the lot before the burly salesman-slash-bodyguard approaches. I tell him I'm here to do business with Carlotta and have to be insistent about it before he disengages his teeth from my ankle and escorts me to the trailer.

"Ah, Will, come in, honey, come in," Carlotta says and dismisses the salesman. "You took your time about getting back to me."

"I've been busy."

She eyes the wound on my head. "I'll say. Bet that hurts. Can I offer you a little ... anaesthetic?"

I accept, telling myself I earned it, I deserve it for having turned the pusher away. She takes two panatellas from a pack, holds out her hand and says, "Well? Where's the dope?"

"I didn't get it, Carlotta, and I won't. You can have your money back."

She paces in front of her desk. "I'm disappointed in you, honey. We could have had quite an enjoyable little partnership." She lets out a heavy sigh. "First Hector disappears, now you quit on me. Hmph. It is so hard to find good help these days."

I hand her the money. "It's all there, you can count it. We're even now."

She does count it, down to the last bill. "It's here all right. But even? Not hardly. There's still the matter of the two hundred you owe me."

"Well you'll just have to wait for that. I'm not running any of your little errands."

She steps up to me and grabs a handful of my shirt. "Honey, life's too short and I don't wait for what I want. You will settle up with me now." She puffs on her cigar, once, twice. "Take off your clothes."

"Huh?"

"Your clothes. Take them off."

"Forget it!"

"I think it's you who has forgotten." She rifles around in her desk, comes up with the plastic zipper-lock bag containing a cigar stub and a shot glass, and dangles it in my face. "Ah, it's all coming back now, I see." She shoves the bag back in her desk. "Take 'em off. Or do I need a member of my sales staff in here to help you?"

"You can't be serious," I say, but my protest withers under her unflinching stare.

I start in on belt and buttons.

"Take it slow, honey, I'm enjoying myself," Carlotta says.

I'm not. This is weird, this is embarrassing. I find myself thinking about Nikki St. Clair. *How does she do this every night?* It's a performance, I remind myself, and detach myself, let the actor put on the show. I focus on Carlotta the way Nikki focused on me.

With her forearm, Carlotta sweeps clean the top of her desk and pats it. "Make yourself comfortable." I lie back. The wood is warm and smooth against my bare butt. Carlotta strips off her clothes and straddles my hips. "Make this good and I just might give you your marker."

Nothing like a little pressure to cause my enthusiasm to flag. I close my eyes and think of … think of … I imagine being with Nikki Saint Clair. That gets the party started but this isn't about me, this is about Carlotta. I take my cues from every shift in her position, pay attention to every little moan. Her skin slickens, her muscles tense, her breath quickens; I work to provoke another sigh, another gasp, a cry.

When it's over, Carlotta says, "Now that was just about worth two bills."

I decline her offer of a postcoital smoke and I ask if I might instead have the little plastic bag of evidence. Before, I was worried about looking guilty of having gone too far undercover. Now that I've resigned, I'm afraid I just look guilty.

She refuses. Putting her clothes back on she says, "I do believe I like having you in my thrall. I've got plans for you."

"Carlotta, I won't be your mule."

Using a framed certificate as a mirror, she pats her hair into place. "I'm not asking you to. That was a mistake on my part, giving you that assignment. Clearly not work you're cut out for. But here's something that is: find Hector for me."

I could refuse, could easily overpower her and take the evidence from her by force but I don't. Her muscle would never let me off the lot.

*****

At this hour on a Friday there's a good chance Grady and Swbyra will be in the office, trying to tie up enough loose ends to have a weekend. Before I can hit the security keypad, the dispatcher buzzes me in with a jovial greeting I cursorily return.

Swbyra claps me on the back. "Will, Will, good to see you, buddy. Say, about that loan—"

"What loan?" Grady asks with a scowl.

"I borrowed a little from Swbyra."

"A little? Man, I could really use that money back."

"What, are you in some kind of trouble?" Grady asks me. "You look a little strung out."

"I'm not strung out!"

"That Zen shit ain't doin' you much good, is it?" he says.

"I haven't been doing it that long, dammit." Or at all, lately. When was the last time I sat? Not since I took up smoking Nearvana cigars with Carlotta Trephino. The memory makes me wince. "I'm not strung out. You're right, though. I am in a little trouble. Someone's shooting at me."

That gets their attention. Swbyra looks dismayed. "Who?"

"When did this happen?" Grady asks.

"Last night, on the Miracle Mile—"

Grady frowns. "Nice fuckin' neighborhood."

"The Mile? What were you doing there?" Swbyra asks.

Looking for Hector.

Fondling strippers.

Dropping the dime on Ace and Spade.

Buying dope. Getting high.

My mouth suddenly goes dry. I can't dump the whole miserable mess in their lap, can't even ask them for help, can't tell them a thing about what I've been up to.

Grady takes out his notepad and clicks on his pen. "Give me the details."

"Why?"

He cocks an eyebrow at me. "You want us to look into it, don't you?"

"Who's shooting at you?" Swbyra asks. "Is it about Hector? Shrike? Did you find out something about Shrike?"

"No, man, it's nothing. I'm telling you, I can handle it. It's nothing." I chuckle, and pray they don't hear the ragged edge of nervousness in it. "It was the Miracle Mile."

"You should stay away from there," Swbyra says.

"I was just ..."

With raised eyebrows they wait for me to explain.

"Looking for this Hector."

"Did you find him?" Swbyra asks. "Did you find Shrike?"

His face close to mine, Grady demands, "Did you?"

"I, uh, no." *God, if only I could tell him.* "Hell, I don't want anything to do with him. I'm not even looking for Hector anymore."

"Good," Swbyra says, "You stay away from him. Leave that to us. About my money—"

"Look, I will pay you back, but I don't have it now. Guys, I got to go."

"Mansion—" Swbyra gives me a pleading look

"You workin' today?" Grady asks him.

"Sure, sure." Lips pressed together, brow furrowed, Swbyra gives me one last look. "Take it easy, huh, Will?" he says, and slouches back to his desk.

A Zen riddle poses this puzzle: A man hangs by his teeth from a tree over a cliff. His hands can grasp no branch, his feet can rest on no limb. From below, someone shouts a life-or-death question. If the man in the tree doesn't answer, he fails; if he does answer, he falls and dies. What should he do?

Hell, I don't know. As for me, between Carlotta and Shrike, it seems I have to keep looking for Hector. The only way to stay alive is to find him.

CHAPTER 15

Ready to retire,
candle flame long extinguished.
The smoke still rises—S_zan

In that spirit, I look sharp about me as I walk the Miracle Mile, jump at anything metallic that glints in the corner of my eyes but no Eternitis with gun ports dog my heels.

Day ends sooner on the Miracle Mile than it does in the rest of the city. The feverish sunset glow isn't natural, it's neon. Business is brisk at the Metro where the dancers have been at it since eleven this morning. The bouncer who knows me as a "special friend" of Nikki's isn't on duty, some other Bluto is, and he is hell bent on keeping me out of the dressing room. I can't badge him and I can't bribe him, I don't have enough money. I could try to bully him but given that he looks like a contestant in a monster truck rally, that's likely to end up hurting me more than him. The path of least resistance turns out to be the cigarette girl. I flag her over.

"Oh I remember you," she says. "You're the shy guy." She arches her back and throws back her shoulders, which pushes her tray out farther. I shake my head.

"What's your problem? Something wrong with the merchandise?"

"I need information more than uh, cigarettes. Is Nikki around?"

"Tonight's her night off."

"Where can I find her?"

"Don't know. Sorry. Sure you don't want something after all?"

"Nah. That's OK."

She gives me an indifferent shrug and sashays off.

Here I am, looking for Nikki again. *Where to begin?* Maybe Lix Gemini knows. He said he was on his way to see her when he found me unconscious in the alley behind the Metro.

Although the handmade "Tattoo" sign is missing from the parlor's door, a thin line of light outlines the drawn window shade. The knob turns but the flimsy door won't budge. Locked with a deadbolt, maybe. I knock.

From inside, a feeble voice calls, "What?"

"It's Will Mansion, Lix."

There's a brief interval of silence, then a rattling at the door. "Hi."

Lix wears a jaundiced white poet's shirt with balloon sleeves and a drawstring neck. Instead of tight leather pants he wears looser brown wool ones, shiny with wear, the legs tucked into jodhpur boots and bloused over the top. A waist-length black leather vest and gold hoops in his piercings give him a gypsy look. He has a dreamy expression and pinpoint pupils, either of which could be from the glare of the task lamp, or drugs.

"Did I wake you?"

"No, I was just relaxing," he answers. He shuffles over to the half-reclined barber chair, climbs on, and stretches out. "An artist got to take a break once in a while. Recharge."

"Sure. Say, you haven't seen Nikki today, have you?"

"You still looking for Nikki? What do you want with her, anyway? Oh, yeah, I remember. That guy you're looking for. I thought you gave that up."

"Changed my mind." I take out a Verve and offer him one. He declines. Not his brand, he says. On second thought, I pass too, and replace the cigarette in the pack.

Lix straightens up, takes a sketchpad and red pencil from the rolling supply cart, and begins to draw. "How come?"

"Just seems to be in my best interest." I saunter around the room looking at the sample tattoos.

"And you think Nikki can help?"

"Maybe. That's what I want to ask her. So, do you know where she is?"

Lix's sketchpad hides his face, but not the rancor in his voice. "Why should I tell you? You went and told everyone I gave her up."

"No, I did not ... Yes. Yes, I did."

"See? Now everyone thinks, 'Lix Gemini, you can't trust him, he's a snitch.'" He raises his eyes over the top of his pad and fixes me with an accusatory glare. "Now how am I supposed to go on living here?"

"I needed to find Hector—"

"Yeah, that's it, isn't it? It's about what you want. Always about what you want, screw anyone else." Lix trades his red pencil for a yellow one and returns to his sketch. "Story of my life. No one ever does, I don't know why."

Yet he helped me last night in the alley. "I'm sorry. I'll make it right."

"Yeah? How?"

"Well, I don't know, I—"

"Unzip your pants."

A five-car pile-up of words forms against the brick wall in my throat. In the silence I can hear Lix's pencil skritch on the rough sketch paper. He looks up over the top of the pad, his expression innocent and serious.

"Go on," he says

I am frozen in place.

"You don't have to take them off if you don't want, just unzip and tuck in the flaps." He slides down off the chair and mimes what he wants me to do. "I just need to get at your navel, actually the real estate below it." He twirls his pencil.

"A ta ... a tattoo?"

"Yeah, a tattoo, what did you think?" He blinks his dark, long-lashed eyes once. "Oh, that?" His lips look very moist. "Is that what you want?" he asks.

"Me?" My voice is a squeak. "I thought this was about what you want."

"What *I* want ..." His eyes get that wistful look again. He picks up his sketchpad and turns it around to show me his drawing. "It's a lotus blossom."

Maybe. But a fierce one. The petals are tongues of flame, their rose color hot with orange undertones. Its yellow heart is a glowing ember. "A lotus?"

"Uh huh. I know what you're thinking: 'a flower, that's a hell of a tatt' for a tough guy like me.' But see, the lotus, it starts off in the muck at the bottom of the pond but then it grows up through the water and finally breaks the surface. A good symbol for you, Will, the way you can't quit nosing around. And if I put it here, below the belt," he pats his own belly, "no one will see it unless you show it to them. It'll be your secret. Our secret."

A tattoo. The man wants to tattoo a lotus on my belly. The lotus, symbol of the pure perfection of the awakened mind, blooming only after it has risen above the murk of ignorance and beguiling desire. *Outrageous.* But temptation tingles my spine and my skin is warm as if Lix's campfire of a lotus already burns there.

"That's what you want to do?" I ask.

"Yeah."

"You like it, huh?"

"Tattooing? Yeah." He lowers his glance, and his voice. "I like getting close to people. Don't get much of a chance to, otherwise."

No, I don't suppose he does. Prettier than many girls, he probably appeals more to men. Maybe that simply isn't his style.

He looks up through his lashes.

It would make him happy, and I'd rather have him as an ally than an enemy on this street. At least, that's what I tell myself. "All right. Where do you want me?"

"You will?" He smiles like a delighted child.

"Hey, you're the best, right? If I'm gonna get a tattoo, I might as well get it from the best."

"I'm the best, man." He pats the barber chair. "Lie down. Stretch out."

With nervous fingers I unzip my pants, skim them down a little, and tuck the ends under as he instructed, then hop up on the chair and lie back. The stiff leather creaks and a torn spot scratches my neck. Shades of being at the dentist's quicken my pulse.

Lix hits a button on his boom box and rock music blares. It's one of those guitarists whose fingers characteristically squeak on the strings, irritating as fingernails on a chalkboard.

Lix picks up a pencil. He leans over me and I pick up the smell of incense permeating his hair.

He presses the pencil point on my skin. "First, I sketch the design."

The pencil tugs and sticks, a stomach-tightening foretaste of the needle.

"Then I get my colors ready." He picks several bottles—the yellow, orange, and pink of a western sunset—and puts them on the swing-out tray. Next, he selects a needle, loads it up with color, and moves toward me.

"Didn't you forget something?" I nod toward the cardboard dispenser pack of latex gloves on the tray.

"No," he replies. "You don't need protection from me, Will. Do I need any from you?"

"I guess not, no." My heart drums double-time against my sternum. "This will hurt, huh?"

"Depends on how much you can take. I'll warn you, though. This ain't no simple design. I'm using lots of colors."

He fans the fingers of his left hand around my navel, positions the needle and begins. Though I consider myself to have a decent pain threshold, this is far worse than I would ever have imagined: stinging, piercing, burning, armies of fire ants with buzz saw teeth relentlessly bite their way through to my bones. The gnawing radiates to my back, my feet, my head.

"Am I hurting you, Will?" Lix asks, his voice a dreamy whisper.

I struggle to rise above the pain enough to speak. "Not much worse than getting shot."

"Yeah, I guess you would know about that. Well, hang on. We've got a ways to go to get the gradients in." He reaches for another color. "You can grunt if you want, it's OK. A lot of people do. They say it helps."

I wouldn't think of it.

"You want something to take the edge off?"

"Like what?" A shot of whiskey, or—

"Actually, I got some Nearvana."

Of course he has. That would definitely take the edge off. I hear a voice that sounds like mine, only breathier, say, "Yes."

"You chip or pop?"

Oh, God. "Chip."

He turns the needle off, sets it on the tray, and steps over to the corner nook. When he returns, he has a crimp of paper with a little powder in the crease. I know what to do with it. Shrike showed me.

When Lix takes up his needle again, I no longer find the sickly sweet chemical smell of the ink nauseating. The guitarist's squealing chord changes don't aggravate me. Lix's petals of flame lick my navel with fiery tongues, but it's OK. With my thoughts no longer obsessing on what Lix's right hand is doing, I can focus on his left, braced against my groin. Strong, sure fingers that definitely know their way around the human body gain purchase on my abdominal plate, oddly soothing in their confidence. The loops and whorls of his fingertips engrave their impressions on my skin.

CHAPTER 16

Her raincoat dripping
In the droplets on the floor,
hundreds of women—S_zan

In the morning, the new tattoo stings and itches. Some pain pills remain from my encounter with the flying pizza and I take a couple of those. Though I'm careful when I pull the tape off the bulky paper-towel bandage Lix applied, I can't avoid yanking out a few hairs, which only adds to the discomfort. The dark scabs of dried ointment, color, and blood that formed under the bandage wash away more easily than I would have thought. Underneath, pink skin puffs around a lotus outlined with a few bright dots of fresh blood.

I stand, then sit, on the bathroom floor, legs folded loosely, comfortably, not pretzeled into any formal posture, and contemplate not my navel but the flesh below it. Though the tile is cold, I feel flushed. Gradually I come to touch my skin, not with my hands but with my mind, feel it stretched over hip bones and across shoulder blades, warm, elastic, alive. A tiny pulse beats just under the skin of my belly. I discover the throbbing also in my legs and feet, chest and arms, even my jaw. Soon I am no longer skin, muscles and bones, but only this pulse, beating, beating. Finally I rise to finish dressing, my entire body astir.

Saturdays really perk at the Kaffeteria. College students sprung from classes and working folk from the cages of their offices nurse coffees and nibble bagels, in no hurry to go back outside into a cold rain. They wrangle about politics and pop stars and the plots of television commercials as though these were life and death issues. Two kids noisily surf the Net on the computer.

I weave through close-packed tables to the crowded counter.

Dunk skids to a halt in his volley. "Will! What will it be?"

"Coffee. Black. Strong." Too little sleep has left me so exhausted, I can't seem to keep from yawning.

"How about a muffin? Frosted cranberry-orange."

Sugar to go with the caffeine. It might give me a lift but I have no appetite.

He fixes a cup and hands it over the counter. "Look at you, man. Where the hell have you been?"

I catch my reflection in a brewer's stainless steel side. The gash on my head from slamming into the Dumpster has knitted badly into a jagged red line. Bags hang under eyes that won't stop tearing. Those eyes stare back as if with the knowledge of some dirty secret. A sly grin turns up the corners of my lips. "Around."

"Yeah, well, there's someone here to see you. A girl. A real babe. Rich, too, I think—she's wearing a ton of jewelry. She wanted someplace private to talk to you. I told her she could wait in my office, OK?"

Heidi! My heart, already racing, beats faster. I lift the hatch in the counter and squeeze through the opening, acutely aware of the scuff of denim against tender freshly-tattooed skin, and open the door to Dunk's closet office.

A familiar head of blonde hair turns and Heidi rises from Dunk's chair. Her dress today is another simple sheath, a rosy canvas for the gold and gemstones she wears.

"Will!"

"Heidi. How did you know where to find me?"

She tips her head to one side and grins. "Cops ... coffee."

"Yeah, but there's also the DayNite Donut Shop."

She waves away the suggestion. "I figured you for croissants rather than crullers. I've been looking all over for you. You were going to call. Where have you been, I've been worried sick?"

"Around." It's all I can do to keep my tone level and matter-of-fact when what I want is for her to kiss me again, embrace this body that still tingles from this morning's meditation.

"The Miracle Mile?"

"Mostly, yeah."

Her frown is half annoyance, half concern. "I thought you were going to stop looking for Hector."

"Changed my mind."

She looks sidelong at me. "You found him, didn't you?"

"What makes you say that?"

"The expression on your face."

"Oh, it's just a great day to be alive, don't you think?"

"A great day?" She glowers at her raincoat, draped over the back of the chair and dripping on the floor. "As for 'alive' ..." She brushes the scab on my head with a fingertip, "What happened?"

"Aw, some inconsiderate moron put a solid object right where my head wanted to go." *Touch me again.*

"Maybe you should take the hint. Maybe Hector doesn't want to be found. Maybe that's why someone shot at you—at us."

The thought had occurred to me that it could be Hector himself behind the wheel of the murderous Eterniti.

"I really think you should stop looking. I feel very strongly about that. How can I convince you?"

Heidi wraps her arms around my neck and presses against me. She says my name, longing and petition crammed into the one syllable, and kisses me deeply. *Oh, yes, to lose myself in her embrace.*

Heidi breaks the contact. "Not here."

Jerked back to reality, I reply, "Of course. Not here."

She collects herself, belts her raincoat closed, then looks up with an impish grin that says "later," and "soon." "Well, I'd better get to work."

"Things OK there? Overshort not giving you trouble?" I ask.

"Mr. Overshort? Nooo, I can handle Mr. Overshort. I think it's you who needs to be careful." With a glance for my banged-up head, she says, "You're certain you won't stop looking for Hector?"

"Retreat's not an option, now." *Not if Heidi is to be safe. Not if I want to stay alive.*

"Then would you keep me informed? So I don't worry. Please?"

"Count on it."

After she leaves, I return to the counter and my coffee and try to think of something other than Heidi.

For example: Hector. *Who wants him lost enough to kill me so I won't find him? Could it be Hector himself?* He could be defending himself against me, thinking I work for Shrike. He wouldn't be far off. Still, he was running before I started to look for him.

Who is he? How did he get from the luxury of Country Club Estates and Shays' Landing to the Mercy Mission? He had a life many would envy: an upscale house, a fine business, money. Apparently, it wasn't enough. Even his wife said so.

Give me more, more, more! It's a soft drink jingle but it could have been Hector's mantra. *Who can blame him?* Zen master Hui Hai observed that our treasure house is within, it contains all we will ever need. Yet even I who seeks enlightenment am seduced away from the hard work of looking there, assaulted all day long by ads on the radio and TV and newspaper, on billboards, on the back of grocery receipts, fluttering out of magazines, choking the phone and the mailbox, promising solace in something conveniently for sale. Brand name food, toothpaste, and underwear will make me powerful, successful, sexy, secure. If they don't, it's not because these are transitory states, it's because I chose the wrong brand. Music and movies and sports and games promise to thrill me more than mere life, distract me from pain.

When those fail there are drugs. Of late Waltann's been consuming commodities he didn't get receipts for: booze, smuggled cigars, heroin. His desperate consumption outstripped his ability to pay. *Is he on the run from Carlotta, from Shrike?*

And what about the theft at Facets? It wasn't long after it that two people died from unnatural causes. Scott Corcoran, Facets' security officer, committed suicide. Monetta, Facets' cleaning lady, died a homicide victim, shot by an alleged mugger on Forbes Road. She should have stayed wherever she fled after the theft. Instead, her return to Paradise City cost the woman her life. I've been thinking the two deaths and the theft are connected but even I'm not sure how, nor even that the guard Corcoran's suicide was suspicious, much less related. Still, something's nagging at me. Something the guard and the cleaning lady had in common, something besides working at the same place. *What? What?*

If only I could think. The synapses won't fire and my body is in turmoil: shoulders ache, stomach knots, muscles twitch with some free-floating agitation as if I were late for an important appointment. Maybe I'm nervous because I'm getting close to an answer. Maybe it's simply time for a cigarette.

I step outside to the alley to light up. In the skimpy shelter of the shallow eaves trough, rain splatters my head and leather jacket and puts out two matches before I get a cigarette lit. I suck the smoke down deep and wait for lassitude, the flood of physical ease with mental exhilaration but it doesn't come. Heart hammering, I raise the cigarette, can barely put it to my lips for the shaking of my hands.

A golden flash streaks past the mouth of the alley and I bolt for the Kaffeteria's rear door before I realize it wasn't the Eterniti but a yellow taxi. *I've got to stay out of alleys, and what's more, I've got to quit smoking. Again.* With firm resolve, I toss the pack away and go inside.

Now, where was I? Scott Corcoran and Monetta. Something their deaths have in common. *What?* Damn, I can't concentrate. Anxiety without name or cause grips me, squeezes me like a giant fist. I can't think of anything except making it go away, achieving some kind of stasis, any kind of peace. I need a cigarette.

Damn again! They're in the alley, getting soaked. Maybe, if I hurry, I can salvage them for one last and final smoke. Just one, to work out this puzzle, then I'll quit, I promise. On my knees, I fish a half-sodden butt from the gutter, break off the dry end, and get it lit. As I smoke, I catch a bum's bedraggled reflection in the rain-swollen gutter's dappled surface. A man from the Mercy Mission! Startled, I whip around but nobody is there. With pounding heart I turn back to the broken image. Eyes shadowed, cheeks drawn in. The face of an addict. My face.

The nervousness, the anorexia, they all add up and the sum total is a Nearvana fiend in need of a fix. I am hooked. The realization chills me more than the cold rain sopping my hair.

Even as I protest "how did it happen?" I know. I took that first hit of Nirvana, liked it, and despite knowing how addictive it is, still took every one I could get after that. Oh, I had reasons, I had excuses, but it was bullshit. The simple fact is, I wanted it. I want it now.

Desire, damned desire! Subtle and patient it ensnared me, one concession at a time: an innocent cup of coffee at first, a drink. As long as I could still say "no" to something I considered myself free, carried unsmoked cigarettes around to prove it, believed it even as I sucked heroin up my nose.

No!

I sit back on my heels in a posture of wretched *seiza,* rattling with the shakes. Rain sluices down my head and neck, seeps past my collar, and trickles down my back.

Desire! Cunning and crafty it seduced me, led me to the brink—

No, it did not lead me. It simply pointed the way and I, so weak of will, went there all by myself, all the way to the edge, ready, willing, eager to jump into the abyss.

Well, damn Desire! Damn what I want. Damn coffee and cigarettes and alcohol and damn Nearvana. I will fight Desire—

No, wait. I can use Desire to free myself. Because there's something else I want, even more than a moment's or an hour's or a whole night's relief from pain. Peace. I want peace. Real, lasting peace.

Yes, this desire thing can be a two-edge sword.

My laughter rings against the brick walls. Crazed, it also has an element of satisfaction and resolve.

Desire is a sword, a two-edged sword. The sword that kills the man. The sword that saves the man.

*****

Back inside, shaking badly enough to shatter, I dry my head and neck as best I can under the hot air blower in the men's room, blot my rain-soaked pant legs with paper towels. I ache but I will not yield. The pain is real, debilitating. It can't be ignored. Fighting it only feeds it. What I must do is go on in spite of it, or rather with it.

Deaf to impatient knocks on the door, I pace around the one-stall room. *Concentrate!* Focus on Scott Corcoran and Monetta. How they died. How they died.

No, not how they died. Where they died. "Some no-tell motel," Mrs. Corcoran said. "Some no-tell motel," Grady said. Out on Forbes Road.

Which motel? Grady or Swbyra could tell me where Monetta was mugged but I can't ask them. I relinquish the men's room to the scowling man dancing in the corridor and dial CleanSweep from the Kaffeteria's pay phone. A recorded message answers. *So much for Monetta, what about Corcoran? Had Mrs. Corcoran said which motel?* If I had gotten the unlisted number when I visited her I could call and ask her. Damn me! I could wait until I'm able to talk to the CleanSweep manager but I can't sit still. I might as well canvass the motels along Forbes.

A picture of Corcoran or Monetta would help. If I were at work, I'd just get one from the morgue ... the morgue! *The Crier* morgue of dead newspapers. There might have been coverage of Corcoran's death, or Monetta's. With a photo. Maybe even mention of the motel.

I sprint into the Kaffeteria, come to a skidding stop at the computer. The same two kids who were there when I first arrived are still joyriding on the information highway.

"Hey, I ... I need to use the computer," I say, panting.

One kid turns his beringed nose up at me. "But see, like, we're already using it."

I appeal to his buddy, a skinny youth who's shaved the sides of his head and gathered the long hair at the crown into a pony tail. "But it's urgent."

Pony Tail looks me up and down. "Get serious."

"This is serious. It's a matter of life and death. I only need it for a minute—"

"Get lost," says Nose Ring.

"You don't understand—"

"I said 'get lost.'" He swivels toward the dining area. "Dad!"

A man in a quilted hunting vest over a Harley sweatshirt looks up, takes in the scene, and rises from his chair.

"Yeah, let's call your Dad over here," I tell the kid. "Let him see just which beach you've been surfing on."

Nose Ring twists back to face a monitor filled with a digitized photo of a naked beauty in full color, most of it flesh. I know there's porn on the Internet. Every now and then the Department wages a campaign to stamp it out.

"Never mind, Dad!" Nose Ring calls. He turns to me. "What do you want, Mister?"

"This will just take a second."

The kid gives up his seat. I key the online address of the Paradise City *Crier*. The paper's home page comes up on the screen. A few hot links later I reach the archived articles I need.

The coverage of Monetta's shooting has no picture nor does it give a precise location. In reporting on Scott Corcoran's death, the paper declined to name the motel. However, there is a picture of him, the same formal portrait I saw in his trailer. His vigorous appearance gives "sixty years old" a good name.

"Dunk!"

"What?"

"Can I print something?"

Dunk frowns. "I don't know. The last time you printed, it was an entire course on meditation and you cleaned me out of paper—"

"Just one sheet, that's all. Please?"

"Yeah, yeah. All right."

I click on "Print." Dunk retrieves the print job from his office and hands it across the counter.

Before I turn the computer over to Nose Ring and Pony Tail, I suggest to Dunk that he get a smut filter for this computer.

*****

Before the interstate came in, Forbes was the main road tourists took through the county, giving rise to a string of gas stations, cafes, and little motels, each with its own evocative name and matching themed decor. Now they're pathetic ruins where illicit lovers tryst and junkies make buys while the ghosts of '50s family vacationers watch in dismay.

Instead of warming up, the morning has gotten colder and the rain has turned to sleet. Forbes is slick and mined with potholes. Potholes aren't the only bumps in the road. Nausea and cramps wash over me like a swollen river lapping its banks. Some waves are so overpowering that they drive me onto the shoulder, clutching the steering wheel like a life preserver. Retching, I stick my head out the door into the rain but throw up only bile. Though the attacks are violent, when they pass, they are instantly forgotten. That the pain does subside is something that's hard to remember when it strikes again.

Traveling slowly, stopping at every little motel along the way, it would be hard for anyone to tail me undetected, so I am confident no gold Eternitis hug my bumper.

The lobby of the Hunting Lodge, the first motel I come to, has brown walls, a faded wine-red carpet, badly rendered coats-of-arms on the walls, and two mangy green velvet armchairs. The front desk man shakes his head at Scott Corcoran's photo. He could be uninterested or lying. I would offer him a ten to see if that changes his disposition but I'm flat and will be until my pension check arrives. *My pension! Oh, what have I done?*

When the heavy set woman at the front desk of the Daisy Patch—decorated in watery yellow, anemic orange, dirty white—looks at the picture, I think I detect a flash of recognition and coax her along. "Sheriff's deputy? Committed suicide?"

"Yeah, I think I remember that. Wasn't here though. Maybe down the road."

"Do you know which motel?"

"No, I'm sure I don't."

"Well, how about which direction, left or right?"

She looks up at the ceiling, thinks hard. "Go right," she says at last.

"Thanks." I start for the door.

"And if that doesn't work, try going left," she calls after me.

Great. I may as well continue on this side of the road.

The Jade Pagoda is a hunk of dingy concrete whose only relationship to jade or pagoda is the oxidized green gable over the office. I park Old Paint, pocket the key, and am about to head for the front desk when something inconsistent with the color scheme catches my eye. Looped around a vacant parking slot's cement bumper is a scrap of yellow ribbon. A yellow ribbon with black lettering. Crime scene tape.

I scan the area that I imagine might have been roped off, then walk it, eyes systematically sweeping from the ground up, feet carefully placed one by one so as not to step on any evidence. Unmindful of the freezing rain and so intent on looking for clues, I nearly collide with the housekeeper pushing her cart on the sidewalk alongside the rooms.

"Lose something, *señor?*" she asks. A short weary thing, she is almost as wide as she is tall, padded in layers of snagged sweaters over pilled double-knit slacks and scarred oxfords. She leans on her cart, grateful, perhaps, for the interruption.

"A friend," I reply. "Scott Corcoran?"

She blinks her sad brown eyes. The name doesn't appear to mean anything to her.

"From the sheriff's department? Died here a few weeks back."

"Oh, *sí*. I remember that. Sad, very sad."

"So it happened here."

"Here. *Sí*."

"And there was a shooting, too. A woman."

"Oh, *sí*. That too. There." She points to the parking lot. "Very sad."

"Did you see it, ma'am?"

"No. It was at night. I work during the day, *gracias a Dios*. I would not want to work where there are dead people."

Neither do I, anymore. "Well, maybe they can tell me something about my friend in the office."

"In the office. *Sí, señor*."

"You have a good day, then, ma'am."

"*Gracias, señor.*"

She pushes off toward the next room so listlessly I wish I had a spare ten just to brighten her day. I turn in the direction of the office and am halfway there when a scream nails me to the walkway.

CHAPTER 17

Just across the street,
grass, trees, toads, the water.
And the moon—Debisu

The *breath. Pay attention to the breath.*

At my back, the Jade Pagoda's block wall feels like sponge. Spangled by snowflakes, the scene before me is a meaningless pattern of dark and light. The visual dissonance warns of an impending hallucination and I have nothing to hold it off with—no cigarette, no drink, no drug—only my resolve to stay present. Death, from which I have run so far and so fast, has found me.

Don't feed the fear, focus not on the emotion but on the physical sensations associated with it: tight chest, shallow, rapid respiration. See that they're not permanent, they wax and wane in intensity. This too shall pass, this too shall pass. Relax. If I slow my breathing, the panic will subside along with it. *The breath, pay attention to the breath.*

This breath brings with it the peaty smell of dead leaves from the woods, the tang of motor oil on wet asphalt. I name these, then remember not to get caught up in naming them, simply acknowledge there are smells and return to the breath.

The shakes and nausea are back. I want a cigarette.

That's Desire again. Note its physical sensations: anxiety, salivation, clamminess. Desire is transitory. The shakes will stop and so will the craving.

This too shall pass, this too shall pass, I intone like a mantra.

Sloppy wet snowflakes plop on my bare head and melt in my hair. The shifting black and white patterns resolve into a striped parking lot, the black ribbon of Forbes Road, and the trees in the snow-dusted field beyond it. My back is cold, even with my jacket on. I'm braced against something cold and solid. The block wall of the Jade Pagoda. Here, on Forbes Road, not Terminal Road. I am still here, not there. And I am alive.

But the poor soul in Room Eight ...

I turn my head just slightly to the right, glance at the door, leprous with flaky white paint, ajar. Through the opening I see a man face up on an unmade bed, his head hanging over the edge.

Please, God, don't let him be dead. But I know he is, I can smell it. More than simply spilled blood or guts or bodily wastes released when muscles relax their hold, it is also that final exhalation hanging in the air, humid and stale.

My next breath brings another scent, something aromatic. It's ... *Don't struggle to name it. Return to the breath.*

I number inhalations, exhalations, barely get to four before shouted thoughts throw off my count. *Run! Get away before Death turns its hot red eyes on you.*

No! Stay. Calm yourself. Beat this thing.

I cut myself a deal. The maid went to call the police, they're on their way. They'll want to talk to me, learn what I know. I will tell them. After that I will leave. I will report to Sister Clyde. Then, done with death, I will go far away. The edge of the forest. Live a long peaceful life.

Yes, the police will arrive soon. Until then I will stand and wait. And breathe.

*****

The red and blue lights on the roofs of approaching cruisers are furred in the falling snow. Tires skid to a stop on slick pavement. Uniformed men step from their cars, take charge of the scene. Secure the area, talk to the maid, to me. If they recognize me, they don't show it. A patrolman tells me, "Wait here, sir. The lieutenant will want to speak to you."

In response, I can only nod, afraid that if I open my mouth, I'll puke.

From squad cars, the calm, gentle voices of the dispatchers alternate with the crackle of attention signals. Preoccupied with their own duties, patrolmen move about with restrained urgency. They do not bother me, standing quietly out of harm's way.

A car door creaks open with the grind of metal-on-metal and heavy footfalls announce yet another arrival.

"Will Mansion." Lieutenant Crowberry's voice is as stiff and resentful as the last day we spoke. "You gonna tell me what's going on or you just gonna stand there with your eyes closed?"

Not completely closed. The point of the lowered, unfocused gaze is to stay aware but reduce distractions.

I open my eyes to a bald, dark-skinned man who knows how to plant every inch of his five-foot-eight, one-hundred-ninety five pound frame for maximum effect.

"Not much to tell, sir," I reply and brief him: the time of my arrival, how the maid found the room, what was touched and not touched. "Didn't want to contaminate the scene."

Crowberry's nod is curt but there is approval in his voice when he says, "You're a good detective, Mansion."

Was.

"Wait here," he says, and goes to confer with the uniformed men, talk to Dispatch. He steps inside the room, emerges a moment later, and tells me little I don't already know, that a man is dead, and recently.

"Of a stab wound," I suggest.

Crowberry responds with raised eyebrows. "I thought you said you didn't go in the room."

An educated guess. I didn't smell gunpowder, which surprised me. That left poisoning, strangulation, smothering, bludgeoning, and stabbing. If the victim had been poisoned, he probably would have regurgitated, but I smelled no vomit. Neither strangulation nor smothering let the quantity of blood I detected.

"Come see for yourself."

If it wasn't for wanting my theory confirmed, I would decline, be done with this and away from here. I follow Crowberry into the room and it is then I get my first close look at Hector Waltann.

The sight is so gruesome I have to turn away. I had forgotten how dead dead people are. Devoid of life they are reduced to organic compounds that decompose, puff, ooze, and stink. Lividity has left the uppermost surface of Waltann's face and arms unnaturally white, while settling blood mottles the lower surfaces, a grotesque marbling. Flies drawn by the siren scent of death crowd the moist places. Waltann's lips are grayish purple and shiny.

When I can force myself to look again, I barely recognize the robust Hector Waltann pictured in the photo Christmas card his wife Marybeth gave me. Cheekbones are sharp planes in a formerly fleshy face that had paled even before death drained the blood from it. Heroin had made him a skeleton even before he died.

Apparently I guessed right. He was stabbed, not blasted with a shotgun. Blood outlines a single slash in the front of his white crew-neck undershirt a few inches above his belt. No hacking administered in the heat of a struggle, this was one neat killing stroke. Someone who knew how best to do damage with a blade attacked unimpeded. Over the undershirt, a finely tailored but dingy, wrinkled white dress shirt is unbuttoned and untucked. Black gabardine slacks are zipped, the belt is buckled, and Waltann still has on his shoes—black leather tasseled slip-ons in need of a shine, not to mention socks. My first thought is he was dressing, or undressing. So he was surprised by his killer. Or they were intimate.

"What we got, Lieutenant?" Grady's voice booms from the doorway. "Mansion? What are you doing here?"

"It's the missing guy I was looking for," I reply.

"Not missing anymore, is he?" Grady leans over the body.

"No." To Crowberry I say, "Can I go now, sir?"

"First tell me everything." Crowberry nods toward the door. I follow him outside to the sidewalk and tell him about Sister Clyde, about Marybeth Waltann, about Marvin Overshort and Facets but stop short of mentioning Carlotta Trephino or her cigar club or the gunshots from the Eterniti. Or Shrike. Or Nirvana. *Not quite everything.*

"Hmph. I don't know. Guy looks like a junkie to me," Crowberry says. "Man could have got himself killed over drugs. You don't know anything about that?"

It's a good possibility. Hector had an enemy in both Shrike and Carlotta. However, I can't clue Crowberry in without incriminating myself. "I've told you everything I can, sir." *Where have I heard that before?*

The lieutenant looks over his shoulder into the room. "Man, you are way ahead of us on this."

"Will that be all, sir?"

"After all this time you've spent looking for this guy, don't you want to get who did him?"

A week ago, when I was fairly certain Hector brought his misfortune, whatever it was, on himself, I may not have cared. Now I'm not so quick to blame him. But let Grady and Swbyra find his killer. They have the resources and the support system. *How could I even consider going back to work when anywhere, anytime, a flashback can whisk me off to Oz?* "No. Lieutenant, may I go now?" Sickness is about to double me over.

"What you can do is get busy finding the doer."

I shake my head. "I resigned."

Crowberry sucks in his cheeks, thinks for a moment. "Seems to me I know something about that. Yes, yes, I got a form on my desk about that right now. Needs my signature. Haven't signed it yet." He looks me in the eye with both barrels. "You want that form signed?"

"Yes I want it signed."

"Fine. Your doc and your shrink cleared you to return to duty. So make this case. Then I'll sign it."

"Lieutenant, you don't need me on this."

"I think we do. 'Cause I don't think we're going to solve it 'less we know everything. Including what you're holding back. Or are you prepared to tell me about that now?"

CHAPTER 18

Dark, silent morning
Geese bark, wind sighs, furnace hums
Wheels thump on the bridge—Soezi

"**I'm** not—"

Crowberry's steady gaze vaporizes any prevarication. "Come on, Mansion, you're wasting time. Got a bunch of flat-footed uniforms in there trampling your crime scene. Better get to it before there's nothing left."

Crowberry waves me into the room. I drag wooden feet over the threshold and he announces, "Mansion's back."

Grady glowers. Swbyra looks anxious, expectant. Probably wondering how to ask me about the four hundred bucks I owe him.

"Lieutenant thinks it was a drug deal gone sour," I say.

Swbyra nods. "You knew the man. Was he using?"

"I have reason to believe he was."

"And what reason is that?" Grady asks.

"Uh, heard it on the street."

That seems to satisfy.

With the intent of looking for needle tracks, Grady and I both extend gloved hands toward Waltann's right arm, withdraw and reach again. Burlesque like that got us all tagged the Three Stooges only this time Grady growls at me. He takes the right arm, I take the left, and we roll up Waltann's sleeves. No tracks. That doesn't tell me much. Waltann could have shot up between the toes, in the thigh, ingested or, as I know all too well, inhaled. The autopsy may tell.

"So this is Hector Waltann," Swbyra says. He points to the monogram on the shirt cuff: HW.

Together Grady and I go through Hector's pockets. An empty eel skin wallet. Small change. Cigarettes and matches. A much-used hanky, a half roll of breath mints, a tube of lip balm. There should be something more but I can't put my finger on what's missing.

The single drawer to the pressed wood night stand holds a Bible and an unopened three-pack of condoms. Did Hector come to this anonymous address for sex? It doesn't smell like sex, just something herbal, cigarettes, sweat, and foul death.

Consumed with anger, resentment, apprehension, and sick to boot, I can barely see. Determined to quell the mental yammering, step by metered step I circle the room. Paying attention quiets the mind, dispels distracting thoughts, helps calm the shaking that rattles my bones.

Drapes of jade green synthetic fabric cover room-darkening yellowed liners. A black plaster ginger jar lamp lies on its side on the thin red carpet, its red paper shade dented, the bulb still valiantly glowing. The double bed with rumpled bedclothes the color of dirty snow is bolted to the wall, the headboard simply a pressed wood panel glued above the mattress. More pressed wood makes up the bureau which is empty.

A plastic ice bucket holds a few inches of clear, odorless liquid. *Water? Melted ice? How long for ice to melt at room temperature?* Hours. So, if it was ice, it was obtained not this morning, but earlier. Last night? For a solitary drink or did Waltann have a guest, his last guest? Though there are no empty bottles, no drinking glasses anywhere, the protective shrink wrap from two of them lies crumpled in the bottom of the wastebasket. I make a mental note to retrieve it, to look in the Dumpster for the tumblers they protected, check for prints.

At command volume Crowberry says, "Grady, you're the primary." He claps his hands once. "Ok, men, ready to roll?"

Swbyra nods vigorously. "Yessir."

"Grady?"

The big man scowls.

"Problem, Grady?"

"Nossir."

"Fine. Report at fourteen hundred." Crowberry turns on his heel and exits the room.

"You do have a problem, don't you, Grady?" Swbyra asks.

"About time he got his ass back here," Grady says, sliding his eyes at me.

"Why are you so hard on him? Cut him some slack, the man had a near death experience."

There wasn't anything near *about it. For a moment I was dead.*

"Life is a near death experience, dammit. Mansion doesn't have the fucking market cornered on mortality. Hell, I'm the short timer. Ah ..." He waves his hand in disgust and stomps outside. I tell Swbyra about the discarded wrappers and tumblers and hustle after the big guy.

Grady stands in the parking lot, smoking a cigarette, his head turned toward an approaching vehicle, the medical examiner's station wagon.

"Where do you want me to start?" I ask Grady, more out of respect for him as primary than a real need for direction. He knows it, but acknowledges the gesture with a slight relaxing of his shoulders.

"Swbyra'll process the scene. You canvass the other people here, see what you can find out about the past twenty-four." He tilts his head toward a small group huddled halfway between Room Eight and the office. To the side of the rubberneckers, two working girls stand whispering under a cigarette-smoke umbrella. One of them lifts her head and catches my eye. Her hard features soften, she looks up through bristly lashes, and smiles shyly. She nudges her friend and she too gives me a smile.

"Mansion, you are a goddam pussy magnet, you know that?" Grady says.

I think of Carlotta Trephino and sigh. This is not the blessing he thinks it is. I acknowledge the girls with a nod and a small smile. They giggle behind their hands.

Grady snorts. "Wait a sec', I'll get an approximate time of death from the M. E." He returns a moment later to report, "Time o' death, middle of the night, early morning."

Nothing that lividity and an inch of water in an ice bucket haven't already suggested.

"He says stab wound's probably the cause since he didn't find any tracks."

Nevertheless, I tell him, let's wait for the drug screen.

One of the rubberneckers strains at the barrier. "Hey, officers, I got to hit the road. You want to talk to me or can I go?"

Grady goes to rejoin the M. E. and I take the impatient man, a trucker who had the room next to Waltann's.

"My sleeper time is up and I got to get back behind the wheel," he says. "I don't get paid for miles I don't run and I need every dime."

"Just a few questions, sir. Look, a man's been killed here."

"Well, I didn't do it if that's what you're thinking."

He could have. He's got the strength in his shoulders and arms to overpower the victim, drive a blade. If I didn't already have a handful of suspects in Waltann's intimates, I'd pay closer attention to his statement. I should anyway. Otherwise I could focus on any one of my likely suspects only to find out too late that Waltann was killed by someone who thought he had the TV up too loud. Knowing is good. Not knowing is better. The open mind is receptive to all possibilities, including the truth.

"I didn't even know who was in that room." The trucker glowers. "When I got into town, I dropped my load and came over about midnight for a shower and some shut-eye. I got a sleeper in the cab, but once every trip I treat myself to a real bed. This was it and I meant to enjoy it. Slept like a rock."

"Could you say whether your neighbor was in his room when you pulled in, sir?"

The trucker scratches his wire-haired head under a Castrol GTX ball cap. "Curtains were drawn. That's all I can say."

Not much help. "How about a car in Room Eight's space? A gold Eterniti?"

He puffs on a cigarette he smokes so nonchalantly. "Not that I recall. Can I go now?"

The best I can do is verify his name, home address and phone number, license, and employer. Given his occupation, they'll have fingerprints plus criminal record and drug use if any on file. If I need more from him later, I should be able to catch up with him through his dispatcher.

The flannel-shirted young man who took the room on the opposite side is an unemployed construction worker. He's been here a week, was out job hunting yesterday.

"And I should be pounding the pavement now. Don't want someone else to get the jump on me," he says.

"Just another minute if you don't mind, sir. The guy next door to you's been killed."

"Yeah, pretty exciting." His eyes are feverish the way people's sometimes get when they ogle a road wreck.

"When did you return to the motel, sir?" I ask.

He answers he returned to his room about six yesterday evening with a six-pack and a bucket of chicken. "Don't remember no car, no." He thinks Waltann's curtains were open.

Like the truck driver, the construction worker claims he spent the night in his room alone. "Got no spare cash for a movie or nothing. I already paid for the room, I figure I'll watch TV and like it."

He fell asleep about eleven, doesn't remember any noise from his next-door neighbor, "but then, it wasn't like I was paying attention. Look, man, I got to hit the bricks."

As with the trucker, I can't stop him. But I get his pedigree and make sure I can find him again if I need to.

The two pros, Rhonda and Champagne, are eager to talk. From them I learn the trucker and the hammer jockey lied. Neither of them spent the night alone.

"Rhonda here only just pre-tripped that trucker before all the commotion started," Champagne explains. Her eyes, though black-walled with makeup, are a pretty pale blue.

Last night, she says, she was with the construction worker from about eleven to one. Afterward, she walked to the Firefly Lounge next door and caught the crowd—"that's using the term loosely, you understand"—just as the place was closing, which was a profitable move for her.

"You don't need the details, do you, Doll?" she asks with an eagerness that says she would share them with relish.

"No, ma'am. Not unless it has something to do with the man's death."

"Well, not exactly. Except that it put me back here maybe around one-thirty or two. And you know, I think I saw someone go into his room."

"Someone. A man? A woman?"

"Yeah, woman," Rhonda chimes in, punctuating the statement with a sway of slim hips encased in a stretchy black skirt no bigger than a loincloth.

"You saw her, too, ma'am?"

"No, Champagne told me," Rhonda says.

"Then maybe we better let her tell it, OK?"

Rhonda pouts in disappointment.

"About the woman, ma'am," I urge Champagne.

"Tall, skinny."

"How tall?"

Champagne shrugs. "Let's see. You're what? Six feet?" She leans in close, her breasts graze my chest. She smells of cigarettes and hair spray. "Five eight, maybe five nine. Long legs."

"What color?"

She has to think. "Black. But you know, I think now she must have had tights or stockings on, because her hands were white."

"Those could have been gloves."

"Mmm, I don't think so."

"What about her face, hair, eyes?"

She shakes her head. "Sorry. Didn't see them. She wore a cape. With a hood. She held the hood closed around her face, that's how I remember the hands were white."

A cape. With a hood. How Hollywood. *A specialist in kinky sex?* With three condoms in the night stand, Waltann was ready for something. "So who is she?"

Again, Champagne shakes her head. "Didn't recognize her."

"Come on, I know you girls are all tight. I don't want to bust her for the date, I just want to ask her some questions."

"Oh, I believe you, Doll. It's just I don't know."

Rhonda suggests, "Maybe she's new in town."

"Maybe."

A long-legged mystery woman in a hooded cape. "You see her again, or you think of anything else, you get a hold of me."

"Can we get a hold of you even if we don't?" Rhonda asks, batting those clotted lashes. Little flakes of black stuff fleck her cheekbones.

"Show you a real good time, Doll," Champagne adds.

"Champagne, do I understand you to be soliciting a police officer?"

She reels back, plants a hand on her hip. "Certainly not. It would be on the house. A professional courtesy, like." She leans forward again. "It would be my pleasure."

"Our pleasure." Rhonda smiles. "We could double."

Champagne drops her voice to a conspiratorial whisper. "You ever have two women at the same time?"

With every brain cell dedicated to imagining that, I can only shake my head and point my feet toward the front office.

"We don't ask people their life story," the front desk man says. "'Specially if they're paying cash. Man wanted a room for the night, we gave him one." He slides the guest register across a countertop so worn the shiny black paint has bare spots.

The penciled entries on the register's dog-eared and yellow pages are smudged. There don't appear to be enough of them to substantiate the business that this place does and they're incomplete. Like Waltann's illegible scrawl they lack home address and vehicle information. It appears the desk is somewhat lax in the record-keeping department.

"The guy in Room Eight. Ever see him before?" I ask.

"Can't say that I have."

"Did he get any visitors? Phone calls?"

"Not while I was on duty. Might want to check with the night man."

"I'll do that. How about a car, sir? Did he have a car?" Because he didn't have any keys. That's what was missing from Hector's pockets: keys. I tap the guest register. "There isn't anything in this column for vehicle information."

"Guess he didn't have a car."

Then how did he get here? Hitchhike? City transit doesn't serve Forbes. Maybe there's a cabbie who could fill in the blanks of Hector's last night. Or did he ride with his killer? And where is the Eterniti? "You're sure? There's no vehicle listed for anyone."

The front desk man touches his upper lip with the tip of his tongue and nods slowly. "Oh. Yeah. Well, uh, sorry."

"So? Did he have a car or not?"

He shrugs again. "Try the night man. He might remember."

"All right. How about the man who died here a few weeks back?"

"Which one? People die here all the time."

Put that in the hotel/motel guide. "Scott Corcoran. The sheriff's deputy?"

"Oh, yeah. What about him?"

"Everything. What room was he in? When did he arrive? Did he stay the whole time or did he go out? Did he have visitors?"

The desk man doesn't appear to be listening. "Hell, I don't know. You'll have to ask the night man."

The night man is taking on oracular proportions. "Thank you, sir. Thank you very much."

I blow out my exasperation in a puff and exit the front office. Grady waves me over.

"Why don't you play Western Union?" he says. "You've met the Mrs. Maybe she'll take it better from you."

Based on my last conversation with Marybeth Waltann, in which she wished her husband dead, this could be the easiest death notification any of us has had to do.

CHAPTER 19

Zafu stuffing shifts
Buckwheat husks rustle
The sound of satin—S_zan

It's not until I turn into Country Club Estates that I realize it
worked: meditating kept me from totally zoning out in front of the
Jade Pagoda. I'm drained, I'm sick, but I'm present.

Marybeth Waltann answers my knock with a drink in her hand. She
wears a pullover top and matching slacks with metallic trims and satin
appliqués, and lots of shiny jewelry. Rather than brightening up her
appearance the gaudy outfit only heightens her dowdiness. I picture
her in a hooded cape but it doesn't work; instead of a leggy mystery
woman I get the image of a hunchbacked and kerchiefed matron.

"Oh, it's you again," she says. "I told you not to come back unless
Hector's dead."

"I'm sorry, Ma'am. That's why I'm here."

Her jaw drops and the arrogance completely drains from her
expression. The hand holding the glass drops to her side, spilling her
drink on my shoe.

"Are you all right, Ma'am?"

"All right?" she echoes faintly. "I don't know."

She drifts back into the house, leaving the door open, which I take as an invitation to follow. She stops in the middle of the living room, turns, and asks me, "How?"

"It's apparently a homicide, Ma'am."

"No." Marybeth shakes her head.

"No? You have another explanation?"

The question doesn't seem to register. Either she's in shock or pretending to be while she contrives her pretense. "Ma'am?"

"When you said he was dead, I thought, a car accident. Drunk driving, something like that. But murdered? How? By who? When?"

"Sometime last night. By who? That's what I'm going to find out."

"Why you? Oh, that's right, you're working for some friend of his." She still seasons "friend" with bitterness.

"Actually, it's in an official capacity now," I say.

"You're a policeman?"

"Detective. Paradise City Police Department."

She gives me a critical look and well she should. I must look a mess, the slacks that got drenched this morning wrinkled and stained, leather jacket water-spotted and reeking of wet cow, shoes dried hard and cracked, and I have neither badge nor ID.

"It's complicated," I tell her.

She shrugs, uninterested. "How did ... it happen?"

"It appears he was stabbed."

"Stabbed. Stabbed?" She shakes her head again, then shudders. "Hector, Hector. What did you get into?" she murmurs. She stands lost in thought for a moment, then says, "Maybe I should call my son, Terry."

"Of course."

"And a lawyer?"

"If you think that's necessary," I reply, barely able to contain my surprise and disappointment.

With a wave of her hand she invites me to sit on the couch and leaves the room. On her return she passes the wet bar and looks at her glass as if noticing for the first time that it's empty. She fills it, then raises the decanter to me in invitation. I shake my head.

When she has settled in the brocade wingback chair, I ask, "Mrs. Waltann, if you had to name someone who could have killed your husband, who would it be?"

"Me."

Is she confessing? Although that would make this the easiest homicide I ever worked, I feel something of a letdown. I want it to be Overshort. My face must reveal my surprise because she gives me a wry smile. "Ma'am, I should advise you—"

"It had to be said. You'd consider me anyway, wouldn't you? The angry abandoned wife who wished him dead? I told you not to come back unless he was dead. Those were harsh words. I didn't mean it literally. You believe me, don't you?"

That remains to be seen. "You won't mind my asking, then. Where were you last night, Ma'am?"

"Here. Alone." Again she gives me that wry smile. "I'm in trouble, aren't I?"

If she truly believed that, she probably would call that lawyer.

"When did you last see Hector, Ma'am?"

"Not since he moved out. I told you that the last time you asked." She pauses to drink. "Why? Why would someone want to kill Hector?" Tears slide down her cheeks.

"I don't know yet, Ma'am," I reply, although I can guess. "Did he have any enemies?" I ask, as if I couldn't already name several. "The son you mentioned. They used to work together at Facets. Did they part on friendly terms?"

"Terry was furious about leaving Facets, but it wasn't Hector he was angry with. It was Marvin who forced Terry out. And just to add insult to injury, Marvin made Hector take out buy-sell insurance."

"And that is—?"

Marybeth sips her drink. "It's insurance that pays if a partner dies or becomes incapacitated or wants to withdraw and the surviving partner wants to continue the business."

Death or withdrawal of partner. The language used in the menacing memos I found in Hector's bedroom.

"The insurance pays the beneficiary, the surviving partner, enough so he can buy the departing partner's share, have total ownership."

Those memos dated back weeks ago. *Was Overshort making a bid for the business even then, based on Hector's absence? Did Overshort foster Hector's disappearance? Has he been trying to keep me from finding the man so he could put in a claim based on withdrawal? Was Hector's scarcity not strong enough justification for the insurance, so Overshort escalated withdrawal to death?*

Murder isn't an unheard-of career advancement strategy and people have killed for much less than what Facets is likely to be generating.

"You know about this insurance for a fact?" I ask her.

She nods. With narrowed eyes she says, "Marvin rubbed Terry's nose in it when he fired him. Hector had to take out the policy as a condition of Marvin's buying into the business. Marvin said if Hector ended up dead, Terry and I would inherit his share of Facets, and Marvin didn't want to be in partnership with either of us, especially Terry."

Under the circumstances, it's a wonder it's Hector who's dead and not Overshort. "I see." I see that Overshort and Marybeth Waltann both benefit from Hector's death. Overshort gets the business at the insurance company's expense, Marybeth gets cash from Overshort. *How much cash? Did Waltann keep up with the premiums or did he let this policy lapse like the others?* "I'll take that under advisement. Meanwhile, Ma'am, you wouldn't have happened to have the Eterniti, would you?" I ask.

Marybeth almost turns up her nose, spite effectively obliterating her grief. "I would sooner walk than get in that car."

Well, where is the car?

I ask a few more questions, get the name of the insurance agent, and leave Marybeth Waltann to sog down her grief.

Before I take this investigation any further, I stop at home to complete the metamorphosis of Will Mansion, ex-cop, into Will Mansion, working detective. In the shower, the lotus tattoo startles me, as though I expected it would have vanished in the transformation. Before the dresser mirror, I knot my tie with sweaty hands. Haunted eyes in a drawn face stare back at me. The only thing missing from this scene is the reluctant hero strapping on his gun belt and loading his revolver. I have neither. All I have is a pawn ticket.

*****

Late on a Saturday, there are few people around the station, so I don't have to explain my official return to my old haunts. Even the Admin. Assistant is absent from her desk. An open door to Crowberry's office says that he is in, and available.

At my approach, he waves me in. Two items lie side by side along the forward edge of his desk. One is the resignation form I filled out in another life. The other is a check, an advance on my pay. He stretches his arms out and pats both. "Thought it only fair to give you another chance, if you're serious about this retirement thing."

He might just as well offer me the Lady or the Tiger. Either way I'll get eaten alive. I take the check.

I brief him on my conversation with Marybeth Waltann.

Crowberry says, "So, the wife and the partner both stand to gain. The question is, would the payoff be worth killing for?"

"I'll see what I can find out from the insurance agent. Assuming that it is—"

"Either of them could have done it."

"Or both of them together."

"So who do you like?" Crowberry asks.

Overshort, but it's likely my personal enmity colors my reaction. "Too early to say," I reply. "The wife has no alibi. I haven't checked into the partner's whereabouts yet." Not to mention Carlotta Trephino or Shrike. There's still the matter of the Eterniti which spends its nights cruising the streets taking deadly aim at me with a yet unnamed assailant at the wheel.

"Do that," Crowberry says. He hands me my shield and ID. "I want Swbyra to look into the drug angle."

I like those assignments just fine. Before I leave the station, I dial Heidi's number. Why I think she will be pleased that I've gotten my old job back, I don't know, but some of that feeling is there as I listen to the phone ring. With considerable disappointment, I listen to the recording and hang up without leaving a message. *Where is she?* Not at work, Facets isn't open late on the weekend. It doesn't take a veteran detective to figure it out. It's Saturday, she's an attractive young woman. She's out somewhere. On a date.

*****

When it is late enough to expect the night man to be on duty, I return to the Jade Pagoda. Lit by stingy forty-watt bulbs and the glow of a small television so old it's almost black-and-white, the lobby appears even shabbier than during the day.

The night man seated behind the counter is more a night youth. Bespectacled eyes and a thin sharp nose point down at a huge volume open on the desktop. He barely glances at my ID. I ask about Hector.

"Oh yeah, the dead guy," he says. His eyes rapidly rebound from left margin to right and back again.

"Did he have a car?" I ask. *Please, tell me he had a gold Eterniti.*

"Could have. I didn't see him with one."

That's definitive. "How about visitors while he was here? Phone calls?" I ask.

"Um, phone calls? There's no phone in the rooms and we don't take messages for guests here. Visitors? Um, yeah, some girl." With his right hand he turns a page. With the left, he taps his cigarette into a red plastic ashtray. Little gray cones of ash on the desktop mark where he overshot the tray.

"Really? Who?" I ask.

"Demi Moore." After a moment, without raising his face, the night kid chuckles and says, "I don't know. Just some girl."

"When did you see her?"

"Um, last night. Around one, two, something like that. I was taking a break. Had to whiz."

"Describe her."

"Can't."

I'm not surprised. He couldn't describe a freight train if it came through the door and rolled over his desk.

"You don't remember anything about her appearance? How about hair color?"

"Couldn't tell. She was wearing a cape with um, a, whatchacallit?" Without raising his eyes from his book, he paints an air portrait, moving cupped hands around his neck and over his head. Ash flies from his cigarette.

"A hood?"

"Right."

"Height? Weight? Tall or short? Thin or fat?"

"Hard to say what she weighed with that cape. But tall, yeah. Long stems sticking out of that cape." He turns the page. Taps ash. "That's all I noticed. I didn't really pay attention. Wanted to get back to my book."

"Did she drive? What was she driving? When did she leave?"

"Shit, man, I'm telling you. I didn't see. I wasn't staring out the damn window, I was reading."

"All right, I'll bite. What are you reading?"

"*The Seeing Hand.* It's an art book." He looks up. "I'm just doin' this to pay for art school. Soon as I graduate, I'm out of here."

"Art school, huh? So, can you draw?"

"Of course I can draw."

"So draw me a picture of the woman you saw."

He gives me a puzzled look. Then with a shrug of his shoulders, he ducks behind the counter, surfaces with a sheet of paper and a pencil. After a few minutes of concentrated scribbling he hands me the sketch. It's not much more informative than his verbal description.

"What do you think?" he asks.

Keep your day job. "Thanks. This will help. Now, how about four weeks ago? Another man died in one of the rooms."

The night youth sighs, rests folded arms on his open book. "Which one do you mean? Lots of men die in our rooms."

What is this, the company slogan? I can see the ad campaign: The accommodations at the Jade Pagoda are so good you'll just die. "Scott Corcoran, sheriff's deputy? A suicide?"

"What about him?"

"For starters, what can you tell me about his activities the night he died?"

The night youth props his chin in his hand, drums his fingers against his lips, rolls his eyes. Finally he says, "I think I saw him walk over to the Lounge."

"The Firefly Lounge?" I ask and cock a thumb to my left.

"Yeah. Maybe he wanted to use their phone. That's what people here usually do. We don't got phones in the rooms and we don't take messages here."

"So you said. What time was this?"

"Might have been nine or ten, something like that. Now if you ask me when did he get back, that I can't tell you. I was—"

"Reading. Yeah, I know." Maybe the staff at the Lounge was more observant. I thank the night youth and exit the office. When I pass the front window, I see he already has a fresh cigarette in hand and his nose in his book.

Within walking distance of the Jade Pagoda, the Firefly Lounge is open for business. There are, apparently, few hours when it is not. A muddy-hued glow from the combination of red, yellow and green neon beer signs reveals unvarnished pine walls, Formica topped tables whose chromed legs show bald spots of rust, a linoleum floor worn in places down to the black mastic. The customers are well in their cups and half passed out. With little to do, the bartender greets me eagerly.

"Whiskey," I tell him, and I would love to drink it. The shakes are back, and it's not PTSD.

I ask if a woman in a hooded cape was here last night.

"In a what?" the bartender asks.

"Never mind. What can you tell me about this man?"

With a scowl, the bartender scans my poor excuse for a photo of Scott Corcoran, Facets' deceased security officer. "Now this guy I remember. Strange duck. Came in alone, sat at the bar alone, didn't talk to anyone. Didn't drink either."

No wonder he remembers the man.

"Until he made a phone call." The bartender points to a pay phone on the wall. "Then he ordered a drink. Couple of drinks. Downed them fast. Then he left. Course, a lot of folks from the Pagoda do that—come in alone. Use the phone. Have a few. Leave. This guy, though, he was big-time nervous. Jumpy. Drank like he was in some kind of hurry. Kept checking his watch. When he left, he was real edgy, like."

Was it the phone conversation that rattled him? Now who or what would shake a sheriff's deputy? "What do you think he was frightened of?"

"I didn't say frightened. Nervous. Like whatever was going to happen when it got to be time, he wasn't sure he was going to like it."

*****

In my dark bedroom, I put a match to a stick of incense, linger a moment to watch the white smoke rise, catch its sweet powdery scent. At this time last night, and the night before that, and the night before that—far enough back that the memory is already dim—a different powder filled my nostrils: Nearvana. My body, ready for more, has already declared war over being denied. Muscles tense and twitch uncontrollably, threatening to secede. My stomach wants to leave my body through my back.

Before struggling into position on the *zafu*, I make a bow, so sketchy any onlooker would miss it. It's a prayer, I think, for success, for strength. My gut knots as if with stage fright. Something is at stake here, and the odds are not good.

Stop. Pay attention. Be here now, not on the Mile, snorting heroin. Breathe.
Inhale, one.
Exhale, two.
Inhale, three.

The shakes are so bad I can barely sit upright. I want a cigarette, need a drink, a fix.

Inhale, one.
Exhale, two——.

Who killed Hector? Not the hookers, Champagne or Rhonda. Sure, they could have rolled him, then killed him. *If so, why hang around the Jade Pagoda to be quizzed by the cops?* Some killers like to revisit the scene of the crime, but that was one brazen performance.

Inhale, one.
Exhale, t——.

Could any one of the men have killed Hector Waltann? Airol Jones? Marvin Overshort? Shrike? All are too tall or too broad to have successfully disguised themselves as a woman, even one in a cape.

What about Marybeth Waltann? I can more easily picture her in her wingback chair, alone, with a drink, in the dark, stewing over Hector than I can in that room at the Jade Pagoda, slicing him with a knife. Besides, she's too short to be the caped mystery woman.

Now, Carlotta Trephino, there's a good possibility.

Stop! This is discursive thinking at its worst. Start again and concentrate!
Inhale, one.
Exhale, two ... oh, screw it.

I push off the floor, flop onto the bed. The plume of scented smoke arabesques toward the ceiling, as sinuous as the mystery woman's cape, writhing like the tattooed snakes on Nikki Saint Clair. My fingertips find the site of my own tattoo, the soreness nearly gone now. Images swirl thick around my brain: Nikki, Champagne, and Rhonda all over me. But the kisses are Heidi's. And the hands, the hands are the sure, practiced hands of Lix Gemini.

CHAPTER 20

In the river
water ripples the branches
leaves drift past the clouds—Soezi

Sunday morning finds me whipped. A night of torment kept me awake and writhing, trying to manage the pain with meditation until I passed out from exhaustion. Fatigued, achy, hot one minute, cold the next, simultaneously wired and dispirited. It's the flu, I tell myself, but I've seen the same symptoms in junkies we've had in lock-up. They weren't coming down with the flu, they were kicking. We always saw that they received medical attention and a modicum of relief, which is more than I plan to do for myself. A guilty conscience insists I suffer. Mindfulness dictates I experience every wracking minute but I am grateful to have been unconscious through at least some of it.

It's late morning by the time I pull myself together enough to brave the day. At 'Lotta Cars for Less, a brisk cold wind hasn't discouraged the shoppers any. I have to fend off rabid salesmen as I weave my way through a lot jammed with cars, looking for and half expecting to find Hector's Eterniti, taken in trade for drugs. I have my hand on the knob of Carlotta's office door when a deep voice behind me says, "Ain't gonna find no bargains in there, Mister."

I whirl around to find Carlotta's heavy-handed sales muscle at my back. He makes it clear that what he's holding in his right pocket is not the Kelly *Blue Book*.

Carlotta's voice comes through the door. "What's going on out there?"

"I want to talk to you, Carlotta," I say before the salesman can answer.

"Will, honey, is that you?" she asks. "Give me five and come on in."

When I'm finally admitted to the office, I find the air is thick with cigar smoke. Carlotta sits enthroned as before in her mauve chair, her feet on the desk. The crystal dish of heroin I'm used to seeing in the middle of the desk is nowhere in sight. Across from her with his back to the door, a man sits in the side chair. He twists around to face me. It's Airol Jones.

"Mansion, right?" he says.

"Right. Helping Carlotta dust her cigars? You help polish the desk, too?"

Jones frowns and Carlotta chuckles.

"Why, Will, honey, I do believe you're jealous." She smokes in short quick puffs that give her an air of nervousness. "Didn't find anything on the lot that interested you?"

"How about something in the luxury department, say, an Eterniti? With a gold paint job. Got anything like that?"

Carlotta smirks. "I wish."

"I'm talking about Hector's Eterniti. You don't have it?" I peer over her shoulder through the window behind her. No Eterniti in the rear lot. "Where is it? Did you sell it? Give it back to Hector?"

"If I had—and I'm not saying I did—why should I tell you?" she asks with a peevish grin.

"Because old drinking buddies don't keep secrets from each other?"

She puffs away in stubborn silence. I flip out my ID. "How about, because it's police business?"

Carlotta lifts her feet off the desk and stands. "I was wondering when you were going to come clean. 'Friend of Hector's,' my ass."

Jones springs from his chair. "You sonofabitch."

"Now how about it, Carlotta? Did Hector take the car?" I ask.

"Hector? Hector's dead."

"And how would you know? Did you kill him?"

She grabs the newspaper from the top of her desk, clenches it in her fist, and waves it in my face. The banner headline flashes: "Diamond Merchant Iced." "I read the paper, honey, and not just to make sure they don't run my ads upside down. That's how I know about Hector. Now I want you out. Get out!" Carlotta points the paper at the door.

"Sure, I can go. But you're coming with me. And all the nice evidence you've got tucked away here. We'll finally get to shut you down, Carlotta, you and your little private club. You, too, Jones. You've slammed your last dunk."

At first round with fear, Carlotta's eyes slowly narrow and a satisfied smile returns to her lips. She reaches into her desk and draws out the plastic bag that holds the shot glass and cigar stub with my fingerprints and saliva. "All the evidence? In that case we'll also have to bring this. Then your buddies in blue will know you were there, too."

Jones heaves a sigh of relief.

Carlotta smiles like a poker player who holds all aces. "If I go down, you'll go down with me, Will Mansion. A dirty cop in the joint. I can see it now. They will eat you up, honey. Yes, they will."

Indeed they will. The threat of punishment I deserve must not sway me from this course. Running from the consequences of my actions has been like trying to swim without rippling the water. "I'll take that chance."

Airol's eyes widen in surprise. "He's kidding, right?" he says to Carlotta.

"You're kidding," she says to me. When I don't respond, she says, "You'd go to prison just to make a bust?"

"Want to make a date to meet on the exercise yard?" I ask her.

Master of the fake on the court, Jones tries a distraction play. "Now why we be sitting around here talking about jail? Let's be smart. Mansion, there's plenty of room on the team for a guy like you."

Much as I'd like to play center for the pros, I doubt he's talking about the Rebels. I shake my head. "Come on, let's go."

"Don't be stupid, man. We'll never go down for this. Carlotta has connections. Tell him, woman."

Carlotta licks her upper lip.

"Shrike not too happy with you these days, Carlotta?" I ask. "Not pleased about your boy Hector dying without paying what he owed?" *What was that debt? Shrike said Hector left him holding the bag but for how much? Must have been a bundle for him to offer my life in trade for Hector's. Now that Hector's dead, where does that deal stand?* "Is Shrike leaning on you to make good on the debt?" Maybe Shrike has the Eterniti. *Where is the damn car?*

"I'm not worried," she says, but she puffs nervously.

"Work with me, Carlotta. You know it'll go easier on you if you do."

"Tell the man what he want to know," Airol urges. "It won't hurt to have him on our side."

"What's your problem, Airol?" Carlotta says. "Afraid of a little heat?"

"Not the heat. But the media'll take me apart and my career will be in the dumper."

"You could always come work for me."

"Woman, I be a star, not a pusher ... of used cars. Come on, what's the big deal?"

"Yeah, Carlotta, what's the big deal?" I ask. "Unless you killed him."

"Killed him? Honey, I thought you knew me better than that. I'm a businesswoman. Why would I kill Hector when he was a good customer? He bought enough junk for two men. No, honey, I didn't kill him and I don't know anything about his car."

"Right."

Carlotta closes the space between us, smiles and fingers my lapel. "I'm telling you, Will, honey, I don't know. I wish I did. You're right, Shrike isn't happy with me. I could put a smile back on his face if I had the car."

She presses herself against me. I find myself measuring her height. Too short to be the mystery woman in the hooded cape.

"Now, can we go back to being friends?" she asks.

"Well—"

"And friends don't arrest friends, do they?" she says.

Not with armed salesmen around. I doubt I'd make it off the lot. Leading in a bizarre fox trot with Carlotta in my arms, I mince backward toward the desk and its plastic bag of evidence. Carlotta anticipates my move and lunges. With Airol guarding me, she makes it to the desk before I do and grabs the bag.

"Sorry, Will. I'd better hang onto this," she says. "Otherwise, you just might go tell your new friends about our little club. Wouldn't you?"

"Yes. I would."

"And I'm afraid I just can't let that happen, can I?"

"No."

She smiles sweetly. "I'm glad we understand each other.

I leave, having given Carlotta the barest for-publication details about Hector's death. She didn't ask many questions, either because she didn't care or she already knew the answers.

*****

At the Canterbury, Old Paint gets its usual scathing glance from the parking valet, but I get the last laugh. I badge him, and steer the vehicle to the prime front parking lot. The lot is crammed. In first gear, I drive up one aisle and down the next, looking for an empty space amongst the Mercedeses, Caddies, Lexuses, Eternitis...

Eterniti. Gold. Right here. *Damn!* Of course, I can't say for certain it's the gunboat that's hounded me, I never got a good enough look but I'll find out soon enough whose it is. I jot down the number of the license plate housed in a Haviland Eterniti dealership frame, then exit Old Paint to make a closer examination. The luxury car is dirty, water-spotted. A wiper-sized wedge is the only clean area in a grimy windshield. I'm about to peer inside when the blare of a car horn behind me draws me away. A man behind the wheel of a Suburban waves his hand at Old Paint as if to shoo it from his path. Reluctantly I leave the Eterniti and park, wishing I had a cell phone or radio so I could run the plate.

Canterbury Bazaar doesn't have a public pay phone, but the restaurant does, in its foyer which at this hour is crammed with Sunday brunchers waiting to be seated. Fortunately I don't have to fend off anyone else wanting to use the phone while I wait for Dispatch. These people all have phones of their own.

The car is registered to Hector Waltann, Columbus Street, Paradise City. No wants, no warrants.

Has the thing been here the whole time? It has been Overshort driving it! I charge off for Facets under a full head of steam.

It's toasty inside Facets and there is hot cider on tap as well as coffee but the cozy atmosphere fails to soothe me. I identify myself to the salesgirl who greets me and demand to see Overshort.

"He's not here."

"How about Heidi Quince?"

"She's not here, either." The clerk's eyes slide nervously toward the commotion at the other side of the room, an irate couple whose complaints can be heard over the Muzak. At the counter, the female of the pair opens a small gray Facets paper bag, removes a velvety plum box, and plops it onto the glass counter top.

"It cracked!" the woman shouts. "It simply cracked as if it were nothing more than bottle glass."

The clerk attending her, a young man whose neck is too skinny for his collar, takes a step back. "Emeralds are not indestructible—"

"But this is ridiculous. It must be paste. I didn't pay five thousand dollars for strass! I was told it was a high-quality emerald."

"I can't explain it, Ma'am, but if there's a problem, we'll correct it."

"Trouble?" I ask my salesgirl.

"Oh, it's nothing," she says.

"Nothing Heidi couldn't fix?"

She smiles apologetically.

"Who did you say originally sold you this piece?" the clerk asks.

The missus pulls a wadded-up receipt from her bag, shakes it out, and slams it on the counter, jostling the baubles in the case.

"Mr. Overshort, and I want to see him," her husband says. "Now get him out here!"

"I'm sorry, he's—"

"I don't care where he is or what he's doing, I want him out here now," the husband yells and pounds the case with his fist.

The clerk looks worried and I don't blame him. If the angry man hits the glass case any harder, it will break.

I step over to the couple and ask, "Is there a problem?"

"Who the hell are you?" the man asks.

I show him my identification.

He turns to his wife. "Who said there's never a cop around when you need one?" To me he says, "Yes, there's a problem. I've been robbed. I paid for an emerald and I got a hunk of glass."

Overshort sold a piece of junk for a fine jewelry price? Just the opposite of what he may have done with the insurance claim after the theft. Then, I seem to recall, he undervalued his inventory.

I open the little box which contains a ring nestled against dark velvet. A big faceted green stone glitters in an ornate gold setting. It reminds me of the one I saw on Nikki Saint Clair's finger when she skimmed her hand down her bare ... I give the image a mental shove. "When did you buy this, Ma'am?"

The missus waves the receipt in my face. "Six weeks ago."

Right after the theft. I pretend to examine the ring while I try to solidify my misgivings about Overshort. Up to this point, I've hesitated to suspect him of wrongdoing, aware that my dislike for him and the way he browbeats the staff, especially Heidi, may prejudice my judgment. Now, between this and the Eterniti, it appears he is up to something after all. Is he passing off imitation jewels as authentic? Why? He could be skimming. *So why not also submit a fraudulent claim to the insurance company? Because an investigation would invite too much scrutiny? Did he need Hector Waltann out of the way for the same reason?* Now that Hector's dead, once the insurance company settles on the death claim, Overshort becomes sole owner of Facets and can run whatever scam he wants.

"Please," says the clerk, his Adam's apple bobbing. "Let us look into this. There must be some mistake."

"Damn right there's a mistake. Now what are you going to do about it?" the angry man asks of us both.

The nervous clerk's glance volleys between me and his customer, unsure of who represents the greater menace.

"No doubt it's just an oversight," I assure the complainant. "But I'll look into it and if there appears a fraud was perpetrated, we will investigate further. Leave the piece with me. I'll find out what went wrong and get back to you." Heidi Quince will be able to tell me if it's a phony.

The husband frowns. "Give it to you?"

A property form, evidence bag, and numbered tag would impress them and I'd have them in the trunk, if I were driving the Crown Vic. "Can you make out a receipt that will document this?" I ask the clerk.

"I really should check with Mr. Overshort first."

"Maybe he should," the wife says.

"You said Overshort was the cause of this problem. Do you really want to check with him?"

The husband rubs his lip with his index finger and the wife studies her shoes.

"Well, fine. If there's no complaint here, I'll be on my way and you can take this up with Overshort, when he shows up. If he shows up." I set the ring box on the counter.

"No, wait," says the wife. She gives me a smile and turns to her husband. "Honey?"

He picks up the ring and narrows his eyes at me. "We just need some assurance."

"Call the stationhouse. Give them my badge number. Tell them what's happening here. It'll be a matter of record."

The husband nods. "I believe I'll do just that. Phone?" he asks the clerk.

He points to one beside the cash register.

The man picks up the receiver. I start to give him the non-emergency number and he says, "Stop. I'll look it up for myself." He gives me a smug, self-satisfied smile and snaps his finger at the clerk. "Phone book."

The clerk produces one from behind the counter. The husband dials. After a brief conversation, he says to his wife, "He's legit."

"All right then." Again I ask the clerk for a receipt.

"I—I can come up with something."

That appears to mollify the angry couple. They get comfortable with a couple of cups of cider while the clerk retreats to the back office. He returns with several pages of documentation: a narrative with dates, names, photocopies of everyone's identification, the ring's description and stock number. We all sign it. The clerk boxes up the ring and wraps it in its little sack which I put it in my pocket.

I take the salesgirl aside. "Where is Overshort?"

She bites her lower lip and glances down to the right.

"Look, it could be nothing, an honest mistake. If it's not, it could look suspicious, you covering up for him," I tell her.

Her glance drifts to the left and she chews her lip on the other side. "He said not to disturb him."

"I don't have to say who told me where I could find him," I tell her.

"He's at the Belleaire Hunt Club," she says, her voice barely above a whisper.

"Thanks. I'll be in touch." Now that I've picked up the scent I'm eager to get down the trail and I head for the exit with long strides. What I hear just before the door closes behind me turns my legs to stone.

"Here's your copy, sir," the clerk tells the angry man. "First thing Monday, I'll have our certified gemologist contact you."

"Fat lot of good that will do," she replies. "It's your so-called certified gemologist who did the original appraisal!"

*****

The Belleaire Hunt Club is, of necessity, out in the boonies. The wind blowing unimpeded across fallow fields rattles the bare branches in the trees along Rifleshot Road. West of the city, two lane blacktop turns to gravel road lined on one side by weedy meadows. The Gin Mill River runs perpendicular under the road and disappears into a wooded tract. A discreet green Belleaire Hunt Club sign alerts me that I'm nearing the facility but I don't need signs to tell me I'm close. I can hear the pop of shotguns even over the road noise and Old Paint's heater. My shoulders hunch, my stomach cramps, and my ears ring. *What was I thinking, coming here?*

The gravel road ends at the club's wrought iron gate. A wide paved drive, neatly landscaped with small junipers and holly bushes, leads to the clubhouse. In the softly lit lobby, cushiony green carpeting muffles noise and contributes to a genteel hush. A young, pretty receptionist stands behind a mahogany counter. Her close-fitting green jacket matches the carpeting. The burgundy and green plaid of the upholstered club chairs is echoed in her necktie. I ask her where Overshort is.

"He's shooting Hunter's Clays."

Competitive shotgunning, like trap and skeet, only the ranges simulate game bird and waterfowl shooting.

Her delivery shifts into something like recitation. "We have two upland ranges for quail and dove hunters, and two waterfowl ranges backed up to the Gin Mill River for goose and duck hunters. Our Hunter's Clay's facilities are second to—"

"And Mr. Overshort is at? ..."

She frowns at the interruption. "Range One, waterfowl," she says.

"Thanks." I turn away from the desk and she says, "Excuse me. Are you a member?"

I show her my universal membership badge. With a look of concern, she asks, "Trouble?"

"I'm not expecting any, are you?"

She doesn't answer directly. Instead she offers to escort me to the range.

The lobby branches off into several corridors. Carved pine signs point the way to the lounge, the restaurant, locker rooms, the pro shop, meeting rooms. Plate glass doors opposite the reception desk open to the outside. "That's OK, I'm sure I can find it," I reply, and I'm across the lobby and out the doors before she can protest. I follow more signs down a concrete path toward the sound of guns. The closer I get, the tenser I become. A cold sweat glazes my skin; nerves and muscles flinch despite my silent chant: *This is not Terminal Road, not Terminal Road.*

The path leads to an open-sided spectator shelter surrounded by fields. The pennant edges of the green and gold vinyl canopy flap in the wind. Cushioned wrought iron chairs ring matching tables. Two of the shooting fields around this observation center are bordered by hedgerows and trees. At the end of the other two fields, the taller trees have been removed in favor of bushes and grasses which only partially conceal the narrow trickle of the Gin Mill River—little more than a brook—beyond.

Overshort stands alone facing a meadow edged by the river. Day-Glo-orange and black shards of broken targets blaze in the dry grass twenty-some yards away. He wears the requisite tweeds, even a cap, but on him the natty threads look like someone else's clothes. Red debris of spent shell casings speckle the pavement at his feet. A Hunt

Club attendant in green and plaid operates the pull station a few yards behind him. Nearby, a rack holds a spare shotgun.

A lone spectator sits at the canopied table, gloved hands wrapped around a foam-topped pedestal mug.

"Hello, Heidi."

Her head whips around not once but twice. "Will! Will, my God, what are you doing here?"

"You said to keep in touch. And I wanted to talk to Overshort."

"Ready!" yells Overshort.

A two-toned composite disk roughly the size of a small ashtray spins out of a trap hidden behind tall grass along the riverbank. Overshort aims, fires, and reduces the clay pigeon to pieces fifteen feet in the air. Completely absorbed in the sport, he hasn't noticed me.

"Nice shooting," I observe through gritted teeth. I clench every muscle trying to hold myself together.

"How did you know we were here?" Heidi asks, pitching her voice over the percussive popping from the next range.

"Someone at the store told me."

A waiter in Belleaire colors stops at our table. "Can I get you something from the bar, sir?" he asks, nearly shouting to be heard over the noise. "An Irish coffee like the lady's, perhaps?"

Whiskey and coffee sounds oh, so good. Or maybe just the whiskey. A nip would keep the shakes under control. Just this one, for medicinal purposes. No, I'm done with lying to myself. "Hot tea would be nice," I reply.

The waiter nods to confirm and goes off to get it.

Heidi hoists her cup. "Should have gotten one of these, you'd enjoy it." She takes a sip and a line of whipped cream clings to her upper lip. She licks it off slowly.

"Ready!" Overshort says.

A fresh bird whirls up high from yet another hidden trap and Overshort nails it despite a sudden gust that alters what might have been a predictable trajectory.

"So, what brings you here?" Heidi asks.

"An official matter. Hector's dead."

At Overshort's shouted "Ready!" Heidi turns her head away and I miss her reaction to my announcement. Two birds spin into the air from different directions and Overshort hits them both. Doubles. I'm impressed.

"An official matter." She chuckles, but her laughter tapers off when I produce my identification. "I didn't realize you were with the police."

"I wasn't. Well, I was. But then I wasn't. Now I am again."

"Maybe it's a good thing you didn't get anything alcoholic. You're not making much sense."

Barrel pointed at the ground, Overshort turns to say something to the attendant and spots me. Sunlight winks off his heavy duty shooting glasses. The barrel of the gun comes up level with my chest. My skull seems to compress, my skin breaks out in goose bumps, and muscles tense from remembered pain and terror more than fear of immediate danger. Using the gun as a pointer, Overshort waves us over. "What are you doing here?" he asks.

Hard to tell if he is yelling from nervousness or defensiveness or simply to be heard over the other party's shooting.

"Hector's dead."

Overshort frowns and removes ear plugs which I wish I had. "Huh?"

"I said, Hector's dead."

There is no missing his reaction as we are face to face, but a steady gaze behind thick shooting glasses gives nothing away.

"Marybeth told me," he says. "Guess you can stop looking for him, huh?"

"Stop looking for him, yeah. Start looking for his killer."

Overshort's features pinch together in a scowl. "What's that to you?"

Heidi clears her throat. "Mr. Overshort—"

"Just butt out, Mansion."

"Mr. Overshort—"

"Police'll look into it—"

I reach for my identification and Heidi says, somewhat more forcefully, "Mr. Overshort!"

"What?" he shouts.

"He is the police!"

I smile in acknowledgment. "Marybeth didn't tell you that?"

Overshort doesn't nod or shake his head, but his angry eyes reveal he's not happy to be caught by surprise.

"So who do you think did it?" I ask him.

He shrugs. "Hell, I don't know. You keep asking me questions about Hector like we were joined at the hip. Look, I worked with the guy, that's all. We weren't close personal friends."

"I guess that's why you're out here the day after his death."

"Where else should I be? Home boo-hooing or something? Like that's gonna bring him back." Overshort tips four shells into the magazine. "No, might as well enjoy myself while I can. With Waltann gone and me the sole owner, I'm gonna be very busy with the store." He is so calm he could be talking about the defection of a part-time clerk instead of the death of a partner whose blood may be on his hands.

"That's why we came out here," Heidi hastens to say. "To do some short-range planning, head off any crises."

"You're having a crisis right now," I tell her. "One of your customers was in the store bitching about being ripped off. Seems someone sold her a fake." I want to show Heidi the gem in question, but not with Overshort breathing down her neck.

"At our s-s-store?" Heidi asks. "Now who would do a thing like that?"

"Actually, they claim it was you, Overshort," I say.

"I'm sure it's a simple mistake," he replies.

"Like the Eterniti?"

"I don't get you."

"Hector's car. It's been in the Canterbury parking lot all this time."

"All what time?" To the man at the pull station Overshort says, "Delay," raises the gun's stock to his shoulder, and yells "Ready." A second passes, then another before a high-flying target emerges from the brush. Overshort reduces it to smithereens. The shell casing falls with a ping a few feet away. He doesn't catch it or even pick it up. In fact, he hasn't collected any of his brass. Maybe that's déclassé at a hunt club.

He tells the attendant "Report pairs," and yells "Ready!" A target flies up and Overshort sweeps the weapon across the sky. No sooner does he fire than another bird appears in the air. He gets them both.

"Good shooting," I say.

"Damn straight it is. I practice plenty. Other guys, you get a cold day like this, they're home sitting on their butts watching 'Outdoor Life' on TV. Not me. I'm out shooting." He reloads the gun, a round in the chamber and three in the magazine. "Pays off. Been known to get forty out of fifty birds and this is a tough course. I like a challenge, though."

Likes to brag, too.

"It's good sport, Hunter's Clays. I like a moving target. Like that one."

I follow his glance to where a tan target has foolishly broken cover just in front of the brush line. No clay pigeon, it's a cottontail.

Overshort draws a bead.

I've shot my fair share of small game but this isn't hunting, this is an assassination. My dad would have had a fit. My first time out he railed at me for just such unsportsmanlike behavior. I fake tripping just enough to jostle Overshort. His shot goes wild and the rabbit runs for cover.

"Hey, you ruined my shot."

"I thought you said you liked a moving target."

"You think it's so easy. Let's see what you can do." Overshort reloads and holds out the gun. I give my mug to Heidi and examine the weapon, a semiautomatic Beretta twelve-gauge. The shell casing I picked up outside the bookstore Wednesday night was a twelve-gauge. Not exactly the weapon Grady said was used on Forbes Road but it is a repeater and Grady could have been wrong about the pump action.

Overshort yells, "Ready!"

Startled, I swing the gun up late, point at the sky with nothing that could be called "aim," and fire. The shot, of course, goes wild and the clay pigeon soars to its apogee before it falls to the ground, still whole. The recoil shoves my shoulder. I think I've pulled a muscle in my back and torquing my body hasn't done my leg any good. My temper flares.

Overshort flashes the same smirk he wore in Knockers when he challenged me at darts. "Hell, I would have thought you'd be good at this, all the practice you get," he says.

I'm good enough, but I get more exercise with handguns. The heat of humiliation burns in my face. This is not a contest I want to lose.

Overshort calls for another target. This time, more familiar with the weapon and the target's speed and trajectory, I feel I may have come a little closer but it's still a miss. Fuming, I lower the gun.

He chuckles. "Third time's a charm," he says and waits, arms folded across his chest.

I pull my handkerchief from my pocket. With a weak smile, I wipe my face and hands, make a show of being flustered. Accidentally on purpose, I fumble the handkerchief and it falls to the ground. Bending down to pick it up gives me a chance to catch a casing ejected from one of my own tries in its folds.

I take my time with the business of stowing the handkerchief and taking up the gun. Meanwhile, I work to calm my breath, my mind. Zen master Shunryu Suzuki taught that the key to right action is to do it without attachment to the result. "If your practice is good, you may become proud of it," he observed. "Pride is extra. Right effort is to get rid of something extra."

What do I want to do here? Prove something to Overshort or nail this shot? Because I can't do both.

I inhale, pull the gun into my shoulder, site down the barrel. I've been trying too hard to aim. Wingshooting's more about holding the gun consistently, maintaining good gun-eye coordination. Hard to do with an unfamiliar firearm. The breeze against my face gives me a hint of the wind's direction and velocity, suggests the spray pattern of shot as it fans out in the air, the twirling flight of the bird. I exhale, release all tension. Before Overshot can get the jump on me, I yell, "Ready!" and swing the weapon up, stretching from ankle to wrist. My arm is the barrel, the muzzle my eye. I see the target and follow it, fly with it. I am one with the wind, the shot, the bird. I am the wind, the shot.

I am the bird.

There is no "I," only the bird.

The clay pigeon explodes into Halloween-colored dust.

Overshort's eyebrows go up. "You learn fast."

"Yes," I reply. "Once I get my target in sight, I'm unstoppable.

CHAPTER 21

Work day over.
Has that clock on the wall
always been so loud?—Debisu

I return the gun to Overshort.

"We'd better get back, put out that little fire at the store," he says to Heidi, and packs up his gear. "And don't you have a killer to catch, cop?" he asks me.

"I'm already on the case. Been working all morning as a matter of fact." If Overshort is going back to the store to destroy evidence, I'm glad said evidence is safe in my pocket. "Just for the sake of argument, where were you last night?"

"With Quince here," he says without hesitation.

Heidi confirms it with a reluctant nod. When I pictured her out on the town Saturday night, Overshort is not whom I pictured her with.

"That it?" he asks.

"For now."

"Well, good luck," he says, and slings his gun bag over his shoulder. Heidi takes the spare gun from the rack.

"Yours?" I ask, unable to keep all the incredulity out of my voice. It's not sawed-off or pump-action either but seeing her with it is still a shock.

"Mr. Overshort thought I should learn to shoot. For self-protection," she replies.

"A handgun you could keep in your purse would serve you better." She shrugs.

"Come on, Quince," Overshort says, "we've got work to do." He stops at the table to sign the tab and heads back toward the clubhouse at a casual pace, Heidi at his heels. Either he's covered his tracks so well he's not worried about me, or he's a consummate actor. He should worry, though. I pat my pocket. *Do I have a mate to the brass I picked up at the bookstore the first time someone—Overshort?—shot at me from the Eterniti?* If I hadn't been too addled to look, I might have a third match from the drive-by after my first meeting with Nikki. One will have to do.

I spend the afternoon working from home. I place several calls to Marybeth Waltann but all I get is her answering machine. Finally I leave a message and call it a day. Buffeted by waves of sickness, I am unable to concentrate on work. My choices seem to be drown in misery or drown in alcohol.

As night approaches, the withdrawal pains I wrestled with last night gather strength like an approaching thunderstorm. I retreat to my bedroom and sit *zazen* with nausea, dizziness, and tension that advance and recede like the swells of a turbulent sea.

*****

Monday dawns clear and dry, the air so cold the sky is more white than blue. Though it's corduroys/leather jacket/boots weather, I put on a suit and oxfords as befits my official status and wish whoever rolled me in the alley behind the strip club hadn't taken my topcoat. I fill my pockets with wallet, keys, handkerchief, and the shell casing I picked up from the street outside the bookstore where Heidi and I were fired on.

The bills and correspondence I took from Hector's condo still litter my kitchen table. Those papers probably contain much information that's material to the case. To use any of them I'll have to explain that I broke into the place to get them. At the foot of the table lies the white vinyl trash bag in which I hauled the papers from Hector's condo. I could shove them back in, dump it in the garbage can for the city to take away, and no one would be the wiser. At a mental crossroads, unwilling to go down either road, I stand in the middle of the kitchen for several minutes not so much debating as waiting for divine intervention. It doesn't come and I leave the mess where it lies.

The station's rear police-only entrance channels me directly into the central corridor and a gauntlet of well-wishers and curiosity-seekers. Some of them haven't seen me since the Terminal Road fiasco and have a lot of catching up to do. When I finally reach my desk, I find it cluttered and dotted with crumbs from someone's brown-bag lunches. Strapped as we usually are for equipment, I'm not surprised to find my desk put to use in my absence.

I clear a space and get busy on a search warrant for the pay phone in the Firefly Lounge next to the Jade Pagoda. In hopes that New England Tel won't put up a big protest or drag its feet, I limit my request to the night of Scott Corcoran's death and the hours he was likely in the bar. A small window of time, a pay phone in a public place, and I'm not trying to find out who made calls or even who answered them, just what calls were made and where they went. Doesn't seem like a big privacy issue to me but the phone company can be jealous of its customer records, especially since those customers tend to sue when they feel their rights have been violated. I must have crossed all the Ts and dotted the Is because the magistrate at least doesn't have a problem with it.

When I return to the office, I place a call to the Waltanns' insurance agent. A recording answers and invites me to leave a message or, if it's an emergency, to call a mobile number. While I doubt my need for answers about Hector's insurance qualifies as an actual emergency, I accept the invitation and wait for a call-back. Not long ago, like this morning, I would have occupied myself during the interval with a cigarette.

Instead, I distract myself by hunting up the file on Scott Corcoran. Just as I remembered, it was Grady's case—the thin folder has a red label. Swbyra is blue and I'm yellow, cause for much ribbing when it was first allotted and which now seems prophetic. I don't expect to find much and I don't, only the beginnings of an investigation into an "unattended death," closed when the medical examiner ruled suicide. The folder holds the offense event report signed by the first reporting officer, a lengthy supplement from Grady detailing the crime scene, the medical examiner's report, and a clearance form officially closing the case. Grady's report describes a motel room furnished like the one in which I discovered Hector, but in less disarray. True to the thoroughness that is Grady's hallmark, he noted not only what he found but also implies what he might have expected to find and didn't. He indicated that the bed was made up, the towel still neatly folded on the towel bar, the sink dry, the drinking glasses still shrink-wrapped, and the bed made up, hinting that the room hadn't been slept in. Further, there was no luggage, all of which supported the M.E.'s finding of suicide.

The Firefly Lounge's bartender told me that after using the phone, Corcoran had returned to his bar stool agitated, filled with dread, and in need of several drinks. *Whom did he call? Did Corcoran make some kind of farewell call to his wife, steel himself with alcohol, then go back to his room at the Jade Pagoda and do the deed?* If I knew now it wouldn't be soon enough. Impatience sets my foot tapping under the desk.

The M.E.'s report recaps some of Grady's findings. The stolen shotgun was found close enough to Corcoran's right side to have fallen from his hand after death. Rigor and lividity were consistent with a recent demise. The postmortem confirmed death from a shotgun blast that tore open a major artery. Yes, that can do some damage. Though the squad room is warm, I find myself shuddering and turn quickly to the firearms investigation. Nitrates were found on Corcoran's right hand and his palm print was on the gun.

Along with the reports are prints of the photographs Grady took. Corcoran's ruined, lifeless body is a pathetic shell emptied of the proud spirit that tempers his posture in his official portrait where he stands with chin up, right hand in sharp salute, left angled away from the sidearm at his hip.

His left hip. Sidearm at his left. Scott Corcoran was left-handed. No way he would have killed himself using his right hand. It's a shot no one would want to have to take twice. *His suicide? A sham to cover up a homicide?* The unused room, the absence of luggage could point not only to a man intent on killing himself but also one planning a meet. The phone call from the Firefly Lounge didn't have to be to bid his wife farewell. It could just as easily have been to set up the rendezvous. More than ever, I want to know whom Corcoran called just prior to his death.

And Monetta, Facets' cleaning lady, fatally mugged in the Jade Pagoda's parking lot ... could her death, too, be as I've suspected, something more than random violence?

I have just pulled up her file on the computer when my line flashes. The dispatcher tells me it's a call from Dessa Barisawski, Waltann's insurance agent. I introduce myself and inform her of Hector's death.

"A homicide?" she asks. Her voice is comfortable, relaxed, amicable, but not obsequious. "That's official?"

"Unless the M.E. uncovers something that proves otherwise," I reply.

"So, not a suicide?"

"No. Why, would you have expected that?"

"Oh, no. Just that it would affect the claim." She chuckles pleasantly. "Thinking like an insurance agent. But thanks for the notification. I can get the ball rolling, contact his widow before she has to call me."

I state briefly my need for details about Hector's insurance coverage and ask if we can meet. She explains she's on the road servicing accounts. "That's why I didn't get back to you sooner. This is the first chance I've had. Look, I haven't had lunch yet. If you don't mind my talking while I eat."

"Not at all. Where should I meet you?"

"How about Benny's?"

"Done and done."

I give her my general description, then head across the river and up Restaurant Row. At the franchise place she specified, I ask the hostess for a booth.

"Smoking preference?" she asks.

"Smok——. No, make that non."

She seats me in a booth just inside the door. While I wait, I order my own lunch. Though I can't remember the last time I ate, I still don't have much of an appetite. I pick at the sandwich, more interested in the parade of other customers. A beleaguered husband and wife come in trailing a mob of noisy, overactive kids. Two older gents take pie and coffee at the counter. Four women loaded down with shopping bags drop gratefully into the next booth and order sundaes. A large van pulls into the handicapped space at the front entrance. I watch with idle interest as the driver's door opens, a ramp extends, and a woman in a wheelchair rolls down and out. She points a remote at the van, the ramp retracts, and the door closes behind it. I'm still admiring the smoothness of the whole operation when the wheelchair woman appears at my booth and extends her hand.

"Dessa Barisawski, National Assurance." Her smile reveals even white teeth and her blue eyes sparkle with personality and intelligence.

Automatically I rise for the lady, then awkwardly stop midway and sit, uncertain of whether one stands for someone in a wheelchair. "Detective Mansion, Ma'am," I stammer.

She casts a dubious eye at the booth and says, "Could we switch to a table?"

"By all means."

From the take-out-order pick-up the waitress calls, "Hi, Dessa. The usual?"

"Come here often, huh?" I ask. Dessa Barisawski nods. "Food's that good?"

She shrugs. "It's edible. But they have a ramp, the aisles are wide, and I can get into the ladies' room."

Suddenly the ache of healing muscles and nerves in my leg seems negligible.

"So, you're a young guy," she says. "You have good coverage, I suppose."

"Actually, no. A man in my line of work ... hold on a second. I didn't ask to meet to get a sales pitch."

"Well, you're on my time," she replies. "The least you could do is listen so I can account for it as a sales meeting."

So I listen patiently while she extols the virtues of whole life and term. Finally I get a chance to ask about Hector's policies. "Did he in fact let his personal insurance lapse by not paying the premiums?"

Dessa Barisawski replies, "As soon as you hung up, I remembered the policy is no longer in force."

"Oh that's diplomatic. What about his business insurance? Did you handle that too?"

"Yes, I did."

"The buy-sell policy, was that still 'in force'?"

"Yes, it was," she says between bites of club sandwich. "The year's premium had been paid in full when the policy was initiated."

"Would the benefit be enough to say, justify murder?"

"Murder? I thought you said——"

"Homicide. Officially. For now."

Her cheeks color slightly.

"I'm not asking you to assess the beneficiary's character, Ma'am," I explain. "I'm just asking about the money."

"I guess people have killed for less," she says quietly. "A lot less."

"And when will the claim likely be settled?"

"Once I get an official death certificate stating definitively it wasn't suicide, a matter of days. Unless, of course, you charge the beneficiary."

That would be Marvin Overshort.

"Will you?"

"It would be premature to comment on that at this time," I reply.

"Now who's being diplomatic?" she asks, but with a smile.

"But the settlement would be worth hanging around for, to see if one, well, got away with murder?"

"Definitely."

I thank Dessa Barisawski for the help and reach for the lunch tab.

"That's OK," she says. "I'll expense it off. That is, if you promise to think about it. The whole life?"

"It'd be expensive, wouldn't it?" I ask.

She shrugs. "It'll only get more expensive the older you get. And you've got a long life ahead of you."

If only I could be as sure of that as she is.

Back at the station, I try Marybeth Waltann again and this time I reach her.

"These messages you've been leaving me about the Eterniti … what's that about?" she asks. She sounds listless.

"It's parked in the lot at the Canterbury," I tell her.

"So? Oh, I guess they want me to move it," she replies.

"No, it's not a problem. I just thought you might want it out of there." Better in her garage rather than at Overshort's disposal.

The silence that greets this suggestion reminds me the car isn't her favorite subject. "Marvin was supposed to box up whatever of Hector's personal belongings are still at Facets, but I haven't been able to make myself go get them yet. I guess I'll pick up the car at the same time. Except, I don't have a key."

"Hector didn't give you one?" I ask her.

Her glare is audible over the phone. "I'll bet Marvin knows where I can find a key," she says.

Yes, I'll bet he does.

I return to the file on the fatal mugging of Facets' cleaning lady, Monetta, shot in the parking lot of the Jade Pagoda between Sunday night and Monday morning a week ago. No witnesses. Hair and fibers found in the car were attributed to Monetta and her boyfriend whose alibi apparently met with Grady's satisfaction. A shell casing and tire tracks. These last two set my scalp tingling. Such evidence is useless unless one has a suspect sample to match it to but I believe I have just such a sample in my pocket.

I clear the computer screen, open a new file, and complete a narrative on yesterday's fake-jewel fracas at Facets. I assign individual evidence case numbers to the alleged-phony emerald and my collection of shell casings—the one ejected from Overshort's gun at the Hunt Club and the one from the bookstore drive-by shooting, along with a note for Grady to compare them with those found at the scene of Monetta's ambush at the Jade Pagoda.

I can't handle the shell casing without picturing Heidi hoisting that spare shotgun. It makes me uneasy, like turning onto a familiar street only to find the road has been widened and all new stores have gone up. "For protection," indeed. What is Overshort up to?

As to my own protection, it's time the old gunslinger strapped on his six-shooter.

Though I push my chair back from the desk, I'm not really done here and I know it.

No, it will never come to this. There's a good chance no one would ever find out.

My conscience is deaf to my excuses. Finally there is nothing left to do but open one last file and swear out everything I know about Carlotta Trephino, Airol Jones, and Shrike, including my involvement. I print it out and drag my feet down the corridor to Crowberry's office.

The lieutenant isn't in. I force myself to stand just inside the doorway to wait. Several minutes pass. I look at the paper in my hand and discover I've rolled it into a scroll. Before I can mangle it any further, I leave, but not before placing the report on Crowberry's desk, edges curling.

CHAPTER 22

Snow is falling
but in the cemetery
fresh flowers abound—Soezi

Twilight gloom pervades the Miracle Mile pawnshop. Nevertheless, the broker recognizes me and seems surprised to see me.

"Not many come back to redeem their stuff, is all," he says. "Gunning for the guy that stung ya, huh?"

"What makes you say that?"

"I notice you're not asking for your camping gear back," he says.

"Look, do you still have the Beretta?" I ask.

"Oh, yeah, I think so. In the back, maybe. I'll go dig it out."

In the back? That figures. He really shouldn't display the gun for sale until the loan matures.

He unlocks a wrought iron security door to a room behind the counter, leaving me to busy myself by perusing what he's got in the case. No guns at all, which is odd. Instead there are cameras, knives, watches, rings, other jewelry. One item in particular catches my eye.

Clanking keys announce the broker's return.

"Here's your piece." He slides the Beretta and its holster across the counter in exchange for my money and receipt.

I buckle it on. "Can I see this?" I ask, pointing.

"Hope you got big bucks, I ain't giving that away." He unlocks the case with yet another key and takes out the large gold and gemstone ring that caught my notice. The cut green stone in its center glitters in the blue light of the overhead fluorescents. It appears to be a twin to the emerald ring the irate customers brought into Facets, the one I just this afternoon checked into Property at the station, the one that reminded me so much of Nikki's. *Is it?* For that I'll need an expert opinion.

"Hold this for me," I tell him. "Promise me you won't sell that to anyone else."

He leans forward, elbows on the counter. "Look, I don't got no layaway plan here. I'm selling that to the first person who comes in with four grand. If that ain't you that ain't my problem."

"I don't have that much on me."

"Come back when you do." He moves to return the ring to the case.

"Wait!" I show him my ID. "I really need that ring. It's in connection with a case."

The broker scrutinizes my identification card. "You get that phony I.D. from Benny the Pen? Like they say, guy's an artist. Looks almost real."

"It is real!"

"But I thought you were ..." The broker's body stiffens and he puts some distance between us. With a raised eyebrow, he says, "If you're a cop, then you know I don't have to give you nothing without some kinda warrant."

"True. But you'll sell it to me?"

He gives me an eager smile. "I said I'd sell it to the first person who meets my price."

"Fine. Let me use your phone."

"What for?"

"To call my lieutenant, get him down here with some cash."

"Your lieutenant," he echoes. "You're serious."

"Oh yes."

He drums his fingers on the counter. "Phone's busted," he says finally.

"I see. Guess all I can do is hope for your cooperation. Maybe you'll come around. I'm a patient man, I can wait." I cross my arms over my chest, let my jacket fall open just enough so my badge will show, and make myself comfortable against the counter.

"Suit yourself." With a smile, the broker places the ring on its shelf and slides the case door shut.

"And when the guy you're selling the guns to comes by, you just go about your business, pretend I'm not here," I add.

Slowly, he turns the key in the lock and straightens. "Don't know what you're talking about." He putters around the shop with occasional furtive glances to see how I'm holding up but he needn't worry. I'm quite happy to stand here and do nothing. I *practice* doing nothing.

Having a cop standing around can't be any good for business, however, and the broker becomes more agitated. When there's a commotion at the rear of the building he says, "All right, take the damn rock. Just get out of here!" He starts for the gate to the room behind the counter.

"Make out a receipt and I'm gone."

"Receipt?"

"I told you, this is all on the up and up."

"All right, all right!" He scribbles a few lines in a padded receipt book and tears out a copy for me. "Now will you beat it?"

"One more thing."

"What!" His eyes slide to the room behind him.

"Who sold you the ring?"

"Goddam!"

"Come on. Either you've got a bill of sale, which I can get a warrant to see anyhow, or you don't, in which case you're in even worse trouble."

"Hey, I told you, I ain't no fence. I got a bill of sale."

I grab a fist full of his shirt, pull his face closer to mine. "You got it from Nikki Saint Clair, didn't you? Didn't you?"

"Shit. Well, I guess it don't matter, she's flown. Yeah, it was Nikki."

"Have you gotten other pieces from her?"

"You said 'one more thing'," the pawnbroker wails. He tugs to get out of my grasp but I hold firm.

"Tell me!"

"Yeah, a few."

"Starting when?"

"Hell, I don't know. Four weeks ago, six, something like that. Then nothing until this."

About that time, according to Carlotta Trephino, Hector dropped out of the Cuban cigar club and took up with Nikki.

"Now go on, get out of here," the pawnbroker whines.

I get because suddenly I am out of time. The pawnbroker said that Nikki had already left town but if I hurry, maybe I can pick up her trail before it cools. The emerald ring is more than a compromising lump in my pocket, it's a millstone around my neck. There isn't time for a detour to stow it in Old Paint much less take it to the station. I jam it onto my left pinkie and turn the stone toward my palm to make it less conspicuous.

Though night has tightened an icy grip on the Miracle Mile I work up a sweat beating feet to the Metro. Urgency fuels me with an energy exhibited by few others on this street.

At the Metro, the bouncer stops my advance on the dressing room. "Where you think you going, fool?" he asks.

"To see Nikki—"

"I don't think so." He clamps my shoulders in two meaty paws and spins me in the direction I've come from.

"You don't understand," I dig in my heels but he has me off-balance.

"Let him go," says a female voice from behind.

The bouncer loosens his grip and we both turn. It's the cigarette girl.

"Better hurry," she says. "Nikki's on her way out."

Nikki hasn't flown, but flight is definitely in her immediate plans. She's wearing clothes, all over her body. A suitcase stands in the middle of the room. An outer garment is draped over the armchair. A black cape. With a hood.

"Will, sugar, come on in," she says. "Nikki was just about to have herself a drink. Pour one for you?" In her haste she knocks over a perfume bottle and a lilies-of-the-valley fragrance fills the air. She holds out a glass of creme de menthe.

The memory of how sickening the green stuff is turns my stomach. Still, a little nip might help me cope with the Nearvana jones. I drink the stuff down. "Where you going, Nikki?"

"Going? Places, Will. Somewhere better than here. Atlantic City, maybe. Or Vegas, where it's warm. Nikki's retiring."

"Where'd you get the money to give up all this?" With a sweep of my hand I include the dressing room cluttered with costumes, street clothes, makeup cases, and props.

She squares her shoulders. "Made it the old-fashioned way: earned it," she says in a misguided parody of an investment firm's slogan. "You see the kind of money Nikki pulls in. They can't throw it at her fast enough."

"Sure. You wouldn't also happen to do a little private dancing on the side?"

She pouts. "Nikki has a few fans who are willing to pay for a personal performance."

"Was Hector Waltann one of them?"

"Who?"

"Did he pay you with jewelry from his store?"

"What are you talking about?"

"Don't play stupid with me, Nikki."

"All right, Nikki knew him. So what? No one got hurt. It was a consenting adult thing."

"One of those adults is now dead."

She plants a hand on a tight hip. "Well, of course he's dead, sugar. Why else would you be asking about him?" She shrugs. "But Nikki can't help you. Nikki certainly didn't kill him. Nikki hasn't even seen him in a while."

"Define 'a while.'"

"Weeks." She pours fresh glasses of creme de menthe. "Have another, sugar."

I sip this one more slowly. "You're lying, Nikki. You've been fencing the stuff he gave you and you sold a piece just the other day." Which is now burning a hole in my fist.

"Nikki didn't fence it, she pawned it. Hector gave Nikki the ring ages ago."

She steps up to me and rests her forehead on my chest. Quickly, I estimate her height to be just about right to match the mystery woman's description. Just about right to stab a man in the gut.

"But Nikki doesn't see Hector anymore. He left her. For another." She repositions herself to look up with big sad eyes while pressing her body against mine. This sandwiches the Beretta between us, but she doesn't comment.

"So you killed him."

"Don't be silly. Why kill him? He was one of Nikki's best johns. Nikki wants him back, not dead." She grinds against me more insistently. "Can't you leave it alone? Nikki didn't hurt anybody."

"I think you'd better come with me." And we'd better go now, while I'm still standing.

"Nikki has a better idea. Why don't you come with her?" She gives me the bump-and-grind I saw her give the pole on stage.

"No thanks." My body is finding it difficult to resist joining this tango.

"Be a better life than what you're living now. Nikki would see you would never want for anything. We could party all night, do whatever we want during the day. Or nothing, just take it easy. The good life."

She fondles me. For a moment I indulge in the fantasy: days spent in languid inertia or dazzled in casinos whiling away the hours, nightlong orgies of mindless indulgence. No work, no stress, no fear, no hunger. Every need satisfied or drugged out of existence. Such a life did the Devil's own three daughters offer the Buddha to divert him from finally achieving release from suffering. He was not swayed, but I am no Buddha.

She takes my fists and places them on her breasts. "Come on, sugar. You know you want to." With thumbs she pries my hands open. "Hey, what's this?" she asks. "It's Nikki's ring! Where'd you get Nikki's ring?"

"You know where."

She peels herself away. The absence of her body leaves me chilled. She steps to the vanity and returns with two glasses of emerald liquid.

"How 'bout one for the road?"

"No thanks." I've had enough. The stuff has gone to my head. Can it really be garden-variety liqueur? With blurry eyes, I spot the bottle still sitting on the vanity next to the booze and cough syrup bottles. Cough syrup. Prescription cough syrup. *With codeine? Which would be difficult for a dupe to detect if disguised by equally sweet, syrupy creme de menthe?* Aw, dammit, Nikki!

"That's too bad," says a gruff voice from the corner behind the dress rack. "It would have been easier for us if you had."

A shotgun barrel pokes out from between two feather boas. The garments part and Marvin Overshort emerges, pink feathers draped across one shoulder.

My head spins from the shock, the alcohol, and the codeine.

"He's armed," Nikki tells Overshort.

"Take it away from him!" Overshort replies. "And get his handcuffs. Cuff 'im."

She frisks me, which under other circumstances I would have enjoyed. "He doesn't have any," she wails.

"No handcuffs? What the hell kind of cop? ... " Overshort looks disappointed. "Well, find something else to tie him up with. Nylons. You got nylons, dontcha?"

"Of course," Nikki says, and rummages around in a corner.

"Hands and feet. Tie him up. Hands *behind* his back, you moron," Overshort says. "You. Sit," he tells me, and with the weapon shoves me into Nikki's vanity chair.

Not the Beretta automatic he had at the Hunt Club, this is a short-barreled, pump-action Winchester. I think I know what kind of game he hunts with this one. In these close quarters, Overshort wouldn't even have to be a good shot to hurt me, so I comply. My knees were about to buckle anyway.

Nikki's chair is low to the ground. Seated with my knees higher than my hips, I feel like a fractious schoolboy sentenced to the corner. Like the hero in some kinky bondage flick I sit in a pink vanity chair while a voluptuous woman at my feet binds me with black fishnet stockings. They make a strong rope—it's not for nothing we use nylon ties as restraints on the force—and Nikki gets me trussed up good, the bindings tighter than they need to be.

"He's got my ring," Nikki says. She points to my hands.

Overshort peers over my shoulder. I keep my fists clenched. The show of petulance only gets me cuffed in the head with the shotgun barrel.

"Get it off him," Overshort says.

On her knees again, Nikki tugs at the ring.

"It won't come off!"

"Shit!" Overshort taps his foot in annoyance. "You got a knife, scissors, something like that?"

Nikki gets to her feet and digs around on the vanity. "Will these do?" She holds up a pair of craft scissors.

"Have to. Cut it off him."

"The ring? With these?"

"Not the ring, dimwit, his finger. Cut it off!"

A plug forms in my throat as I picture myself slumped in this pink chair, blood spurting from my mutilated hand like water from a hose.

"Nikki can't do that!" she says. "You cut it off."

"I'm holding the gun! All right, I'll get it later."

I don't like the sound of that "later."

"Now get Quince," Overshort says. "I'm gonna need both of you."

His words penetrate the codeine fog. *Heidi help?* Overshort's hold over her is that strong?

"Now wait just a minute, sugar. Nikki was on her way out of town when the pawnbroker called. You said, 'Hold him till I get there,' and Nikki's done that. So, see ya around."

"I said Quince and I could handle him if you got him drugged up, but you didn't. Now you'll have to help get rid of him. Don't screw with me, Nikki. The sooner we take care of him the sooner we can all disappear. Now go get Quince!"

Nikki pulls on her cape and takes off as fast as her high heels will carry her. Overshort stands spread-legged, shotgun pointed at my chest. I don't want to look at it but I can barely hold up my head. The nylons are so tight they're cutting off the circulation to my hands and feet. I can feel them tingle. There might be a chance later. Overshort won't do me here. He means to move me, and maybe I can make a break for it in the process.

I shift in the chair. My cramped position has set off waves of pain in my thigh. "Just what exactly is the game, Overshort? Fake jewelry?"

"Yeah, fake jewelry. I buy crap, sell it for serious cash. Easy. Yeah. I do the ordering, I handle the books. Both sets."

There's a knock on the door and Overshort admits Heidi. She strides toward me with the same confidence I saw in her that first time when she crossed the Facets lobby to greet me. Gone is the elegantly dressed delicate female who clung to me, the damsel in distress, if she ever was. Instead, garbed in a black jacket, slacks, and sturdy shoes she stands with chin up, shoulders back, and looks down her nose at me.

"The chumps aren't any the wiser," Overshort says. "They get paper certifying the junk is the real thing from our gemologist here."

"You were in on it all along?" I ask Heidi. My speech sounds slurred.

She smiles. Her green eyes are hard as glass.

To Heidi I say, "You set me up at the bookstore. You told him I'd be there." And to Overshort, "It was you in the Eterniti."

"Ah, the Eterniti. That was a stroke. Didn't want to use my car, or Quince's, in case someone saw me. Even if they made the Eterniti, so what?"

"I warned you about looking for Hector," Heidi says to me. "I begged you to quit."

"Before I got wise to what you two were up to, the way Hector did."

Overshort laughs. "Are you kidding? Hector didn't have a clue. He was so busy fucking himself up he didn't know what was going on. It was his boy, Terry, I was worried about. He really was a gemologist. But all I had to do was fire him. He didn't even fight to keep his job. No backbone. Like father, like son."

"Marvin, do you really have to tell him all this?" Heidi asks.

He can't help it, he's a braggart. If I keep stroking him, I can probably get the whole thing. And if I keep talking, maybe I can keep from passing out. "Having a spare remote for the car helped, I guess."

"Found it Hector's desk when I moved into his office. Enough of this yak. Time to go. Get up."

The struggle to stand on cramped legs and bloodless feet insensible as blocks of wood brings me to my knees.

"You fuck!" Overshort says. "What's the matter with you?"

"Feet fell asleep. Can't walk. I think I broke my ankle trying to stand."

"I'll untie him," Nikki offers.

Yes!

"Not a chance!" Overshort says.

Damn!

"And just for insurance ..." He swings to whack me in the head with the gun barrel. I see it coming and turn my face, take it on the ear instead of the temple. It rings my bell but good and I keel over.

In a codeine-and-concussion stupor, I hear Overshort as if from a great distance. "We'll have to carry him out to the car. Heidi, hold the gun on him. Shoot him if he moves. Nikki, take his feet." Overshort grabs me under the arms. Nikki grasps my feet and gets tangled up in her cloak.

"Dammit, Nikki, ditch that stupid rag."

"It's cold outside."

"Then find something else."

The tall, red-headed figure of Nikki hunts through the clothes on the rack and selects a blue Windbreaker and matching cap. *The Pizza Boy at Hector's condo?*

Overshort and Nikki get me horizontal. They carry me out the back door, Nikki tottering on her high heels, to the waiting Eterniti.

"Put him in the trunk?" Nikki asks, panting.

"Nah. I want him where I can keep an eye on him. In the back seat. Get in the back with him. "Keep that gun of his on him."

Won't do her any good. Not loaded.

"Quince, you drive. I'll tell you where." Overshort directs her north, away from the Mile, onto Forbes Road.

Forbes Road. Jade Pagoda. Scott Corcoran. Monetta. *Me, next?*

"I owe that pawnbroker for tipping us off," Overshort says.

I am back in the pawnshop, where the pawnbroker claims the phone is busted. I see myself leave, see him call Nikki and Overshort, give them the head's up. Next I picture my first visit to the Metro. Nikki asks for five minutes alone in her dressing room. While I wait, Overshort leaves her dressing room, gets in the Eterniti, fires on me in the alley.

"Nikki's been good to him," she replies.

Overshort says, "You're a tight little bunch, you Miracle Mile folks. Share everything, dontcha: news, drugs, lovers?"

"Now you shut your mouth about that," Nikki says.

Overshort laughs. "He's gonna miss that good Facets merchandise you were fencing for Hector."

It would be so easy to succumb to the pain and intoxicants. I struggle to hear and understand. *Hector was ripping off his own place? Did he commit the theft?* No wonder it looked like an inside job. And no wonder Overshort discouraged the insurance company and the police from taking a close look.

"Well, if Hector's dead, that kind of shuts off that supply, doesn't it?" Nikki says.

Facets' cleaning woman and security officer ... did they catch Hector in the act? Did Hector kill them, making the murders look like a carjacking and a suicide? Between his personal assets and Facets' inventory, Hector has run through a lot of cash. That must have been some heroin habit.

"Got shut off the minute I stopped buying genuine stones. Funny thing, that dealer Hector was scoring from never noticed," Overshort says. "Wonder what Hector's latest squeeze is gonna do for dope now that Sugar Daddy is gone."

"Like Nikki cares." Her tone is sour.

Oh, so the Nearvana wasn't all for Hector. Carlotta did say he was buying enough for two. So who was this lover?

"Don't this heap go any faster?" Overshort asks. "Let's get there already."

There? Where? I open my eyes a crack. The sky is dark. Gone is the neon brightness of the Miracle Mile, the daylight-yellow glow of the city's sulfur lamps. We're somewhere rural.

"With Hector dead, it's sort of the end of that gravy train for us, too," Nikki says.

"Yeah, whoever wasted Hector did me no kind of favor. Now I gotta deal with Marybeth and his insurance people, not to mention this dude. What do I need with that noise? 'Bout time we got out of town anyway, the way Mansion's been poking into those little personnel actions we had to take."

Personnel actions? Does he mean the cleaning lady and the security officer? Did Overshort kill them? He said "we." He and Nikki? He and ... Heidi?

"Put a lid on it, Marvin, for God's sake," Heidi hisses. Her voice is full of menace.

"What?"

"Mansion's hearing every word."

Overshort twists to eye me over the back of the seat. "Mansion's out cold. Even if he's not, it don't matter. He won't be telling anyone. OK, turn here."

"Here?" Heidi echoes.

I share her befuddlement. We don't seem to be anywhere, just a cul-de-sac off Riverside Drive. Heidi stops.

"Get us down closer to the river," Overshort says.

"Be serious. There's no pavement. From here's it's just graded. This isn't an off-road vehicle."

"Do it!"

After a moment's hesitation, Heidi takes us at a crawl over rough terrain. After a few yards she stops again.

"I didn't say 'stop,'" Overshort yells.

"If I go any farther, we'll get stuck," she replies firmly.

"Great. We'll have to carry him the rest of the way," he says. "Quince, guard him. Nikki, take his feet."

Nikki and Overshort lift me up as before and tramp through the underbrush, Heidi close behind with the shotgun. Nikki stumbles in her high heels, drops my feet. Overshort swears, demands her shoes, and tears the heels off.

A few yards later, the river comes into view. They mean to drop me in and I tell myself this is good, I'm a decent swimmer. I don't mention it will be cold, I'll be weighed down by my clothing, and hampered by the restraints. The chance that I'll get very far, very fast is slim, but I'll take it. Before I can imagine what my first move should be when I hit the water, Overshort stops. He and Nikki dump me, not in the river but in the grass.

"What?" Nikki asks.

"I'm just thinking. He might come to in the water. Maybe we should plug him first," Overshort says. "Nikki, where's that gun of his?"

Good idea. Shoot me with an unloaded gun. That would give me a chance to run—if I weren't trussed like a turkey, if I weren't numb from codeine and creme de menthe. If I could feel my feet. I've got to get him to untie me.

Overshort pulls the trigger. The gun makes an unproductive click. "Shit," Overshort says. "What the fuck's the matter with this? Nikki, take this piece of shit. Heidi, give me the shotgun."

He jacks in a round, something I've done to impress an offender with my seriousness. It works. I cringe; my head goes light.

"Shit, he's awake," Overshort says. He nudges me with his foot. "Mansion, you awake?"

"Yeah, Overshort. What are you going to do? Shoot me here in cold blood, Great White Hunter?"

"Oh, I forgot," he replies, a sneer in his voice. "That wouldn't be sportsmanlike. Ok, have it your way. Stand up."

This time I don't have to feign impairment. I can get to my knees but can't get to feet I can't feel.

"Stand or I will shoot you right here!"

If I look up it will be into the barrel of a shotgun and then I will lose it entirely, so I keep my head bowed.

"Nikki, untie his feet."

Nikki kneels down beside me and tugs at the bindings. As the ties loosen, I wriggle and shift to make the process of freeing me take as long as possible, buying time to get some circulation back in my feet.

Finally, Nikki announces success and waves the nylons in the air. Slowly I raise a knee and put weight on one foot. What must be gallons of blood rush all at once into parched vessels. My legs threaten to explode. Savage pins-and-needles make me whimper.

Overshort says, "Get up, you fucking wimp!"

Still moving a muscle at a time, I struggle into a crouch, the pain so crippling it threatens to topple me again. On screaming legs I rise to a standing position which brings my chest up against the muzzle of Overshort's gun.

CHAPTER 23

My vision blurs and my gut flips. I'm zoning out. I'm as good as dead.

"Ladies, we're gonna shoot ourselves some waterfowl here tonight," Overshort says.

With me a sitting duck. Despite the cold, I'm drenched in sweat.

Sounding detached, Overshort says, "This'll be like a delay round. Mansion, after Quince here yells 'Ready,' you'll have up to three seconds before I start firing. You won't know how many seconds, though." He lowers the gun.

I won't gamble on three. On still wobbly legs, I take off, limping, running blind. Zigging, zagging, I try to stay low but pain makes a half-crouch agony and I straighten.

"She didn't say 'Ready,'" Overshort yells and the first charge explodes to my left, lead hail. Startled crows take to the air, squawking. I catch some shot in the shoulder, yelp with pain but I don't stop, don't slow. I run squats, torturous squats. Nikki shouts, "Did ya get him?" and I charge even harder through the foliage. Birds abandon their roosts, small animals flee my advance—squirrels, a raccoon, a fox? Roots trip me, the moss is slippery. Bushes whap my legs, low branches scratch my face. With my hands tied I can't push them aside, can only keep my feet going and head down, pinballing from tree trunk to tree trunk.

Or are the tall structures on either side of me buildings, the surface under my feet asphalt? Where am I? Is the haze before my eyes riparian mist or gun smoke? Am I at the river's edge or on Terminal Road? Running from Overshort or Shrike? Unable to use my arms for balance, I skid into a tree. I break my fall with my birdshot shoulder, waking angry nerves that adrenalin had put to sleep, and clench my teeth against the pain.

"Did ya get him?" Nikki calls again.

"Shut up! I can't hear," Overshort hollers back.

Hear. Of course! He can't see in the dark any better than I can, he's aiming by ear. If I take him at his word, that he's not much of a field shooter, he won't be good at this. *Now, how to make tracks without making noise?*

Afraid to make another move, afraid not to, I stand frozen. Overshort gets off another shot. It grazes by so closely that I can feel the heat, smell the powder, hear the pellets punch wood and snap twigs.

"Where is he? I don't see him," Nikki says.

"Shut up!" Overshort fires twice more in a sweep which I escape by mere feet. There's a second of relative silence while he reloads. He fired four shots. *Was the gun fully loaded before he started shooting? Damn, I wish I knew!*

"He's getting away," Heidi cries.

"If he does it's your fault," Overshort replies. "Why didn't you yell 'Ready?'"

Why didn't she?

"Well, where is he?" Nikki asks. "Do you think he's trying to make it back to the car?"

I haven't been, although I could probably find it. I've been running roughly parallel to the river. To reach the car, I'd have to break cover. Besides, once there, what would I do? There's no way I could get into the car much less drive with my hands tied, couldn't get loose in time to make an escape. But Overshort might not see it that way. I scout out a stone and punt it toward the road with a kick worthy of the Superbowl. It costs me a lance of pain but the stone clears the bushes and crash-lands into the grass a satisfying fifty yards away.

"Yes," Overshort hollers, and blasts his way through the brush toward the sound.

I sprint in the opposite direction, plant my feet heel first, a hunting stealth technique. My newly-wounded shoulder burns. I feel light-headed and wonder if I've lost a lot of blood.

"Where is he?" Nikki's voice is faint.

Overshort says, "I was sure he ... I heard him!"

"Must have been an animal," Heidi says.

"An animal?" Nikki echoes with alarm.

"A chipmunk or something, Nikki, dammit," Overshort says. "Back the other way. Nikki, use that damn gun of his, huh? Shoot anything you see." His voice is already close.

I hear an abortive click. Nikki wails, "It's still jammed!"

My amusement is short-lived. I have run down a blind alley. An impenetrable thicket bars the way ahead. The hunting party rapidly approaches to my right and rear. To my left, the river courses in its bed, dark as cold coffee. There is only one way to go.

No time for second thoughts. I roll into the water. The shock of the cold immobilizes, steals my breath, and stuns my muscles, but it clears my head. I had some vague plan to hide in the shallows, submerged just under the surface but I am already in deep water. Saturated shoes, holster, and clothes pull me down like lead weights. I toe off the shoes but with my hands bound can do nothing about the holster or the jacket. With outraged muscles in knots and tortured lungs gasping for air, I frog-kick to the surface, try frog-kicking upriver, away from Overshort. The jacket slides off my shoulders down onto my arms, snags at my bound wrists and slows me like a parachute. I have to stop every few seconds and lift my face out of the water to breathe. I could be running up a down escalator for all the headway I'm making. From my apartment window, the river never looked this fast. *How do salmon do this upstream swimming?* Out of breath, I stop to rest, kick to keep from sinking.

"Mansion, you can't hide," Overshort yells. "There's three of us and only one of you and we have all the ammo." He fires off a few rounds to prove it.

Heart pounding, I renew my efforts to swim. Instinctively, my arms try to stroke and I find that the same water that turned my jacket to dead weight has made the stockings binding my wrists flaccid. I work them loose. Lightning bolts of mind-paralyzing pain accompany the return of circulation to my hands but it's not as bad as having to put weight on numb feet. I shed the jacket and holster.

I start to swim in earnest and find no power at all in my left shoulder, only pain. The entire onus of stroking falls on the right arm which is not up to the task and I pull to one side like a car with a bad alignment. I use the worthless left arm as a rudder and swim that way until the sounds of the hunting party become reassuringly more distant.

Adrenalin has carried me far but now I've exhausted even that. It's is all I can do to keep moving. Teeth hurt from chattering, ears ache in the cold air. The water, at first too cold to taste, now coats the back of my throat with the flavor of dead fish, rotted wood, old tires, fuel oil, and God knows what pollutants. I have swallowed so much it swells my stomach.

My plan had been to swim upstream and come ashore at the boat launch where the scullers put in. Now that seems an impossible dream. I'm sore all over and tired, so tired. The urge to stretch out and simply float for a while is irresistible but the minute I quit struggling against the stream it washes me back toward where I started in half the time it took me to swim it.

All I can do is "go with the flow." I turn and float downstream.

As I near the point at which I entered the water, I hear the three pursuers shooting along the bank. I breathe deep and dive. The deep water is even colder than at the surface and I have to force myself to stay under its dark cover. Finally out of breath, I surface a few yards downstream, float quietly with the current and listen for the hunting party. From the sound of it they don't appear to have moved far or noticed I've passed them. Encouraged, I renew my efforts to swim, this time aided rather than impeded by the current.

Not for long. Fatigue returns with a vengeance and I long to sleep. It's hypothermia. The danger is I'll fall asleep without even realizing it. If I do, I'll drown or Overshort will catch me but I'm too tired to care. A nap, just a tiny nap ... I'm not even aware that I've fallen asleep until I try to breathe under water and have to struggle back to the surface, spewing river water and stifling a gag.

I fight to stay awake the way I do when I meditate, by paying attention to each moment, to each breath. In and out, in and out. It's hard work. It's said that the mental effort made by Zen monks meditating in their frigid mountain caves generates so much body heat they can turn ice into steam.

A sensation of acceleration jostles me from reverie. I'm moving faster, much faster. No, the water is moving faster, carrying me with it. *Why?* I raise my head and get my bearings. In the distance, light close to the bank silhouettes tall buildings. *Where the hell am I?*

The buildings are the profile of the Shays' Landing condominium townhouses. In building it, the developers straightened and narrowed the river's natural contours, causing the water to run faster.

If I can make it to the condos, I can find help. Someone to call the police, and an ambulance. I swim toward the condo across the current but it's too fast, too strong for a one-armed, one-legged paddler. The bank could be miles away instead of yards.

Fighting the river drains me. The current carries me away from the bank, toward the middle of the river, downstream and away from rescue. My next chance is miles away where the river runs under the bridge to come within feet of my own Riverbank Road, but I won't make it. My leg, my shoulder, my swimming arm are limp noodles. Sleep. Sleep now.

Relaxed, I slip down, down. All is pleasant—until imminent drowning awakens the instinct to survive. I stroke back to the surface, renew my struggle toward the bank ... and hit the wall, literally and figuratively.

Energy depleted, in dismay I flounder before the retaining wall the Shays' Landing developers installed to shore up the riverbank and prevent erosion. Even with my arm extended straight up, the wall's top edge is still six inches past my fingertips, six inches that could be six hundred. The river bottom is too far below me to push off from.

In despair, I look down river for an easier beachhead but I know this is it. I have to make it here, there won't be another chance. Digging deep into my muscles, I frog-kick, trying to propel myself up and out of the water but with each try I fall increasing short of the goal, groaning in desperation. Long scrapes sting in stripes from shoulder to waist. My shirt is shreds.

Scrapes. *What scraped me?* Kicking, fighting currents that want to drag me downstream, I probe the sheet pilings. Below the surface a brace runs horizontally across the interlocking sheets.

I'm no mountaineer but I have done a little rock-climbing. I can do this. To make myself as light as possible, I pitch my wallet and keys onto the bank, wriggle out of my shredded shirt. Though cold air glazes wet shoulders, the sensation of water against bare skin is liberating. I breathe, imagine myself weightless and slick, picture myself a torpedo breaking the surface tension of the water, the grip of gravity. Putting everything I have into one mighty kick, I propel myself up against the piling. Toes scrabble for the brace, not quite wide enough to stand on. Half-pushing, half-pulling, I stretch to scale the sheet piling. My fingers contact ...*a rope?* I tug on it. A piece comes off in my hand and I nearly lose my perch on the brace.

It's not a rope but some kind of vining plant. *Wild or part of the Shays' Landing landscaping?* Either way, it might be just enough help. I stretch my good arm, elongate my torso and my good leg. My fingers find the dangling plant. Pulling with my good arm, pushing with my good leg, knotted muscles screaming, ready to tear, I clamber up and over the wall and collapse, gasping, onto the grass. I puke river water until I'm empty, then retch dry heaves. Lightheaded, I rest until the cold on my back warns me that I can't relax, won't be safe until I get shelter and get dry. Pocketing my wallet and keys, I creep toward the light. Crawling with a bad leg and worse shoulder is impossible so I get to my feet and lurch ahead.

To no surprise, the Shays' Landing main gate is locked. As I stand there struggling to stay upright, the headlights of an approaching car advance down the road toward me. I raise my arm to wave, then stop, suddenly paralyzed. *Overshort? Could he have seen me go into the river, followed my flight downstream?*

The car slows. I scuttle back toward the river. There's a loud thud behind me. I hit the dirt. Headlights cut an arc along the end of the street. The white of headlights turns to the red of taillights as the car turns one-eighty and goes back the way it came.

When they have vanished, I return to the gate by cautious inches. Now a stack of *Criers* tied with plastic twine lies at its foot. The slow-cruising vehicle was the newspaper carrier's car, the thump the sound of the papers hitting the sidewalk. Soon, I realize, someone will come to distribute them throughout the complex. Until then they will dry me, cover me. I drag them over to where sheltering junipers hug the brick wall, work the papers loose, use some of them to blot wet clothes and the rest as blankets. Just before I fade out I catch the headline: SMOKIN' DEAL—CAR LOT TORCHED.

After what seems like an hour but is probably just a few minutes, heavy footsteps approach the gate from within the complex. A flashlight beam on the pavement precedes the clank of the automatic gate.

"Oh, Lordy, look at this mess, newspapers all over," a deep female voice says. "Damn kids, I catch 'em I'm going to—hey! Hey you!"

Who, me? I want to say. My mouth opens but nothing comes out except a croak.

"Move along now. Folks pay too much to live here to have bums sleeping on their sidewalk." The woman steps into the light. A puffy brown parka with a Security Service patch on the sleeve makes her short, wide body even stockier. She waggles her flashlight at me as if the beam itself will push me away. "Move along now or I'll have to call the police."

"I am ..."

"Say what?"

"Police." Under the soggy newspapers I fumble with icicle fingers for my wallet.

"Now you stop that. Don't be doing that here," she says. "I told you to stop!" She produces a cell phone and calls the police before I can reach my identification.

I lie back and wait for them to arrive.

CHAPTER 24

In the window glass,
mockingbird's worst enemy!
This guy just won't quit!—S_zan

Before the first cruiser arrives, I've gotten out soggy but sufficient identification. It reassures the security officer enough for her to leave me unguarded while she runs to get a blanket and her thermos. Hot coffee revives me enough to give a sketchy report to the first-responding patrolman. He springs into action, calls for another car and an ambulance. I give him the make, model, and tag numbers of my abductors' vehicle, Hector Waltann's gold Eterniti.

"I don't know if the three of them are traveling together," I say, my voice barely above a whisper. Despite the coffee, my throat is raw and sore. "If they've split up, Quince has a green BMW. I don't know what Saint Clair drives. She might be headed for Atlantic City or Vegas."

"That's OK, sir, don't worry about it. You just take it easy, we'll find them," the patrolman replies, then sets into motion the machinery that will apprehend Overshort and Company.

The paramedics who follow close on the heels of a second cruiser find me weak but lucid.

"I can walk," I tell the young woman in white who wheels a gurney to my side, although when I move I find that muscles driven to their limit have set up hard as concrete. Scratches, scrapes, slices, punctures and bruises compete to see which can make me scream.

"Sure you can, but why walk when you can ride?" the EMT asks. To her partner she says, "On three." They transfer me to the gurney and slide me into the back of an ambulance.

"I've briefed your lieutenant," the first responding officer tells me. "He'll meet you at the hospital. He says you have a lot of explaining to do."

Compared to where I've spent the last eight hours, the ambulance is toasty and I want nothing more than to sleep and escape the pain. Instead, the paramedics poke and prod and pepper me with questions all the way to the hospital.

In the ER, they cut away ruined clothes stinking of river bottom. A nurse points to the emerald ring on my finger. "Want to hold onto that, or do you want us to put it away for safekeeping?"

I figure I'd better hold onto it so there's no question about breaks in the chain of custody.

The doctor on duty is one of the team who brought me back from the dead the night of the Terminal Road shootout. He directs the nurse to prepare an injection. "Just a little something for pain," he says.

"No. No drugs," I tell him.

"You've got to be kidding," he replies. "The way you look, you've got to be hurting."

He's right about that. But the pain at least lets me know I'm alive, and I've had enough of narcotics.

"A local at least while I operate," he says, and I let him administer that.

"You don't plan to make getting shot a monthly occurrence, do you?" he asks while he meticulously picks pellets out of my shoulder and back. Out of the corner of my eye I see him step away to admire his work. "The wounds themselves aren't too serious, not like this was." He gently pats my thigh and instructs me to roll over. Offhandedly he says, "The tattoo is new. Mind if I take a look?"

"Go ahead."

"I wouldn't have figured you for a body art man. No signs of infection here, at least. You got good post-operative care."

"I'm a fast healer."

"Well, good. This latest injury shouldn't give you any problems, then. Oh, there'll be a degree of residual neuralgia, but you have some familiarity in that department."

"Yes."

"Watch the wound and lacerations for infection. Interesting first aid technique you used, keeping them irrigated and chilled, but I would have chosen something other than river water." He applies antiseptic to the front of my body which couldn't be any more scraped if I'd tried to Brillo myself clean. As a fresh blanket of pain spreads across my skin I wonder why he didn't simply set me on fire.

"We'll keep you twenty-four hours or so, get you started on a course of antibiotics, get your electrolytes in line. You can take it from there. Nothing that rest won't fix. A lot of rest. Understand me?"

He doesn't have to tell me twice. If everyone would just leave me alone I'd start right now. To find the pauses between the mayday signals from the besieged battleship of my body I need to concentrate, to work with the pain.

"See me again when you want to be cleared to return to duty," the doctor says, "although frankly, I'd advise finding another line of work."

"I'm considering it," I reply.

He chuckles and waves me into the care of an orderly who wheels me out. A puffy-eyed Lieutenant Crowberry stands just outside the Emergency Room door. This is no social call. He has questions and I won't be allowed to sleep until I answer them. He follows us wordlessly to the ward, waits while a pretty nurse with bright red lipstick gets me gowned, tucked in a bed, and hooked up to an IV. Her white uniform reminds me of the costume Nikki St. Clair wore the first time I saw her.

"After you've had a chance to rest some, I'll come back and help you get cleaned up better," the nurse says. She lowers her voice, says, "Can't wait for a closer look at that tattoo," and gives me a wink before departing.

"It never quits with you, does it, Mansion?" Crowberry sighs. "Do I have your attention now?"

All I want to do is snuggle down in these clean white sheets and pull the blanket over me. "Lieutenant, I'm beat."

"You'll want to hear this. We've got an APB out for Overshort, Quince, and Saint Clair. It won't be long before we get them."

Get them? Oh, right. Once I'd escaped them, I pictured them riding off into the sunset, or perhaps more accurately the sunrise, and the further they got away from me the better I liked it. Of course, our relationship has only just begun, albeit on a different plane. I only hope when I next see Heidi that I can hide my hurt and humiliation.

Crowberry spots a chrome-frame side chair with a split-pea green vinyl seat and pulls it over to the bed, settling in for a long stay.

"Mansion, what the hell were you trying to do?"

"My assignment, sir. Find Waltann's killer."

"I didn't say 'single-handed.' It's not a one-man job. That's why we have a team to work on it. Maybe you've heard of it, we call it a 'squad.'"

I am too tired to parry Crowberry's jabs. "I wrote a   report—"

"Ah, your report. Something about heroin and cigars I recall. Wildest shit I've ever read in a report. I checked that out. Yeah, looked into it myself personally. Funny thing, though. When I got to the car lot, I found it had been burned down."

The headline on the papers I wrapped my cold wet self in this morning crawls across my brain like an electronic billboard: SMOKIN' DEAL, CAR LOT TORCHED. Hope bubbles in my blood like fizzy tonic.

"So, no stogies, no tequila, no smack," Crowberry says.

"No plastic bag with a cigar stub and a shot glass?" I ask.

"If there ever was one. Which I have a hard time believing. Yeah, that was some wild shit." Crowberry laughs but his face is stormy. "Nope, not a shred of evidence. Too bad Airol Jones didn't know that when we went to interview him." Crowberry laughs again and this time his whole face joins in. "You know, he may be a hard charger on the court, but off it the man's a creampuff. It was just no problem cutting a deal with him to give up Carlotta Trephino."

Crowberry shifts on his chair. "Now what about this fraud at the jewelry store? What the hell has that got to do with anything?"

"Everything, sir," I reply, but I don't have the energy to elaborate. "The murder of the cleaning lady."

"Oh, yeah. You left Grady some chicken-scratch about shell casings."

The one Grady collected at the Jade Pagoda where Monetta, Facets' cleaning lady, was fatally ambushed. And the ones I palmed at the Hunt Club and the bookstore. "There were matches."

"Yes there were."

I name the evidence case numbers I assigned to the bookstore sample and the parking lot ambush. Crowberry nods.

"They were from Overshort's gun." I suggest a scenario. According to Monetta's boss at Clean Sweep, the cleaning woman went AWOL for a time, then reappeared, explaining she had fled because she was upset about the theft at Facets. Thinking the crime would be pinned on her, Monetta may have bolted after the theft, then worked out that Hector had burgled his own store, and returned. She contacted Overshort, maybe to be helpful, or possibly for blackmail. Either way it cost her her life. "Overshort killed her."

"Or someone using his gun did," Crowberry says, not ready to cut me any slack.

"And he killed Corcoran, the security officer. Not a suicide. Murder. Similar scenario."

Crowberry nods. "We've reopened the case."

"But Overshort didn't kill Waltann. Neither did Quince. Nor did Saint Clair, despite her having a black cape. They wanted Hector scarce, not dead."

He leans forward in his chair. "So who did?"

"I don't know, Lieutenant." What's more, I don't care. My brain is pudding, my body hamburger. I want to sleep.

"But you'll find out?" It's as much a plea as a command.

"Lieutenant, I've been drugged, hogtied, kidnapped, hounded through the woods at gunpoint, shot, and nearly drowned. I don't have to be told twice but apparently you do. I quit." I let my eyelids fall nearly shut.

Crowberry remains seated.

Playing possum, I watch him through my eyelashes. We wait each other out. At last he gets to his feet. "You'll find out," he says with a chuckle. "I know you. A good horse'll run at the shadow of the whip."

I close my eyes completely and try to sleep but the unfamiliar sounds, the stiff bed, and the pain conspire against me. The stink of the river gives way to the sharp smell of disinfectant so strong it hurts to breathe. The harder I try to sleep, the more it eludes me and the more desperate and exhausted I become until the effort of trying to be with the pain, ride its tides, finally wears me down into unconsciousness.

It isn't hunger, pain, or thirst that wakes me. It's an irritating rasping noise, like mice in the walls. I crack open an eye. Carlotta Trephino sits in the side chair, filing her nails.

"Honey, no one has a right to look that good in a hospital gown," she says.

"Carlotta. I understand your place made headlines."

"Ah, the fire. Yes, seems Shrike is tad upset with me about Hector." She studies her manicure, gives her left ring finger an extra swipe. "You'll excuse me, honey, won't you? Got to do something with my hands since they won't let me smoke."

"No, they won't. Nor snort, either."

"Hmph. Speaking of which, you know I never would have sent you to Shrike if I thought you were going to turn righteous on me."

"I'm sure."

"You're a regular Boy Scout, Will Mansion." Carlotta gets to work on the nails of her right hand. "Seems the gemstones Hector was paying Shrike with were fake. If I'd been able to find Hector, I would have encouraged him to correct that mistake, but the man had to go and die and leave Shrike holding the bag—a bag of marbles for all the stuff is worth. Apparently Shrike thinks this is now my problem and lit up my car lot to call it to my attention."

"What a shame."

"Yes, a great loss. Especially the trailer. I had some things in my desk I wish I could have saved."

"Like a shot glass and a cigar stub?"

"Yes, like that. You lucked out, Honey. So much for insurance. Ah, there are few safeguards in life, especially the kind I lead." She sighs and whittles another nail. "Well, it was obviously arson, so now there's investigators crawling all over the place. I can't get a thing done. I'd take a vacation—a long vacation, way out of town—but I've been told to stick around. Little matter of a certain cigar club. Some bright-eyed ADA is accusing me of non-payment of import duties or some such nonsense."

They're going to try to get her in civil court. Not a bad idea. It worked with Al Capone.

"So why are you here?" I regard the silvery nail file with trepidation. It's sharp-pointed, and in the right hands, could do some damage. Like stab a man?

"I was hoping you could put in a good word for me. We're still friends, aren't we, Honey?" When I don't respond, she takes my silence as negative. "I see. One thing I don't understand. Why ever would you bust us when you knew you would go down too?"

I could tell her what I've known for some time but haven't had to articulate until now: karma. What goes around, comes around. There's no escaping it. Not for her. Not for me. Not for anyone. Not in this life. Not in the next.

"Like I said, you're a regular Boy Scout." She opens her purse, drops in the nail file, and closes it with an angry snap.

From mule to Boy Scout in a single week. Now that's what I call right living.

Carlotta isn't long gone before a familiar face peeps inside the door.

"Hey, buddy," he calls softly.

"Hey, Swbyra."

He edges into the room and lowers his lanky body into the side chair. "You keep coming back here, they're gonna start charging you rent."

"What can I do for you, Swbyra?"

"No, no, it's what can I do for you?" He scoots forward on the chair until his knees almost touch the bed. "I would have come to see you sooner but we've been trying to settle the dust you stirred up. In fact, it's not settled yet, but Grady said he'd hold down the fort so I could get over here. He'll be along later."

As if I haven't suffered enough.

"We got Overshort and Quince in custody. They were on their way to Bradley International. Would have made it, too, if it had been closer."

Sometimes not having a local airport is a real liability.

Swbyra gives me that picket fence smile. "Man, you are something. You wrap up in one night what we've been working on for fuckin' weeks—months, even. The cleaning lady's ambush at the Jade Pagoda, Corcoran's bogus suicide, that whole drug ring. We've got Carlotta Trephino where we want her now, yessiree."

"Yeah, but look where it got me."

"True," says Swbyra, sobering. "So how you doin'? You OK?"

"Nothing rest won't fix right up, according to the doc," I reply, but Swbyra doesn't get the hint. He remains glued to his chair.

"And you deserve it. So, anything I can get for you? Water? You got plenty of water?" He lifts the lid of the jug on the bedside table.

"I'm fine. Look, there is something you can do for me."

"Name it."

"Go down to the hospital property locker, get my stuff out."

"No problem."

Swbyra dashes from the room and I grab some winks until he returns with a yellow clasp envelope. Inside are my keys, my badge, my wallet—itself zipped into a plastic bag because it's still damp.

"Thanks. And take custody of this, will you?" I twist the emerald ring off my finger, still somewhat shriveled and pruney.

"This little sparkler looks just like the one that goes with the report you did on the Facets fraud complaint," he says.

"It's supposed to. Or, that one's supposed to look like this. Hector Waltann gave this to Nikki Saint Clair. She pawned it for getaway money. I think you'll find this is the real McCoy. I'm betting once Overshort got control of the store and got rid of Terry Waltann, he bought cheap imitations that he sold as the real thing and pocketed the difference." When Hector burgled the store for jewels to trade for drugs, he got a bunch of glass instead and made an enemy out of Shrike. "With Quince as a certified gemologist vouching for their authenticity, they would have gotten away with it except someone went and got a second opinion."

"Some scam. I'll be damned. Killing Waltann wasn't part of it?"

"No, I don't believe it was."

"So who did?"

"I don't know." Maybe Marybeth Waltann deserves a second look. Or Shrike. The very thought of him makes my skin pucker.

"Well, soon as you're up to it, we can get back to work on it."

"Start without me."

"Make me laugh, 'start without me,' that's good. You said I could do two things. What's the second one?"

I hand him my keys. "Could you bring me some clothes? You know, like the last time? In the ER, they took—"

"Oh, yeah, I know the drill. Shoes?"

"Yeah, shoes."

"Shaving gear, too?"

"Sure." Rounding up all that stuff should keep him busy.

"I'll be back before you know it."

A small price to pay.

No sooner do I drop lids over eyes grainy with exhaustion than Grady shows up. The little side chair creaks under the big man's weight.

"You just missed Swbyra," I tell him.

"That a fact? We got Overshort and Quince charged with fraud, assaulting an officer, and two counts of murder. Wanted to make it three."

"Could have made it three—three assaults on an officer."

Grady frowns. "What the fuck are you talking about?"

"That shooting I was telling you guys about. Behind the Metro?"

His frown deepens. "You've known about Overshort for over a fuckin' week and you didn't say anything?"

"I didn't know. I wasn't sure who was behind it, not until yesterday."

"You could have filled us in."

"I tried to, Grady, but—"

"But what?" He's using that tone, the one that says, "don't fuck with me, slimebag," which he employs to good effect on suspects.

"I just ... I thought I'd get a little more to go on, that's all."

Up to this point he has been motionless in the chair, but now he bunches his shoulders. His already-broad upper body seems to swell. "Is that what you're planning to do with Waltann's killer? We wanted Overshort and Quince for that, too, but the lieut' says you nixed that."

"I just don't think they did Waltann, that's all."

"So who the fuck did?"

"I don't know."

His big hands grip the chair arms. "The fuck you don't. You've been on this thing for weeks. You gotta have some idea. Why won't you tell us?"

"Because I don't know!" The heat of his anger sparks my indignation. "And what's more, I don't care!" I rise halfway to sitting. "I quit. Q-U-I-T, quit! What part don't you people understand?"

Tension puts my body back on full alert. Bells clang, whistles shrill, and I collapse against the pillow.

"If you knew what was good for you, you would!" Like air from a leaky balloon, the anger vents out of him. His body seems to deflate and he sounds weary. He picks himself from the side chair and plods out the door looking as tired as he sounds.

I've worked up quite a head of steam fighting with Grady but when that dissipates I am even more feeble than before and drift off. When I wake, I find that while I slept, someone turned off the overheads. Sunset veils the room in golden light. Apparently Swbyra has come and gone. My keys rest on the bedside table next to my badge and the door to the cupboard at the foot of the bed stands ajar to reveal a set of clothes and a pair of shoes.

Someone is sitting in the side chair.

"Lix?"

"Come to check up on you." He sits rigidly in the chair. His wavy hair falls to the cowl neck of a bulky black sweater topped by a quilted vest, purple with lime racing stripes. The sweater is snagged and years have worn the sheen off the vest parka. Like everything else I've seen him in, it has the look of a costume. This ensemble gives him the appearance of a ski bum on a decidedly downhill run.

"How did you know—?"

"OFFICER DOWN. Big news."

"How'd you know where to find me?"

"Ain't like there's a hospital on every corner."

His voice is stiff, almost petulant, and doesn't invite casual conversation. We sit in silence for a moment. The gloom deepens.

"You lied to me. Again," he finally says.

"I didn't—"

He picks up my badge, tosses it lightly in his palm. "I asked you if you was a cop. You said 'no.'"

Though I might have expected, even preferred anger or resentment, he sounds only wounded.

"It's hard to explain. I've sort of been drafted."

He thinks that over for a minute. "Like a deputy. In a Western."

"Kind of like that, yeah."

He gets comfortable in the chair. "So how are ya?"

"I'll live."

"That's good."

"That's better than good, that's great. And I aim to keep it that way."

He favors me with a small smile. "Great. Yeah."

Another few moments pass in silence that is neither tense nor awkward, but rather companionable.

"The doctor said you did good work, Lix. On the tattoo."

"You told him about me?" he asks eagerly.

Well, not in so many words. *Why not let him think so if it makes him happy?* "Nice post-operative care, he said."

"Nice post-opera ... ," Lix echoes. "Yeah." He nods, a small smile on his face.

"You're the best."

"Damn straight." He nods some more, then his smile fades. "So, you gonna keep on doing this cop thing?" He takes up tossing the badge again.

"I don't know. Someone killed a guy—"

"Hector."

"Yeah. I want to find out who did it."

"Why? He's nobody to you. You said. Unless that was a lie, too."

"No, you're right. He's nobody to me."

"So is it, like, some mass murder thing?"

"I don't know. Maybe. I need to find out more about it."

"So you're gonna keep looking." He holds the badge toward the window, catches the sunset glow on the shiny surface and wiggles it, making sundogs on the wall.

"I want to know."

"Bad enough to sleep in a pine box?" he asks.

"Um, maybe not that bad."

"Good. No, great." His smile broadens. White teeth gleam against lips that look glossed with licorice. "I don't like thinking about you being dead." He lays the badge on the bedside table face-down. "Be seein' ya, Will Mansion."

"See ya, Lix Gemini."

He leaves the room as silently as he came.

Night settles on me like a blanket. I lie in the dark and wonder, what will I do? The job is not done. There is still a killer out there. Crowberry, Swbyra, and Grady all take it for granted I will shoulder the charge again, talk as if I have no choice. Only Lix Gemini sees the danger, sees it as I do: a choice between long life and early death.

Just thinking about it makes me sweat, though the room is cool. My heart accelerates, muscles tense. Like paint fumes, the hospital smell is making me brainsick. It triggers associations. I feel the queasy, room-spinning warning signs of a flashback. I've got to get out of here.

The nurse enters the room, turns on the light, and catches me sitting up and picking at the tape over the needle that tethers me to the IV stand.

"Ready for that sponge bath?" she asks with a cheerful smile. "Hey, leave that IV alone."

"I want out." The imperative to flee is stronger than the conviction that there's no place to run to.

"Oh, no way!"

"The doctor said I could leave when I felt like it and I feel like it now."

She props her hands on curvaceous hips. "Doctor said twenty-four hours and it hasn't been nearly that."

"He said to rest and I'm not getting any here."

"I don't understand, you have the room all to yourself."

"Yeah, but you wouldn't believe the parade of people that came through here today. I'm not hanging around for more."

"There's a 'No Visitors' sign on your door."

"That didn't stop any of the ones I got. Now I want to go home." I wiggle the hand with the IV needle. "Get this thing off me."

With obvious reluctance, she releases me from captivity. "You're sure I can't give you that sponge bath? For old times' sake?"

"Thanks. Some other time."

"If you're going to wash up, you should let me help you. You shouldn't get your bandages wet."

"Really, I'm fine. Thank you."

She shrugs and continues on her rounds.

Forget about bathing. Simply getting dressed is an ordeal. My body has completely seized up: my trunk is stiff as a double-starched shirt, my shoulders are a steel I-beam. Spine and hamstrings seem to be several inches shorter and I can't bend past a fifteen-degree angle. Inch by painful, creaking inch I get clothes on. Swbyra brought everything I need—underwear, socks and shoes, jeans and a sweater, the leather jacket that, like me, has seen better days.

I get myself discharged, submit to a wheelchair transport to the front door, and hail a cab.

CHAPTER 25

After the rain,
white clouds drift in the gutter,
flow down the storm drain-Soezi

A Zen riddle asks, how does a man proceed forward from the top of a hundred-foot pole? *No doubt the answer is simply to step out, preferably with arms thrown wide open to embrace the consequences.*

So it is that come morning, buoyed by something more like recklessness than actual bravery, I dress for work. In the shower, the water could be acid on my punctured abraded skin. There's never a nurse around when you need one. I could use help getting the unbandaged parts of me clean while keeping the dressings dry. As I drag a razor over my cheeks, I wonder why don't I just run my face up against a retaining wall?

Wheel-less without Old Paint, I cadge a lift to the station from a cruiser. After the first congratulatory backslap connects with my aching shoulder I learn to stick my hand out preemptively. When I finally pass the lieutenant's office, Crowberry's businesslike nonchalance is a relief. "Mansion, aren't you supposed to be in the hospital?" he asks bluntly.

"Ready to return to duty, sir."

"I doubt that."

"I'm definitely not up to a foot chase. A nice desk job is what I had in mind, sir."

"Are you up to bouncing this Waltann murder?"

I nod. "Laurel and Hardy around?"

"In Booking. They got back from Atlantic City this morning with the stripper," he says. "I couldn't see as how it was going to take them both to handle her, but ..." He opens a drawer and lays an evidence bag on the desktop. It contains my Beretta with a tag looped around the butt. "The men found it in the Eterniti. Apparently it was never fired, correct?"

"Correct, sir."

"So is it material to the case? Used as a club, anything like that?"

"Overshort threatened me with it. Wasn't much of a threat since I knew it wasn't loaded."

Crowberry purses his lips. "Guess that's one way to avoid getting shot with your own piece." He puts the bagged weapon in his out tray. "It'll be in the Evidence Locker until the case is adjudicated. Better get yourself another sidearm. And I'd recommend loading it this time."

"Yes, sir."

Noise in the corridor drowns out his next words. Grady and Swbyra crowd into the doorway of Crowberry's office, baggy-eyed and wearing twelve-hour-old five o'clock shadows.

"OK, Lieut', we got her all tucked in, but she was a handful, oh baby," Swbyra says breathlessly. He yells, "Will!" and takes a long step forward, arm outstretched, about to go for the shoulder. I head him off at the pass with a handshake.

"You back already?" Grady asks.

"That's using the term loosely," Crowberry says. "We'll put him on a desk for a while."

"We got the stripper," Swbyra reports with a big grin. "Has she got a thing for you, buddy boy. Kept asking if you were OK and I don't think it was 'cause she was worried we'd be charging her if you weren't."

I manage a weak smile.

"I can't believe the hospital discharged you already," Grady says.

"Guess they needed the bed for a sick person."

"Hmph. Well, I hope you have some good ideas about who did Waltann 'cause the lady swears she had nothing to do with it." To

Crowberry he says, "I don't know what it is with this bunch, Boss. They'll own up to damn near everything else. But snuffing Waltann? No go."

"Fortunately, we are not out of suspects." I remind them that Marybeth Waltann stood to gain from Hector's death and doesn't have a decent alibi. "And then there's Shrike. The gems that Hector traded him for dope were worthless, he owed him big bucks. Maybe Shrike tried to collect and ... well, you know the words to that tune."

"We need to shake that fucker's tree," Crowberry says.

"Easier said than done, Boss," Grady replies. "Shrike is harder to flush than a stopped up toilet."

"Mansion got to him," Swbyra points out.

"That was when he thought I was part of Carlotta's organization," I reply. "Now I'm just another cop. Shrike wouldn't let me see his shadow."

"He may not know that," Swbyra says.

"He's got to know it. He and Carlotta are tight."

"Then he might meet anyway for a chance to take you out before you can do him more damage," says Grady.

Now there's a comforting thought. "He might not even still be holed up at the theater," I reply.

"We can scout that out first," Swbyra says. "Mansion?"

"Check that," the lieutenant replies. "Didn't you hear me? I said Mansion's holding down a desk. Take Grady."

"Boss, it's got to be Mansion," Swbyra says. "Shrike won't open up for any of us."

"I don't think he's in any shape to play decoy."

"He doesn't have to be in shape. Just get them to open the door, disarm the security system. I'll take care of the rest."

Grady shakes his head. "Sounds risky to me. Look what happened the last time. Swbyra got hosed and if it wasn't for Mansion—"

Swbyra says, "It'll be different this time, I promise you. I got to have this chance. Got to. It could be the last."

Crowberry regards me with a steady gaze and Grady glares. A puppy wanting to ride in the car couldn't look more hopeful than Swbyra. Maybe he thinks he'll make it all up to me by doing it right this time, by getting Shrike once and for all.

"What do you say, Mansion?" Crowberry asks.

What I remember of the theater's interior and its security system isn't much of an asset. Even if I did recall something useful, I could easily brief another man. Yet over the past few weeks, the Terminal Road shootout has replayed itself on the screen of my mind in gruesome slow motion with the sadistic persistence of the Zapruder film. There's no reason to believe it won't continue to do so. Maybe rerunning that episode will consign it permanently to the vault. To not have to jump at shadows, Shrike's shadow... We wouldn't make the same mistakes this time. "I think it's our best chance."

Grady is detailed, under vehement protest, to follow up on Marybeth Waltann. That's fine with me. I don't know what's been eating him, but I don't want to attempt this recon with him staring daggers at my back. Swbyra goes off to put a plant on the theater and marshal backup forces—a veritable platoon in full riot gear, he promises. Meanwhile, I equip myself with handcuffs, body armor, a new Beretta, and rig.

At the range, the stiff leather, the weapon, feel exceptionally awkward and unresponsive. My shoulder protests every pound of recoil. The fact that I'm the one making the noise doesn't make the gunfire less disturbing. Though muffled, each shot leaves me quaking until I can barely hold the weapon steady. I'm about to give up when I get a call from Swbyra.

"Shrike's here," he says.

"Where?"

"The theater."

"So he hasn't set up shop somewhere else?"

"No, he's here, I'm telling you. Get your ass over here, now."

"Now?"

"Fuck yes. Now!"

"Grady?"

"I called him, he's on his way. But we got to make our move, now."

"Backup?"

"Here. I'm getting in position. I'll take the back door."

The retreat position, if Shrike decides to run. In this case the "back door" would be the theater's front entrance. Facing the street and boarded up, I doubt it'll see much action. If he feels cornered, Shrike is more apt to lure us inside, which would be walking into a shooting gallery. Under other circumstances, Grady would lead the charge, the way he did on Terminal Road. It's got to be this way, though. I've got to be the one to flush Shrike. I'm the bait. He's not likely to open the door for anyone else, unless it's someone from his organization.

That gives me an idea. Against the fading light I race back to the station. I borrow some gear from Ace and Spade's stash: a leather cap and long coat not unlike what the King Phil Nearvana dealer wore, and darken my face and hands with copier toner.

On the Miracle Mile, I pause at the package store opposite the theater to scope out the scene. Miracle Mile's shop-window lights only deepen the twilight. The sidewalk in front of the coffee shop and theater is empty. Swbyra's team must be keeping people off the street. Swbyra himself must be holed up close by where he can monitor the action.

Across the street, the theater hunkers silently on the corner. Graffiti'd plywood sheets cover the once-celebrated Art Deco doors and the windows in the ticket booth. Yellow glows through cracks in the white paint that coats two street-side clerestory windows. A light's on inside.

I dart across the Mile to the mouth of the alley. Gun at the ready, I peer down its narrow length. By day it is more revolting than in the disguising dark. The wet stinking piles reveal themselves to be waste—animal? human?—and dead things. Cats' and rats' eyes glitter from piles of crumbling boxes. A tawny streak reminds me of the fox-like stray dog from the Mercy Mission. In the vacant lot behind the theater, the night breeze stirs weeds that are tall enough to conceal the forces I suspect Swbyra has hidden there.

As I inch down the alley hugging the theater wall, sweat soaks my shirt and not because I'm warm in the body armor. My lungs are empty, my head hollow and light. I used to take the door with temerity but no more. Across the alley, nothing betrays the presence of backup at the coffee shop.

In the dusky light I've got a better look at the theater's side door than I did the first time. It's been reinforced with riveted metal plates. The narrow eye-level rectangle is fitted not with wire glass like the coffee shop but with a metal panel. No one can look in, or out for that matter, although those on the inside with the advantage of the video surveillance camera. Its red light glows in the eave trough's shadow.

There is no handle or knob, no getting in without being let in. No getting in without standing directly in front of the door, a target for whoever's on the other side.

Inside I hear a rumble of voices, like a conversation. From the way my courage sinks I can tell I had been thinking I'd face Shrike alone.

Chin tucked, cap pulled low on my brow, I step into the camera's range. If there is a secret knock, I don't know it, can only pound the door with my fist and see what happens. A metallic click jolts me. Just in time I realize the sound was the door lock being released, not a weapon being readied. I flatten myself against the wall to the right. The door moves outward a few inches, nudged by someone inside? Pale, strobing light flashes across the crack in the door, and the sound of conversation is louder. *Could I have slipped into flashback mode? Am I hallucinating?* I wait for bullets or attackers to come flying out but nothing happens. Shrike does not appear. The next move is mine and it has to be to step through the opening.

I cross the threshold.

Flickering light, though not strong, strains my dark-adjusted eyes. At first I think I am hallucinating. Then I realize it's coming from the front of the theater, from the screen where, incredibly, a movie is playing. A black-and-white Western.

With a pneumatic sigh, the door closes and clicks locked behind me. Dark holes reveal where a crash bar was once bolted to the steel. Now, there is no handle at all. A five-button access control panel guards the exit. Not only is there no getting in unless someone inside unlocks the door, there's no getting out unless someone operates the panel.

The status light glows green. The word "armed" pops into my head. *From where?* The article in *Modern Locksmith* that I read in Secur-It's office pictured a keyless system like this. To disarm it and unlock the door, giving Swbyra and backup access, I have to push the right buttons in the right sequence. The way Shrike did when he and his second escorted me out. Do I recall the sequence? If I hadn't been high on Nearvana at the time, I might have a better chance.

I remember more of the article than I do of the code. This system has a feature to defeat working out the sequence by punching buttons randomly. The correct sequence must be completed within a preset interval after the first button is pressed. Otherwise, the system levies a five-second penalty before I can try again. No time like the present to start with what I think I remember from my last visit.

As I stand with my fingers poised over the buttons, the flickering light of the screen picks out the glossy-painted numbers on the surfaces of the keys and tiny particles of dust around them. Around some of them, not all. Not around the ones that have been used. Fingertips have wiped the dust away. That narrows my choices. Now all I have to do is work out the sequence.

"Hey, man, what gives?"

The voice comes from Shrike's second-in-command, standing in the side aisle just above the door, TEC-9 held limply at his side.

"Nothin' much," I reply, trying to sound like the King Phil dealer. With my head down, I can't scan the whole theater, but from what I've seen, Shrike isn't here. "Shrike around?"

"Upstairs." The second takes a step toward me. "What you doin' messin' with the door? You ... hey, you ain't Skins!" He jerks his weapon up but I am already charging. I barrel into him. We go down in a tangle of big coats, caps, and armament, struggle to separate and get the upper hand. He finds his feet before I can get to my knees and whips the TEC-9 around, spitting bullets. Under the line of fire, I roll into his legs, sweep him off his feet. He lands on his butt, gun arm outflung. Bullets puncture the stage's apron and the merchandise arrayed on its edge. He brings the awkward weapon forward but I'm faster with the nimble Beretta and from my knees, aim for body mass. Screaming, Shrike's lieutenant claws at his gut and falls back.

Keeping him covered, I grab at his weapon and wrench it away. He puts up little resistance. His screams have already become whimpers. I hurt him bad. If I don't get help for him soon, this man will bleed out.

Where is Swbyra? Where is backup? They could be just on the other side of this door, unable to get in. I take another stab at the control panel with no luck. Maybe there's another way out. Beretta in my right hand, TEC-9 in my left, I start up the aisle toward the lobby, trying for both speed and caution. A shot from behind sends me diving for cover between rows of seats where I huddle until I realize it was a sound effect from the movie.

The door from the lobby opens. A dark figure in a sweeping coat starts down the aisle and I'm face to face with Shrike.

"What the fuck's going on here?" He spots his second lying supine near the exit door. "Hey!"

"He jumped me," I reply, backing down the aisle.

Shrike squints in the light from the screen. "Hey, you ain't Skins … Mansion? Stop your ass right there." He steadies the barrel of his Cobray, already pointed at my belly.

At this range, Kevlar won't save me, but neither will a poplin raincoat protect Shrike from my bullets, so it's a stand-off. It's up to Swbyra. *Where the hell is Swbyra?*

"Man, you some kind of suicidal motherfucker," Shrike says.

"So are you." I wiggle the Beretta, note with pleasure that Shrike's glance follows the movement. Easily distracted.

"You scratched my man!"

"Damn, he never gave me a chance."

"Neither will I."

Before he gets off a shot, I take cover between the seats, crawl backward in the musty, narrow space, palms sticking to the tacky floor. Maybe I can get to the center aisle, get to the lobby. *And then what?* "Wait! Give me a minute!"

Shots whine overhead and I can't tell if it's real or from the movie.

"OK, be that way. You're under arrest for the murder of Hector Waltann."

"You stupid fuck, you want to die for that? I didn't kill him," Shrike shouts back. "That bitch Carlotta I might. You for sure. But why I want to waste Hector?"

I'm prepared to believe him, especially since he's stopped shooting at me. "He stiffed you."

"So how do I collect if he dead? You so stupid you deserve to die." Shrike sends a spit ball of bullets in my direction for punctuation.

"I can do you just as quick," I reply, but reserve any punctuation of my own. Who knows how many rounds are left in the TEC-9. "Talk to me and we both get to live."

Shrike says, "You forget. I got backup."

Damn, there's more? "You think I came here alone?" *Where is Swbyra?*

"You stupid enough to come here in the first place," he says, but he sounds unsure.

"Tell me about Hector. If you didn't kill him, who did?"

"I don't know, man, maybe his poke." His tone is less abrupt, almost conversational. I push up from the floor high enough to see him. "Another hype. Hector was buying more smack than he could do hisself and live."

"And paid you with fake jewels."

"Don't fuckin' remind me. But I didn't do him!"

"So if you didn't kill Hector, you've got nothing to fear from me. Just come downtown, we'll talk—"

"Then you let me loose to come nail me some other day?" He fires off another round.

"There isn't going to be another day. Not for me. I'm history. They know about me. About the Nearvana."

Shrike's teeth show white in the light from the movie screen. His gun arm is slightly relaxed. "Yeah, and you liked it, too."

And God, I could use some now. This was much easier to do stoned.

The door opens and a tall, thin form fills the side aisle. Shrike's backup? Prepared to fire in both directions, I risk a glance over my shoulder.

CHAPTER 26

Outside the tearoom,
fine flavors still on my tongue,
cigarette smoke cloud–Soezi

It's Swbyra!

"Told you I had back up," Shrike says. "Hey, my man."

Swbyra trains his weapon on me. It's all I can do not to say, "Huh?"

"Why didn't you tell me you was a cop instead of giving me that shit about Carlotta," Shrike yells at me. "We could have come to some kind of arrangement like with my man here."

"You're with him?" No wonder Ace and Spade haven't been able to find Shrike. Swbyra's been tipping him to their operations. And no wonder the Terminal Road bust went bad. Swbyra took the back door not to head off Shrike's escape but to engineer it. When he came barreling around the side of the house, he wasn't fleeing Shrike, he was clearing the way for him. When I got hit running for cover after knocking Swybra out of his path, I thought it was Shrike doing the shooting, but maybe not. Maybe it was—"

"What this arrest shit?" Shrike asks Swbyra. "You supposed to keep shit like this from happenin' to me. Here Mansion just jig his ass right on in here."

"You're the one who let him in," Swbyra reminds him.

"Yeah, well, you be the one to put him out."

"Put him? ..."

"Waste 'im," Shrike says, and starts back up the aisle.

A wave of cold flows down my back leaving puckered skin in its wake. Swybra doesn't move.

"I said waste him," Shrike yells. "Are you my man or what?"

Still Swbyra doesn't move.

"Aw, useless fuck. I got eleven-year-olds worth more than you," Shrike says and shoots Swbyra. He falls back, firing. Before anyone can aim at me, I hit the floor. Shrike doesn't mess with the secured exit. Covering his back with blasts from the Cobray, he races up the side aisle toward the lobby. With the Beretta, I fire after him but half my attention is on Swbyra, now flat on his back. Shrike takes cover behind a row of seats and retaliates. Still in a painful crouch, I scrabble over to Swbyra and drag him to the foot of the first row. "Are you hurt?"

"Yeah."

There is a small hole in his quilted jacket. When I peel the jacket away, I find a bloodier hole in his vest. I don't want to think about the projectile that drilled through it.

"Backup! Why can't they get in? How'd you get in?"

"Shrike ... let me in ... service entrance. Backup ... there is no backup."

Bullets punch into and carom off the seats. I fire back, then lie alongside Swbyra. "Does Shrike know?"

"Yes," he hisses.

"Swbyra ... why?"

He doesn't answer right away. "Nearvana," he finally says.

Swbyra a junkie? That can't be. He's a good cop, thorough, on target, always right there. Except for those migraines—

Oh, God, no. The migraines weren't migraines.

I risk rising enough to peer over the seats and spot Shrike in the center aisle. He shoots at me and I shoot back, sending us both diving for cover.

"Get 'im, Mansion," Swbyra hisses.

"Get him? Are you crazy? Dammit, if he'd stop trying to kill me, I'd let him get as far away as he wants. I just want to get out, get you some help." Swbyra is in bad shape. I know what will happen if I don't get him an ambulance soon.

Swbyra grasps my ankle. "You'll have to kill him. He won't run. Not and leave you alive." His voice is thready.

As if to prove Swbyra right, Shrike unleashes another round. Gunfire from behind is hard to ignore. "It's only a movie, it's only a movie," I keep telling myself, until one entirely too-real round whizzes past my ear. Shrike's second, not so dead he can't try to finish what Swbyra wouldn't, is up on one elbow and firing a pistol. A drop gun! In response to the new threat, a fresh wave of adrenalin floods my system. Before I can return fire a shot rings out from Swbyra's direction. Shrike's second jerks back and falls flat.

"Go!" Swbyra yells hoarsely. "I got your back."

Like he did on Terminal Road? Can I take that chance? My thigh screaming, I crabwalk up the aisle, scrunching behind seats whenever Shrike fires. He reaches the swinging door to the lobby and slams on through, leaving me in the clear. I gamble on standing upright for which my leg and shoulder are grateful.

"Swbyra?"

No answer. Once through the door, I inch up the yard-long alcove just shy of a lobby darker than the theater's interior. No light projected onto a white screen here and I can't see a thing. It's a dead end! Worse, a trap, with Shrike out there somewhere just waiting for me to show myself.

Panic makes me so lightheaded I can't think. I take a deep breath, then another, and strain to see. This time I can make out details I couldn't a moment ago. Encouraged, I stand still, breathe slowly and deeply, direct all my energy to my eyes, and find the darkness a shade less total. Cracks in the paint opaquing the clerestory windows let in some street light. The illumination is just enough.

Directly opposite me is a wall. The front door angles off it to the right. Another door gives access from the lobby to the ticket booth. About six feet to the right of the ticket booth there's yet another door, possibly to an office. The service entrance from Miracle Mile is to the right of the office, and at the far right are the restrooms.

A glass pane in the office door reflects light coming from something directly across from it. I can't tell what for certain without leaving the safety of the alcove and stepping into the lobby, but I can guess. If my memory serves me, the concession stand is to my right, opposite the ticket booth. Something there is picking up the light from the clerestory windows, possibly the candy case's glass front, or the mirror behind the concession stand. Whichever, it reflects back onto the office door glass.

A small green light glows steadily on the wall next to the service entrance door. The security system is still armed. Shrike could have already escaped, rearming the system as he exited in order to slow me down. Or, he could still be here, waiting to get me out in the open. He could be hiding in the ticket booth, the office, either of the restrooms, or the concession stand. From any of these positions, he's got the drop on me the minute I leave this alcove to step into the lobby.

Maybe I should go back into the theater and take my chances with the control panel at the exit door. I don't like the odds. There's no cover at that position. All Shrike would have to do is open the door from the lobby and he'd have me directly in his sight.

As I'm considering my options, I notice a detail I missed in the reflected light on the office door glass. A dark shape. A shadow.

Shrike. Behind the concession stand. Knowing where he is helps, but not much. He still has the advantage the minute I break cover. I've got to flush him out of his bunker.

A diversion? No. If he didn't fall for it, he'd have my position. If I were him, I wouldn't even move. With that Cobray, I'd just blast me through the wall between us.

Good idea. Praying I've got ammo left in the TEC-9, I step back and drill the wall between me and the concession stand. Sheetrock flies and glass tinkles. A second later I see a rain-coated figure dart across the lobby, making for the service entrance.

"Shrike, stop! Drop your weapon! Drop it!"

He whips around. "Your ass!" he yells back and ducks into the men's room under covering fire from the Cobray.

He shoots at me, I shoot at him. It's ridiculous. We're both with our back against the wall and nowhere to go. We don't have unlimited supplies of ammo and it's just a matter of time before one of us runs out. My TEC-9 clicks dry first.

A high cackle rattles across the silent lobby and Shrike steps into the smoky haze, Cobray aimed in my direction.

Giving me no choice but to drop him with the Beretta.

Before he even hits the ground, the sound of a tree being felled whips me around. With the squeal of splintering wood, the front door caves in and a phalanx of men in riot gear crash through behind a battering ram. The lead man, poised like a tackle, sees me, sees Shrike crumpled near the service entrance, and hollers at me, "Drop your weapon! Get down on the ground!"

"Grady, it's me," I yell back.

"Down on the ground!" he repeats, his revolver pointed at my chest.

"Oh, God, don't shoot, it's me, I tell ya. Mansion!" Kneeling, I lay both guns on the ground. With one hand at the back of my neck, I push my cap off with the other, swipe at the black toner on my face.

"Mansion?" Grady says. "Hold your fire." He takes a step closer. "It is you! Are you OK?"

"Yeah, but Swybra isn't. We need an ambulance, now. We've got one officer and two suspects down."

"Cover Shrike," Grady tells an officer. "Get an ambulance," he tells another. "You two, secure the scene. The rest of you, fan out, see if there's more of them."

"Sir, he's still breathin'," reports the man at Shrike's side.

Grady grunts. "Swbyra?"

"Follow me!"

In the theater, Shrike's second lies still near the exit door. Guardedly, Grady approaches the supine junkie. "He's dead," Grady announces.

He joins me at Swbyra's side. He lies moaning in bright light. The movie over, closing credits crawl down the screen. Swbyra's weak, but alive.

"Saved your ass, didn't I?" he asks. "We're even now, huh?"

"Yeah, we're even."

"You OK?" Grady asks me.

"Just." My healing wounds feel ripped wide open, I'm drenched in sweat, but I am alive. "Thanks, Grady."

One of the uniforms administers aid to Swbyra while the other bleats our location into his radio. "Code 20. I mean 30. Oh, God, officer down!"

"Swbyra," I murmur. "He's been using! Grady, I can't believe it."

"Hell, who the fuck knows anymore? I thought someone might be on the pad. Was thinking it was you, the way you been acting so fucking weird."

Let's not go there. "I guess I've been wondering the same thing about you. What took you guys so long to get here?"

"Hell, you're lucky we're here at all. I get back from interviewing Marybeth Waltann and go to see what kind of plan Swbyra put together and man, there is no fucking plan. No fucking backup, no nothing. So I tell Crowberry and he goes fucking ballistic. Tells me to commandeer what I can and get my ass over here. Not a moment too soon, huh?"

"Not a moment too soon," I breathe.

While Grady checks on Swbyra, I go to stand over Shrike. This is the moment I've longed for: Shrike at my feet, vanquished. I wait to be suffused with a sensation of closure, of release, of confidence that I'll be all right now, but it doesn't happen. I feel only uneasy.

The paramedics and Crowberry arrive almost simultaneously. The ambulance whisks Swbyra and Shrike away. Crowberry takes my report, his face going as gray as campfire ashes, his jowls sagging lower as Swbyra's duplicity unfolds. Grady helps me retrieve Old Paint from where I left it parked near the pawnshop. So disreputable is its appearance it survived two nights on Miracle Mile unharmed except for a missing hubcap.

I take myself to the E. R. Swbyra and Shrike have already been admitted to beds where they will remain under guard until they're well enough to be booked. The doctor examines my leg, re-bandages my shoulder, and gives me a vial of pills for the pain. I don't plan to take them but I accept anyway; I need a new talisman.

There is still work to be done. This evening's events have generated a ton of paperwork. Even worse, I still don't know who killed Hector. I offhandedly remarked to myself at the Jade Pagoda it could be that one of Hector's neighbors at the motel took a deep disliking to him. After all this, his death could be the result of random violence.

Still, what about this secret lover, the one Nikki alluded to, the one Hector dumped her for? The one Shrike implied Hector was buying drugs for? Could that be the mystery woman in the hooded cape the hookers and desk man at the Jade Pagoda claimed they saw? We might be able to pry a name out of Nikki

Saint Clair or Overshort. If so, it can wait until tomorrow. They're not going anywhere. I, however, am headed home.

Main Street has such a nightmarish quality it makes me think I've taken a wrong turn and ended up back on the Miracle Mile. Skeletons, Angels of Death, mummies in winding sheets throng the sidewalks. Oh. Hallowe'en.

Like the rest of downtown's stores, the Kaffeteria's front window is decorated with grinning orange jack-o'-lanterns, booing white ghosts, and leering gray skeletons, their mouths garishly lit by the yellow light from inside. The silhouettes on the glass indicate the place is packed. I'm in no shape to party but I'm too wired to sleep. I'm also not eager to be alone with my thoughts about Swbyra.

The chalkboard on the easel just inside the Kaffeteria door advertises today's special beverage as Witch's Brew and the Daily Muffin as Devil's Food. My nose must be functioning normally again: I can smell sweet cinnamon and rich French roast.

Behind the counter is Juan Valdez. The brim of a wide straw sombrero tilts down over his face and shadows shoulders draped by a brown burlap poncho.

"I'll have the special," I say.

He raises his face. It's Dunk. "Will!"

"Juan."

"What are you doing here, man, I thought you were in the hospital? I tried to come see how you were doing but they wouldn't let me. Said you couldn't have visitors."

"At least none I would have wanted, so I left. Seems I came to the right place." Around me, Dunk's clientele wear costumes that run the gamut from elaborate to simple, manufactured to homemade, and represent all the popular icons. There's a trio of Madonnas—the media darling, not the Holy Mother—in various incarnations; an impeached President, a dead Princess, a bandoliered and pinstriped gangster, an oft-married movie star, characters from the latest Disney film. There's even a man in an Airol Jones jersey. There's a lot of cross-dressing; all three Madonnas are men. Spirits are high and so is the noise level.

"Nice outfit, Juan," I tell Dunk.

"*Gracias,*" he says with a twirl of his store-bought mustache. "Eet ees my own design. Made the poncho from a bean bag." He fans out the burlap to reveal "COLUMBIA SUPREMO" stamped in black block letters across his chest. "You, I see, came as a street dealer. What is that, some kind of little police in-joke?"

"Some kind of. How about some of that Witch's Brew to go?"

"Not for you, man. You need something far more palliative. Here, munch a muffin while I fix it."

Ruffed in orange paper, the Devil's Food muffin is black and fragrant with chocolate. A little frosting goblin on the top winks at me with chocolate chip eyes, smiles with a mandarin- orange-slice mouth. Dunk sets before me a large foam cup of tea. The chestnut aroma tells me it's brewed from green, not black, leaves. Familiar puffs of popped brown rice float on top.

"It's *genmaicha*," I say.

"Not just any *genmaicha*," Dunk replies. "It's my latest recipe: tea and rice with lemon grass, black cohosh, and ginseng. You'll feel like a new man. Maybe even want to stick around for the wet T-shirt apple bob."

"Sounds tempting, but I'm packing it in for the night." I snap a lid on the tea.

"Help me think of a name for the tea, Will," Dunk calls. "ZenBlend? BuddhaBrew? SereniTea?"

Shaking my head, I elbow my way through the crowd. A magician sweeps past me in a black cape, taking me momentarily aback. The cape has no hood and the magician's a man, not a woman. What did I think, that I'd find Hector's killer right here under my nose?

Home, I drag myself up the stairs, trudge through the kitchen, and head straight into the tub to soak what isn't bandaged and sip. Dunk was right; the tea is restorative, although not quite enough to return to the Kaffeteria for his Halloween party. Too bad; a wet T-shirt apple bob ... what a concept.

For the first time in days, I have an appetite. The chocolate muffin a mere drop in the bucket of my hunger, I amble into the kitchen where the only thing edible is peanut butter. No bread, and even the crackers are stale. I perch on a kitchen chair, suck peanut butter off my fingers, and regard the tabletop, still littered with the papers I took from Hector's condo. The trash bag I hauled them away in is on the floor and I drop the papers in one by one.

To my hand comes the half-folded sheet of paper I've picked up several times but never examined. The paper's coarse grain and eggshell color, before only tantalizingly familiar, is now telltale. Even as I open it I know what I expect to find. The light, sure strokes of a pencil sketch raise the hairs on the back of my neck. It's incriminating evidence that a man disguised as Pizza Boy sneaked into Hector's condo to retrieve: a sheet of paper torn from his sketchpad with his custom design for a tattoo. For Hector Waltann. By Lix Gemini.

CHAPTER 27

The match flares, goes out.
Longer lasting than the flame,
its heat on my cheek—Debisu

Tonight the dingy "Tattoos" sign hangs on the cardboard rib cage of a dancing skeleton with accordioned crepe paper arms and legs. I push through the door and am greeted not by the usual tinkling bell but by a banshee howl, no less eerie for being recorded. Satanic heavy metal music blares and cigarette smoke fogs the air.

"Lix!" I call.

"Who's that? Is that you, Will?"

I follow the sound of his voice and find him hunkered down on the floor near the corner nook. His pale face is flushed, his eyes squinty.

"I'm glad you're here, Will. Will, you got to help me. I don't feel so good."

He doesn't sound good, either, his voice hoarse and listless, overpowered by the loud music.

"What's the matter, Lix?"

"Oh, I'm hurting a little. I need a little something, you know?" He takes short, avid puffs on a cigarette to ease the pain of craving something stronger than nicotine.

I do know, all too well. His nose runs, his eyes tear, his skin crawls, and muscles twitch. He's tense and achy, nauseated. "Your regular supplier out of business, huh?" I ask.

"Yeah, you know something about that, don't you?" he says with a feeble giggle. "But you can get some stuff for me, can't you?"

"Because I was holding once before? You knew I was because you found it on me when I was unconscious behind the Metro, the night Overshort shot at me. You were the one who rolled me." It was Lix who took the heroin Carlotta had sent me to buy from Shrike. He took my topcoat and my cigarettes, the ones Overshort gave me. That's why he had an open pack of Verves in his nook, although later he told me they weren't his brand.

He gives a weak shrug. "You was just a bum then. It was a good score for me, fifteen bills worth of horse. I didn't know there'd be more to it."

"More junk? I told you then that was something special. I'm no hophead, Lix."

"You say. I seen you suck the stuff down." He shifts nervously and drags long, black-enameled fingernails across his cheek. "Anyhow, that's not what I meant. I meant about us. Helping each other. I helped you. Now you help me. Will, you got to help me." His voice is a raspy whisper, his throat rubbed raw by the smoke. He hugs himself to keep his body from shattering.

"Why should I? You lied to me, Lix."

He looks up at me with bleary eyes. "Huh?"

"About Hector Waltann. You said you didn't know where he was but you did. The condo at Shays' Landing. You not only knew it, you had a key for it. You threw the pizza at me. You were Pizza Boy."

He looks down, his bent knees tick back and forth. "Yeah. There was something of mine at Hector's. The way you was asking about him, I knew I had to get it back fast. Hell, I knew he'd ditched the place. Shrike was watching it. But I figured nobody'd pay attention to a pizza man showing up."

"The blue jacket, the cap?"

"Got it from Nikki. Them girls at the Metro always have clothes for dressing up. Like this." He waves his hand over his costume, a sheer pink blouse with billowing sleeves under yet another vest, this one pink satin; a net skirt over black leggings. "For Halloween. I'm a fairy, see? It's a joke. I had a crown here, somewhere." He pats the floor around him.

"The black cape with the hood? You borrowed that from Nikki, too, didn't you? The night you killed Hector. You were the caped woman at the Jade Pagoda."

"Aw, Hector was damn near dead already. All he wanted to do was fuck and get high. He was wasted, man."

"Fuck ... with you?"

"Yeah, with me." He smiles. "Like I told you, I'm the best. Hector knew it. That's why he didn't want me to leave him. But I wanted you."

"Fresh meat. With a pocket full of smack?"

He presses together lips dark as plums. "It wasn't just that. I liked you. You liked me, I could tell. When I touched you"

Goosebumps sprout along my back.

"I didn't set out to kill him," Lix says. "He said he had a little stuff for me. After I did it, I told him we was through but he didn't want to hear it. Said he'd do anything to keep me but you know, there wasn't nothing more he could do for me, see. He was a mess. Broke, strung out, sick." He pauses to drag on his cigarette. "I did him a favor, really. Put him out of his misery. Now I'm free for you."

"For me? You got it all wrong, Lix. Get up."

Lix stands and staggers toward me and I catch the fragrance of patchouli, arresting as incense, seductive as pheromones. The powdery, woody, aromatic scent sparks my recall of rain-soaked semi-consciousness in the alley behind the Metro when Lix rolled me for my stash. It was patchouli I smelled when Lix bent over me to apply my tattoo, which now stings as though infected. I would have made the connection then if I hadn't been stoned. *Damn!* Should have recognized it lingering in Room Eight of the Jade Pagoda. Might have noticed it when he visited me in the hospital if my sense of smell hadn't been crippled by river water and disinfectant.

"I'm arresting you for the murder of Hector Waltann, Lix Gemini."

He shakes his head sadly. "Nah, I can't let you do that. It wouldn't work. See, I'm not like other people."

"Maybe not like other people. Like other murderers, you are."

"No, Will, you don't understand. I'm really not. I'll show you."

He removes his vest and the sight of him stuns me. Under the veil of the pink blouse, high on his rib cage are breasts, small and neat as a young girl's. Not mere adipose pouches but true breasts, round and smooth as nectarines.

"You're ... a woman?"

He pulls the blouse over his head, which lifts his chest. His nipples are crimson points on those tiny breasts. He runs his hands down his body, over his breasts, his torso, his belly. "Yes. And no."

What is he—she?—talking about?

His hands move down to skim the skirt and leggings off narrow hips. He steps out of them and stands before me naked and frail. Below a pale flat hairless belly is a penis of sorts, about the size of a thumb, small as a baby's but tumescent and dark red. "See? Not like other people."

No. Not like anyone or anything I have ever seen, so aberrant as to seem made, not born. I should be horrified, repelled. Instead I am riveted, not by the sick fascination that draws audiences to side shows and slasher movies, but in awe.

"You can have me, Will," he says. He holds his hands out. "I can be everything to you. Woman. Man." His voice is a husky purr. "Both at the same time."

Both at the same time. Countless permutations.

"You in me. Me in you."

Both at the same time.

"I am the best. Hector knew it. He gave up everything for it. He begged me not to leave him." He licks his lips. "You want me, don't you?"

A woman who is a man. A man who is a woman. Awestruck, I keep forgetting to breathe. Oxygen-deprivation is making me dizzy. I gulp smoky air.

"Think about it, man."

I can't. It's madness. With shaky hands, I hold out a set of restraints. "Put on some clothes, Lix."

"Put my clothes on?"

"Some street clothes." I won't take him down to the station dressed as a fairy. He wouldn't last five minutes in lock-up. "I want you to come with me."

"Anywhere, Will. I'll make you happy. You'll never need anyone else." He pads barefoot to a cardboard box.

"Come on now, Lix. It's time to go." I try to keep my voice level, to project resolve, authority, but to me I sound pleading, apologetic.

He turns away from me and bends from the hips to rustle in the box, displaying the perfect globes of his buttocks and the dark secret between his thighs. The staggering sight paralyzes my vocal cords but maybe it doesn't matter. I have said what I came to say, what I had to say, and he is pulling up his jeans. The zipper rasps, his elbows saw back and forth as he works the top button. His shoulders come up and he turns to face me—with the apple-carving knife in his hand, the blade held flat, the better to slip between my ribs.

"Lix," I say, my voice soft, "do you really want to kill me?"

"I don't want to but I ain't going to prison. Can you imagine what that would be like for me?"

Yes, I can. Before they kill him, they'll toy with him, little boys pulling the wings and legs off a fly. It would be hell. If it were me, I would kill to avoid that. I don't doubt he will. I could go for my gun but it wouldn't matter. At this range he can rush me faster than I can draw.

The tape deck howls. Spectral light, herald of a PTSD flashback, begins to strobe. Killing Shrike, solving the mystery of my own shooting, hasn't cured my fear of death.

No, I will not go spinning off into space! A panic attack has its own weird energy: accelerated pulse, shallow breathing, tense muscles. *Relax. Breathe deeply! Be here, now. Be here! Now!*

I smell scents—smoke, sweat, patchouli. See flickering lights—not hallucinations but the bright and shadow of the studio. The twisted sylph at its center is not an apparition, it's Lix, naked from the waist up, his phenomenal chest rising and falling with each breath.

The breath. His attack will come with an exhalation. He'll take a breath, and then he'll pounce. Look for it and be ready. Watch his chest rise. Fall.

Rise.

Fall.

Rise—

He lunges. There's nowhere to run so I don't back away, I go forward. Head down, I dive under his lancing arm, roll into his legs.

He tumbles over my back and into the color cart. Bottles torpedo him and crash to the floor, carpeting it with glass shards. Lix flings the cart at me. Barely on my feet, I catch it to deflect the blow and almost toss it aside. No—I hold it in front of me, an awkward, long-legged aluminum shield. We face off on a floor treacherous with spilled ink and splintered glass. His grinning mouth a dark smudge, his body smeared with ink and striped with bloody scratches, Lix lashes out. I parry with the cart. The knife sings dully on the cart's top shelf. Lix stumbles with the recoil, giving me just enough time to flip the cart around, top against my chest. With Lix caged in its legs, I can keep him at bay, shield myself from his stabbing arm yet get in close enough to kick out at his knee. I hurt him enough to drive him screaming onto a bed of glass and still he has the knife. He kicks and slashes at my legs. I trap him under the cart and lean on it to keep him pinned while I grab for my gun. The casters betray me. Lix wriggles and squirms, the cart flies out from under me, and I fall on him. He embraces me, his knife arm targets my back. I jam the gun in his side and fire.

CHAPTER 28

Sitting on the step,
sipping my morning coffee,
my head in the clouds—Soezi

I could sit and watch the river forever. It's peaceful to watch the river do what a river does, flow to the sea, never questioning what might happen when it gets there, never seeking something more. Never mind that, bareheaded here on my stair landing, I'm cold. Only my hands, wrapped around a cup of tea, are warm. Tea, not coffee, although my forehead already booms with a caffeine-deprivation headache.

Caffeine isn't the only drug I've had to kick. I've withdrawn from heroin, the hard way, cold turkey, with nothing to support me but my Zen practice.

Ironically, a lifetime's cigarette habit is harder to quit. The unquenched craving for a smoke tugs constantly. Like background music in a movie, it's not the main theme. Still, it does lend a certain tone to the action. It will, I expect, for the rest of my life, a life I'm ready to live.

I have some decisions to make. That I have been more alive when facing death than I was when running from it hasn't escaped my notice.

But I can't sit here forever. Those who preyed on Hector Waltann are dead or in custody but there's still work to do. Paperwork, mostly, but work nonetheless. Before that, though, I have one last task to complete, one that will take me back to Miracle Mile.

*****

I can't bathe and dress without noticing the lotus tattoo, can't notice the tattoo without reliving the moment I shot Lix Gemini at a range beyond close—intimate. I can feel his lips against my ear, hear his scream echo in my skull. His body spasms against me as the bullet, my bullet, penetrates. The recollection makes me shudder so I try not to think about it. More than ever, I want to learn to banish discursive thoughts.

I could have the tattoo lasered off but I won't. Lix was right; it is the perfect symbol for me, a reminder not only of my commitment to transcending the enslavement of desire but also of my weakness and fallibility. Besides, it's beautiful. For all else that he was, Lix was also an artist.

Northbound on Miracle Mile, I drive past the liquor store, a thrift store, the massage parlor, the adult bookstore, reach the Metro on the corner and stop, taken aback. Somehow I traveled the entire block and drove right past Sister Clyde's Mercy Mission. *How could I have missed it?* It was between the liquor store and the massage parlor. Going too fast, I guess. With a shrug I hang a left onto Putnam, make a U-turn, turn back onto Miracle Mile, and go south for another pass, slower this time. Metro, adult bookstore, massage parlor, thrift store, liquor store. At the corner of Main and Miracle I stop, baffled. *Missed it again! How did I do that?* I glance back over my shoulder, try to figure out what I'm doing wrong. An impatient honk behind me prods me onward. I pull another U-ey and head up the Mile once more. This time I stop in front of the liquor store, park Old Paint, and take to the sidewalk.

Yes, here is the liquor store, right where I left it. Next to it is a thrift store and next to that, the massage parlor. This thrift store, I don't understand. It's right where the Mission was, should be.

I go inside. It's dimly lit and close with the must of old clothes, cardboard, and rust. On rolling racks like the one Nikki had in her dressing room, limp dresses in faded florals, coats missing buttons, and slacks shiny in the seat dangle from bent wire hangers. Pitted percolators, toasters with frayed fabric cords, and incomplete sets of chipped dinnerware fill the dusty shelves that line the room.

At the room's center, a glass showcase is sparsely filled with costume jewelry and watches. An old man in a plaid golf cap stands beside a mechanical cash register. I introduce myself, show the man my ID.

"Sister Clyde here?" I ask. Maybe the Mission went belly-up since I was there last and the sister has gone into the thrift-shop side of the good works business.

"Here? You mean, like work here?" the man asks. "No one work here but me." His dark brown eyes regard me candidly.

"Maybe she's a contributor. Brings you stuff from her church?"

"If she do, I don't know her. And I know all the auxiliary ladies. Brotherhood men, too. Elks, Moose, I know all them all. Good people. But a Sister Clyde? Nope, don't know no Sister Clyde," the man says with certainty.

I describe her to him, but he shakes his head.

"There a problem with this Sister, Officer?" he asks.

"No, no problem at all. I—I have something to tell her, that's all." At a loss even for what to ask next, I look around the room as though something of the surroundings will inspire me. "New business here, sir?"

"Nossir. Not new at all. Been here fifteen years."

"Fifteen years? At this location?"

"Yessir. There a problem with the store?"

"No, really. No problem. I just ... you're sure?"

The look he gives me seems to say he's beginning to doubt my sanity, but he politely replies, "I'm sure."

"Well, uh ..." I don't know what to say. *This is the right place, I'm positive. The right street, the right address. Just days ago there was a Mission here.* "Mind if I look around?"

With a wave of his arm, the man says, "Be my guest. You have a question about anything, see something you like, I'm here to serve."

I amble around the room, pick up a tarnished silver picture frame here, a radio with a dull Bakelite case there. My survey only leads to the conclusion that this is nothing but a thrift shop, and one that could have been here for fifty years as easily as fifteen. There's got to be an explanation but I can't even begin to come up with one. My brain is stultified by dust and mold. Finally I can only turn to go.

"Well, uh, thank you, sir."

The man taps the bill of his cap. "Sorry I couldn't help."

So am I. Feet attached to a body that suddenly feels like a stranger's drift toward a door that I fully expect to open onto a rabbit hole to Wonderland. My eyes skim over cardboard boxes of loose buttons, tube socks, yellowed linen hankies with torn lace—and stop. From a box near the door I pick up an object, turn, and hold it up.

"What can you tell me about this?" I ask the man in a voice I can barely keep steady. "Do you know where you got it?"

He squints at the object, then leaves his post by the cash register to take it from my hand.

"Where I got it? Couldn't say. Once stuff's here, I'm more concerned with gettin' it gone than where it come from. It's a collar, sir. Like from a coat." He rubs the brown fur between his thumb and forefinger. "Fox, I think."

Fox. A small quick animal who was with me at my lowest moments—binging on Nearvana, shirking Sister Clyde's challenge, running from Overshort, from death. Fox. A character in ghost stories Zen masters tell of dead disciples reincarnated in foxes' bodies, penance for their faintheartedness. Fox. A fur collar on the coat of a nun assigned hard duty for lack of conviction. A sage old woman who was here, and now isn't.

I don't want to alarm the old man, so I wait until I get outside and close the door behind me. Then, I laugh.

ABOUT THE AUTHOR

"What if?" Those two words all too easily send Devorah Fox spinning into flights of fancy. Best-selling author of The Bewildering Adventures of King Bewilliam epic historical fantasy series including *The Redoubt*, voted one of 50 Self-Published Books Worth Reading 2016, and *The Lost King*, awarded the All Authors Certificate of Excellence. She also wrote the historical thriller *Detour*, co-authored the contemporary thriller, *Naked Came the Sharks*, with Jed Donellie, contributed to *Masters of Time: a SciFi/Fantasy Time Travel Anthology*, and *Magic Unveiled: An Anthology*, and has several Mystery Mini Short Reads to her name. Born in Brooklyn, New York, she now lives in The Barefoot Palace on the Texas Gulf Coast with rescued tabby cats and a dragon named Inky, and writes the "Dee-Scoveries" blog at http://devorahfox.com

Connect online:

Email: devorahfox@aol.com

Facebook: https://facebook.com/DevorahFoxAuthor

Twitter: @devorah_fox

Smashwords: https://www.smashwords.com/profile/view/mbapub.